ONE FOR
SORROW
A CLEMENTINE CARTER MYSTERY

ALSO BY JOANNE TRACEY

ONE FOR
SORROW
A CLEMENTINE CARTER MYSTERY

JOANNE TRACEY

First published in Australia in 2024

by Joanne Tracey

https://joannetracey.com

Copyright © Joanne Tracey 2024

Print ISBN 978-0-6459587-5-1

Epub ISBN 978-0-6459587-3-7

Cover design by Louisa West

A catalogue record for this book is available from the National Library of Australia

For Deborah

PROLOGUE

Last night, I had the dream again – the one I'd had every night for the last week.

It always began the same way: me swimming at the local leisure centre, gliding through the clear blue water, following the black line below. Stroke after effortless stroke, the water supporting my body, keeping it afloat, the repetitive action soothing my mind. I reached the end of the pool and performed a neat tumble-turn, pushing off the edge to glide into another lap. This time, the black line began to get further away and then further still until I could no longer see it, not even as a wavy line in the distance. On I swam.

The water became almost green, and far below me, the sand was speckled with sea grass, a little at first but then a forest, waving and swaying in the current. Weaving through the sea grass was a dugong, sometimes hovering across the top of the grassy grove, stopping every so often to feed. The water was now thick and the current heavy, my stroke laboured, yet I knew I had to keep going. If I didn't, I'd sink.

That's when the dugong flipped around to look at me, and it was no longer a dugong but a mermaid, her emerald lips matching the streaks in the black hair streaming behind her and some of the scales in her luminescent tail. Even in my dream, she reminded me of someone I used to know.

Most nights, the dream ended there, but last night, the mermaid swam towards me – so close I could touch her – and paused, beckoning me with a crooked finger to follow. I'd heard all the stories about mermaids, how they lured sailors to their deaths, yet still I followed, the seagrass giving way to a sandy bottom littered with white shells, some large, some small, some broken. Beams of sunlight through the water formed patterns on the sand, and rather than forcing my way through the current, soft waves pushed me closer to a shore I still couldn't see.

It wasn't long before I could stand to walk onto the beach, one I recognised from my childhood, and on it were what looked to be a castle and four figures, the second of which was sitting on a throne on a patch of grass, the sea rushing around the grass but never quite making it to her feet. As I drew closer, the standing figures became flatter yet more distinct, and then the tarot cards became clear: the Tower, Death, the High Priestess, and Ten of Pentacles, with the central position occupied by the Queen of Cups. But instead of the queen, the card wore the face of my aunt Rose.

I turned away for a second, less than a second, and as I

did, a wave towered over me and broke on top of the card figures. When I looked back, they were all floating, heading out to sea – except for the Queen of Cups. She was lying on the patch of grass, her eyes open and sightless. Beside her lay another card – the Fool.

CHAPTER ONE

'Twenty percent of the company value plus sixty percent of the house and we sign and walk away. My client does, after all, need a place to live.' Andi Shaw pressed a red-tipped finger into her cheek, lifted one shoulder, the green silk of her blouse rippling, and stared defiantly across the polished timber boardroom table at me. Every part of her posture was designed to bluff me into accepting her offer.

Beside me, Marta shifted in her seat. If I glanced sideways, I'd see her hands trembling in her lap, the beginning of uncertainty in her brown eyes, so I didn't. Instead, I slowly and deliberately gathered my papers from where I'd spread them in front of us. I met and held Andi's steady gaze. 'That's a shame because we're not budging.'

I cast a disdainful stare at the man sitting beside Andi. Roman had stalked so confidently into this boardroom less than an hour before, and now his eyes skittered away from mine. 'Do I need to remind you your client left the marital home for the first time prior to my client registering her company name? She has built this business from the ground up with minimal financial or emotional assistance from your client. If your client is looking to my client for a house deposit, I'd suggest he approach his bank instead. In the full and final settlement, we are, however, prepared to offer him a cash settlement to acknowledge the two years they were together and thirty percent of the sale proceeds of the marital home – even though my client provided the original deposit and has been solely responsible for the payment of the mortgage for the past three years. Your client is also welcome to any furniture and other goods he'd like to take from the home.' I leant forward, my forearms resting on the smooth wood. 'You and I both know that's more than he's entitled to.' I paused for half a beat before continuing, my attention now on Roman Cametti. 'This is a generous offer, Mr Cametti, and certainly more generous than what I would've advised my client to make to you.' As Roman would've opened his mouth to say something, Andi held her hand up in warning.

I passed across a slip of paper on which I'd scribbled a figure.

Andi reached for the slip and opened it, her eyes widening slightly. 'I'll need to consult with my client.'

I leant back in my chair, tapping my pen on the buff manila folder. 'Naturally, but you should know the cash settlement portion is on the table until the close of business today. You can use the meeting room across the hall. We'll wait for you here.'

Marta and I sat silently until they left the room. 'Do you think he'll sign?' Marta's voice, normally so strong and certain, wavered.

'I do.' I opened the folder and pulled out an agreement I'd prepared earlier. 'He knows he won't get a better deal, no matter what he originally asked for. I am, however' —I smiled gently— 'concerned about you. Are you sure this is what you want?'

Marta took a deep breath. 'Are you married?' I shook my head. 'Have you ever been married?' When I gave a small nod, she asked, 'What was your divorce like?'

I attempted to prevaricate. 'It was a long time ago.'

'But what was it like?' Her voice had almost a desperate edge to it as if she wanted me to reassure her that the acrimonious divorce we were finalising for her was completely normal.

'It wasn't pleasant,' Conceding the truth brought it back without warning. 'We were both young and didn't have much to fight about, but even so … No.' I tried to push aside the memories of that time. 'It wasn't pleasant, but then again' —I laid my hand gently on her arm— 'divorce isn't meant to be easy. The vows were serious, so unwinding them should also be serious.' I let out a half laugh. 'I often think divorce is as hard as it is so we can be doubly sure it's what we really want. So I'll ask again, are you sure this is what you want?'

She nodded jerkily. 'Yes, Clem, it's what I want.'

'Then that's what we'll get you.' The boardroom door opened again, and Andi walked in, followed by a subdued Roman. I waited until they'd sat. 'Do we have a deal?'

Andi looked across at Roman, whose focus was on a water glass he was pushing around on its coaster. 'We do.' Andi pushed her black-rimmed glasses firmly onto the bridge of her nose. 'We're ready to sign.'

Roman's head snapped up. 'Can I say something first?' He directed his question to Marta.

She glanced first at me and, at my nod, answered him. 'Okay.'

'Do we really want to do this, Marta? I love you – I've always loved you.' His hands were open, beseeching. 'I know I've behaved badly in the past, but I've changed, and I'm asking for the chance to make it up to you.'

'But—' Marta twisted her fingers.

'I know what you're going to say – you've already given me a second chance – and a third chance too – and I wouldn't blame you for not wanting to give me another, but you and me, babe' —he shook his head, a wistful expression on his handsome face— 'we're magic together. We always have been, and we could be again.'

A sob escaped Marta's lips, and inwardly, I groaned. Across the table, Andi grimaced. Suppressing an unprofessional chuckle, I reached for Marta's arm. She shook it off and leant further forward in her seat as if to hear him better.

'I love you, babe.' His smile was sheepish. 'In every kind of way.' Good God, the man was quoting Harry Styles. 'What do you say? Let's forget about all this and just go home.' When Marta turned to me, confusion on her face, he added, 'If I'm being honest, I think I was jealous of your success and the way it shut me out.'

So now his infidelity was her fault?

Roman was still speaking, his words spilling from his mouth. 'I never wanted a divorce. I just wanted you to notice me again, to pay me the same attention you gave to your work.' He brushed away a tear from dry eyes. 'Let's put this behind us and start again. It'll be just like when we were first together … What do you say, babe?' He stood and stretched his arms out to Marta. 'You do still love me, don't you?' Fear had crept into his voice, and I couldn't believe Marta was falling for it.

Neither, it seemed, could Andi who mouthed, 'Oh my God.'

'Yes, Romy, I still love you. I've never stopped.' And she was out of her chair and running to him as fast as her stiletto heels could take her. He caught her and, bending her over his arm in an exaggerated Hollywood style, kissed her thoroughly.

When he finally released her, she scuttled back to where she'd been sitting, picked up her Louis Vuitton tote and turned to me. 'I'm sorry, Clem, but I love him. Send me the bill.' Addressing Andi, she added, 'Send me both bills.'

We waited until they'd left the room arm in arm before collapsing in laughter.

'Give that man an Academy Award,' Andi managed between chuckles. 'You know she'll be back, don't you? Do you want to make a wager about how long it lasts?'

'And next time, he'll have a valid claim against the business,' I said with resignation.

'You're right, of course.' Andi rested her hand on top of her burgeoning belly.

'How long have you got to go?' One of those women who combined beauty and brains, pregnancy had only enhanced Andi's bloom. With her long black hair, prim black-rimmed glasses and dressed in an emerald silk blouse with a form-fitting black skirt, she made pregnancy look both professional and sexy.

She rose to her feet, sighing heavily. 'Six weeks, but it's getting harder to walk in these heels.' She grimaced and placed one hand in the small of her back. 'Todd says I should give in and put the Louboutins away. What's next, though? Sensible shoes? Perish the thought.' She shuddered. 'On another note, how's Miles?'

'Good, I think – not that I've seen much of him lately. He's been working on a major acquisition and has been back and forth from Singapore for the last few months. He's home tomorrow, though – we're heading to Bali next week.'

Her clear green eyes narrowed. 'That'll be nice – you

probably need the break, but how are you about him being away so much?'

I shrugged. What could I say? Andi and Todd had only been together a few years so were still in that first flush of love where everything was new and exciting. Plus, they were expecting a baby together – a honeymoon baby, she'd said. Even if I had told her that in our case, absence hadn't made the heart grow fonder, she wouldn't have understood. 'I'm getting used to him not being there.'

'I see.' Maybe she understood more than I was prepared to say.

Crossing to the rain-spattered window, I looked out. Below, Collins Street was a sea of colourful umbrellas as workers spewed out of office buildings to commence their commute home. The plane trees were beginning to change colour, but in today's drizzle, the fiery colours were muted and dull.

Roman and Marta emerged hand in hand, Roman taking Marta's umbrella from her and opening it above them before pulling her towards him and kissing her deeply. How long had it been since Miles had kissed me like that? Months? With a strange emptiness inside, I turned back to Andi. 'Do you ever wonder if this is all there is?'

Andi frowned, her hands full of papers she was placing back in their respective folders. 'What? Helping clients you know you'd never date in a heartbeat extricate themselves from marriages so they can be unleashed onto a whole new set of unsuspecting women? Actually,' she mused, 'I probably would've dated Roman back in the day and believed him when he told me that either a) he wasn't married or b) he was separated or c) she didn't understand him.' Her chuckle was that of a woman lamenting past mistakes while also grateful she'd moved past them and found her forever man. She walked over and stood beside me, watching the couple below. 'I know what you mean, though. They'll be back, and next time, you won't be able to get away with a settlement as low as you almost did today.'

I nodded absently and watched the pair as Roman opened the taxi door he'd hailed, sweeping his arm around with a 'your ride is here, ma'am' flourish and taking her umbrella as she slid inside. I'd seen it all before – he'd love bomb her for the next few weeks – months maybe – until she was more in love with him than ever. He'd then begin to involve himself in the business she'd built, little by little. Yes, they'd be back, and next time, he'd be pushing for a percentage of Marta's company – and would get it. I rested my forehead against the glass. Was this what I'd worked for? When had I become so cynical? Ten years ago, all that had mattered was reaching partner status. But now I was there, what else was there? Another, what, two decades of helping rich people uncouple at the least possible expense to themselves? Sure, it was lucrative, but what did any of it mean? Was this really all there was? Although the glass was cool against my forehead, an image of a sun-filled room flashed through my mind, the light so bright the colours were faded. Why had that phrase – is this all there is – brought back that image? And why now?

'Hey.' Andi's voice was soft. 'We do good as well, you know. We fight for our clients in a way they wouldn't be able to fight for themselves.' I cast her a disparaging look. 'Think of all the women we've helped back on their feet after years of trust and love comes crashing down around them, and think of the kids we've protected through appropriate custody orders.'

'And think of everyone we've helped screw over haven't deserved to be screwed over ...' I shook my head. What was the point of talking about it now?

'Clem.' Andi was serious now, her hand resting on the small of my back. 'You're one of the best in this business. The pre-nups you draft are legendary and if, God forbid, I ever needed to get a divorce, it's you I'd come to. No one fights for their clients the way you do, and as far as I can tell, the only reason you're not a *senior* partner here is because there's no room in the boy's club. If ever you wanted to move on, you'd be snapped up in a heartbeat.'

My smile was grateful. 'Ignore me, I'm having a moment.'

Understanding the conversation was over, Andi changed the subject. 'You are joining us tonight, aren't you?' She'd returned to the board table, the rustling of papers telling me she'd resumed packing her things.

I groaned and turned to face her. 'Sorry, I completely forgot!' Once a month or so, a few of us got together for a drink in a bar in the city. We were all lawyers for Melbourne city firms, and these meetings were our only chance to let off a little steam with other women who understood the pressure we were all under. 'But yes, I'll be there.'

'You have to be.' A mock stern expression filled her face. 'After all, it's your birthday we're celebrating. When is it? Tomorrow?'

My birthday, I'd almost forgotten that too. 'Yes. Of course I'll be there.' I grinned widely, shaking away the uncharacteristic melancholy.

'Great.' Andi placed the last of her folders into her Ted Baker tote bag. 'See you there – usual place, usual time.' With a little wave, she was off.

Back in my office, my assistant, Meera, was waiting with a fistful of messages. I glanced at my watch and sighed. 'Give it to me in order of priority.' I softened my words with a resigned smile.

'Miles called. He said not to bother calling him back – he'll catch up with you later. Stephen needs to see you before you leave—'

'Do you know why?' It was never good news when Stephen, our managing partner, needed to see me. I cast my mind back through my caseload, looking for the possible reason and came up blank.

'No, sorry.' She didn't appear at all sorry. 'And your father's called twice. He's asked that you call him back as soon as you can.'

I grimaced. With Dad, it was always important – until I spoke to him and it turned out to be not at all important. He would, however, continue to call until I rang him back. 'Okay, got it. You head home, and I'll take it from here.'

Meera lingered in the doorway. 'How did it go with Marta?'

'We had them ready to sign and then' — I rolled my eyes— 'he convinced her to give him another chance.'

'You're kidding! After all he's put her through, she believed him?'

Meera reminded me of how I'd been at twenty-five – ambitious, keen and so absolute – although I don't think my ponytail was ever that high or that perky. She had yet to learn the world wasn't black and white but rather endless shades of grey ... so much grey. I shrugged. 'What can we do? The heart wants what the heart wants.'

Meera frowned, her smooth forehead slightly furrowed. 'She's mad. But at least this way we'll get two sets of fees out of her.' As quickly as the frown had appeared, it was gone, a grin in its place. 'When she's back, I mean.'

My laugh was rueful. 'That's one way of looking at it. Now, you get out of here. I've got drinks with the girls tonight so won't be too far behind you.'

I closed the door behind her, catching my reflection

in the mirror behind it. Thanks to a good hairdresser, my mid-length chestnut hair was still free of grey, the layers, highlights and lowlights giving softness to what otherwise would've been a too-square jaw. Did I look almost forty-four? Patting the underside of my chin with the back of my fingers, I had to admit the skin was softer there than it used to be, but other than a few lines around my hazel eyes and in my forehead – neither of which were too deep – my skincare regime was working. When I smiled, the dimples in my cheeks made me look younger, so maybe I should just smile more. But what was there to smile about? As quickly as the thought slid into my mind, I pushed it aside, reopened the door and made my way down the hall to Stephen's office, knocking once before letting myself in.

'Aaah Clementine, thanks for dropping by.' He got up from behind his desk and walked around to meet me. Tall and slim, Stephen wore his Italian suits and silk ties with flair. Although we'd started with the firm at the same time, Stephen was always going to get to the top before I did. It wasn't just that he'd been to the 'right' private schools and had the 'right' network, he also had the right attitude and look. Stephen was, to put it simply, the whole package, and now he was managing partner.

Stephen selected a Waterford crystal flask two-thirds full of amber liquid from the tray on a shelf in the maple bookcase. 'Can I tempt you?' At my nod, he poured a small measure into two wide glasses in the same cut crystal and held one out to me.

'Thanks.' I took a sip, closing my eyes briefly as the whisky warmed its way down my throat and across my chest, and sank into one of the red leather chairs opposite his desk. He took the other.

'How did it go with Cametti versus Cametti?' His tone was conversational.

'We were about to settle, and then Mr Cametti persuaded his wife to give the marriage another chance. So they're back on, and the settlement is off.' I took another sip of the whisky, inhaling the rich, smoky, peaty fragrance.

'That's unfortunate.' Stephen cradled his glass, a pensive frown marring his urbane features. 'I was hoping that one would go to litigation.'

'You know I prefer to settle than go to court,' I reminded him. 'It's a much better process for the client.'

'But not as lucrative for us. What's the likelihood of the reconciliation lasting?' I waggled my hand in a so-so motion. 'So it's likely she'll be back? Good.'

Smiling at his cynicism, I nodded. 'I'd say so. In the meantime, I'll call and see if she'll consider a postnup. Not that I think she would, but it's worth a try.'

'Good idea.' He drained his glass and stood. 'Another?'

'No, thank you.' I reached forward to set my glass on the desk before sitting back and crossing my legs. 'What did you need to see me about, Stephen?'

'Are you sure you won't have another?' He held his

glass up.

My heart beat faster, a ripple of foreboding running through my chest. 'Do I need another?'

'No, not really.' He sat back in the chair and crossed one leg over the other, lightly resting the whisky glass on his knee, his overly casual posture doing nothing to quell that foreboding. 'Are you aware of the matter involving Helen Bouras?'

'Helen? Mark Pollock's junior? Didn't she leave a month or so ago?' What had Meera said? Something about it being a quick exit … 'What has she to do with me? I barely knew the woman.'

Stephen tipped his glass to the side, tracing the angles of the crystal with his fingers. 'It seems as though her departure wasn't as clear-cut as it might have been.' His words were slow and measured.

I sighed. 'Please don't tell me Mark—'

'No, nothing like that.' Stephen was quick to jump on my unspoken suggestion of any harassment. 'She's made a complaint about work pressures and unreasonable hours.' He shook his head in exasperation or disbelief – I couldn't decide which. 'You and I both know the race to achieve the most billable hours is part of the deal, and we've all been there, but Helen is making an issue of it.'

'Riiiight …' I still wasn't sure what she had to do with me.

'We'll need to be careful with the hours we ask our

associates – in particular our juniors – to work, at least for the time being. It's a box-ticking exercise, you understand.'

I inclined my head to let him know I did, indeed, understand. 'You want me to keep an eye on Meera's hours?' There had to be more he wasn't saying.

He didn't answer immediately – his attention focused on the play of light on amber as he slowly turned his glass. 'It's also about annual leave. Fair Work makes a big deal about all employees taking a holiday each year – and that includes salaried partners.' He shifted his eyes to mine. 'And that's where you come in … You currently have eight weeks' annual leave accrued in addition to your long service leave entitlements.'

'And …?'

'And we need you to take it.'

'I'm taking a week from close of business tomorrow, remember? Miles and I are off to Bali.' His eyes flicked away from mine, but before they did, I caught something in them that made the hairs on the back of my neck prickle. 'Are you sure that's all there is?'

'Absolutely.'

His single-word answer should've been reassuring, but there was something in the tautness of his jaw and the way his eyes couldn't meet mine that had my antennas on alert. 'How much of this leave do you need me to take?'

He placed his glass on the desk and stood to walk back around to his computer. Sitting, he tapped at a few keys.

'We need to get your annual leave down to below twenty days if we're to demonstrate to the commission that we're serious about work-life balance.'

I couldn't help the laugh that escaped me. 'You're joking, right? We've never been serious about that.'

He had the grace to flash me a sheepish grin. 'I know, but we must be seen to be doing the right thing. Besides, how long has it been since you had a holiday?'

'God knows. Bali will be our first proper break in a few years. With Miles being away as much as he is …' Miles was an equity partner here at Marshall and Hale, and we could rarely get our respective acts together regarding holidays, usually making do with the enforced two-week closure over Christmas.

'Yes, it would make it difficult, but surely there's someplace else you want to go. Europe's nice at this time of the year – my social media is full of people in Italy – and everyone seems to be on the Amalfi Coast or Greece.'

I squirmed in my chair. 'On my own? Miles is too busy to get away for longer.' A thought occurred to me. 'He must have as much leave as I do – does he need to take it too?'

'Being an equity partner makes it different.' He sighed and added with a too-bright smile, 'Is there anything you want to do around the house? You've been working very hard …'

'We live in an apartment,' I reminded him. 'There is nothing to do around the house.'

He pushed away from his desk and stood again, a sign that the meeting was over. 'Well, I'd suggest you find something to do as you'll be on leave for the next month. And before you ask, cashing it out is not an option.'

I stood too, pulling my tight navy skirt down as I straightened. 'When does this leave of mine start?' I searched his face for a sign that there was more to this than ticking some box on a Fair Work checklist. Nothing.

'You were already redistributing your caseload as it is, and Meera will be reallocated to Mark Pollock – he's still recruiting – so there's no reason you can't simply stay away for longer.'

My breath caught in my throat – there *was* something more to this. 'Stephen, what's going on? Am I being investigated for something? Has one of my clients made a complaint?'

His face tinged pink, and again, he couldn't meet my eyes. 'You're not being investigated for anything; none of your work is in question. We simply need you to get your leave down quickly.'

'Is the firm being investigated?' All my spider senses were on alert. There was something he wasn't telling me.

The colour spread to his ears, and eventually, he spoke. 'All employees benefit from four consecutive weeks' leave a year.' Opening the door, he added, 'I'll let you get on with your evening.' As I would've pressed the subject some more, Stephen shook his head slightly to signal for me to leave the matter alone. 'I'm sorry, Clem; I can't say more than that.' As I walked out, he called, 'Have a good night.'

I lifted a hand in farewell but didn't reply.

CHAPTER TWO

Drinks with the girls turned into dinner, and although I laughed at the right times and contributed to the conversation when I should have, I found myself preoccupied with the meeting I'd had before leaving the office.

'Hey,' Andi softly scolded when I was a little slow to respond to something she'd said. 'What's on your mind?'

I snapped back to attention. 'I'm sorry; what did you say?'

Andi waggled her finger. 'Not fast enough, Ms Carter. What's going on? You're off on holiday on Monday, so you should be excited. Is it pre-birthday worries or something more? You're not yourself tonight.'

A stab of remorse ran through me. These women were some of my closest friends, and we didn't get to catch up nearly often enough, yet here I was, wasting the time we had dwelling on something that could yet turn out to be nothing. 'Sorry, I had a weird conversation with Stephen tonight, and I'm trying to decide if it's something or nothing.'

'Try us.' Lara was a corporate lawyer, mother of two and the eldest of our little band of legal renegades. 'If you can't tell us, who can you tell?'

'Go on,' encouraged Goldie. 'Andi's right, you're not yourself tonight.'

Taking a breath, I launched into a recap of the afternoon's conversation. 'I know I should be grateful he's telling me I have to have a month off, but I can't help wondering if there's something else happening.'

Lara nodded slowly. 'I know what you mean, although it could be a box-ticking exercise – especially if this junior has made a complaint to Fair Work. The best way to counter that is to prove they're actively concerned with ensuring employees at all levels have proper breaks from work, but …'

'Other than the senior partners, I probably do have the most accrued leave. I've certainly been there longer than most people, so perhaps that is all there is to it.' I wasn't sure who I was trying to convince – them or me.

'But your instinct is telling you something different.' Andi absently twirled the straw in her mocktail, her brow furrowed in thought.

'Exactly. I asked him outright if I was under investigation or if any of my clients had made a complaint, but he categorically denied it.'

'Did you ask if the firm was being investigated?' Goldie was always quick on the uptake.

I hesitated slightly before answering. 'I did, and he repeated that this was an issue about annual leave.'

Lara chewed at her bottom lip. 'I think you're right – something's going on, and while it mightn't be anything to do with you, it might involve something you know and they need you not to compromise yourself—'

'Or them,' interrupted Andi.

'Or it could be about someone you know,' suggested Goldie.

The table was quiet for a few seconds as we all absorbed her meaning. 'You're talking about Miles, aren't you?'

Goldie lifted a shoulder in response, the others silent as I considered and then discounted the possibility that whatever this was about involved Miles.

'How *are* you two?' Lara broke the silence.

I caught the eye of a passing server and indicated we needed fresh drinks. Although I contemplated avoiding an answer, as Lara had said, if I couldn't talk to these women, who could I talk to? 'About as well as a relationship can go when one party is never in the country and when he is, is attached to his phone or his email. Don't get me wrong, Miles has always been like this, so I knew what I was getting into, but we've been together seven years, and just lately, I've begun to wonder—'

'If that's all there is?' Goldie finished my sentence.

There it was, that phrase again. I nodded mutely,

wanting to tell them that these days we rarely talked and rarely touched – our apartment was somewhere for Miles to sleep in between flights, meetings and calls – but the words stuck in my throat. Goldie rubbed my arm in sympathy, somehow knowing what I couldn't say. The delivery of our drinks was, however, a timely distraction.

'Or we could all be wrong and this is just about finance needing to reduce leave accruals before the end of the financial year.' Lara shrugged. 'I, for one, would love to be told not to come to work for a month. On which note, I think we have a duty to Clem to come up with some activities for when she's back from Bali.'

'Or maybe some holiday destinations,' added Goldie. 'You don't want to waste your time staying at home.'

'Speaking of which,' said Andi. 'I'm knackered, so as soon as I finish this drink, I'm heading home.' She yawned to illustrate the point. 'Anyone who tells you this last trimester is a breeze is lying.'

'But you're blooming,' protested Goldie.

'About the only thing that is blooming is my sex life. I don't think I've ever been this horny … well, except for when we first got together … and then there was our honeymoon.' A wicked smile floated across her face. 'Maybe it's because we have to be more creative – I'm not exactly flexible at the moment. All I'm saying is don't discount doggy-style.'

As I shook my head and laughed, Goldie stuck

her fingers in her ears and proclaimed it was 'too much information'.

Lara, however, didn't hold back. 'Really? With each of my two, I didn't want him anywhere near me … although maybe it was that I didn't want *him* anywhere near me.' She laughed, and we all laughed with her, but as we did, we knew the humour was to hide the fact that Lara was still hurting from the pain of a separation that had blindsided her – and an impending divorce she didn't want.

Goldie put her arm around Lara's waist, Lara resting her head against Goldie's shoulder. 'I need another drink,' she muttered.

'And that's my cue to love you and leave you.' Andi kissed us all goodbye and fluttered her fingers in a wave. 'Happy birthday, Clem!'

By mutual agreement, we moved to the bar next door for 'just one more'.

'What's going on over there?' I wondered aloud. In a dimly lit corner, a woman sat at a small card table covered with a crimson velvet cloth.

'I think she's doing tarot readings.' Goldie's face lit up. 'What fun! Let's have one.'

'Oh yes, let's!' Lara clapped her hands. 'Maybe she can tell me when that dick of an ex-husband will agree to the settlement he's been offered.'

'I don't know,' I said slowly, unsure why I was holding back. Again, the image of that sun-filled room flicked into my brain.

'It's just a bit of fun,' said Goldie. 'I'll go put our names down.'

'Do you believe in it?' Lara asked once she'd gone. 'Tarot, astrology and the like. It *is* just a bit of fun, isn't it?'

I took a sip of my wine before answering. 'Yeah, it's a bit of fun … You know, my aunt is an astrologer. She dabbles in tarot too.'

'For real?'

I traced a drip of condensation on the outside of my glass. 'She works at a New Age shop in her town.' I smiled softly as the sun-filled room was again before me. This time, though, the picture was clearer: me sitting on a rug on the wooden floor, my long legs splayed out, charts and other papers full of symbols scattered on the floor and across the top of the well-worn wooden dining table.

Goldie had returned in time to hear what I'd said. 'You never mentioned that.'

'It was a long time ago.' My smile was pensive, my mind on hazy summer beach holidays, on another life. I hadn't thought about those days in years, possibly decades … Why had the memories surfaced today?

'Well, it's your turn first, so you'll have to let us know whether she's any good.' Goldie chuckled, a twinkle in her eye.

I approached the woman at the table with some trepidation. As cynical as the years in family law had made me, the lost and lonely teenager who'd turned to my aunt for advice was still within me.

'Hello, dear,' the woman greeted me. From a distance, I hadn't been able to place her age, but up close, dressed in layers of lace, with reams of silver around her neck and on her wrists, she would've had to be sixty, maybe older, maybe younger. 'I'm Glenda. What's your name?'

'Clementine. Clementine Carter.' My voice wavered as my heart hammered. Why on earth was I nervous? 'Everyone calls me Clem.'

'Then that's what I'll call you too.' Her smile was gentle and reassuring. 'Your friend said it was your birthday in a couple of days?'

'Yes, tomorrow.'

She nodded and reached for her phone. 'You're an Aries … I don't suppose you know your time of birth?'

'I was adopted, but my aunt is an astrologer and she worked out my birth time.' I wrote the details on the sheet of paper she pushed across to me.

'She rectified it?'

'Yes, that's the term she used,' I said.

As she tapped the details into what I assumed was an app on her phone, I suppressed a smile at how much things had changed. Back when Rose would plot charts for clients, neighbours and friends, she'd hand draw them, consulting a book called an ephemeris which contained all the planetary positions. At the time, it seemed like an awful lot of palaver, and as much as I soaked up what she had to say about planets and signs and the aspects that influenced their behaviour, I never had the patience to draw charts myself. All my practice was on charts Rose created for me – even after I was ready to read them myself. An involuntary smile came to my lips as I wondered whether she now used an app or still painstakingly performed the calculations as she used to.

Glenda looked up from the phone and turned it towards me. 'You said your aunt is an astrologer so I assume you've seen your chart before?'

I nodded. 'I have. She taught me how to read them but I've forgotten most of it now.' I laughed nervously and took a sip of my wine, unwilling to disclose that for a time that's how I too earnt an income. It was, after all, another life.

'You'd be surprised at how much you do remember – with your chart placements, you could probably do this for a living.'

I laughed uncomfortably. 'I doubt that very much.'

Rose's voice came to me from across the decades. *You're naturally intuitive, Clem – don't ever forget that.*

Glenda said nothing but smiled enigmatically as if she'd heard the voice in my head. 'Have you ever heard of the Uranus opposition? It's something we astrologers refer to as one of the midlife crisis transits.'

Another memory floated through: my aunt talking to someone – a client? *Be grateful he's just bought a sports car, dear*

– it's a lot less expensive or hurtful than another woman.

I nodded again, seemingly unable to do anything else, my brain reacting to the words Glenda used as it would to a language I hadn't spoken for many years.

'It's something that happens to everyone between the ages of forty-one to forty-four, but the easiest way to explain it is you can find yourself feeling quite restless and questioning who you are, who you want to be, the choices you've made and whether this is all there is.' She narrowed her eyes, and it felt uncomfortably like she'd eavesdropped on my conversation with Andi this afternoon. 'It's that which is in play when you hear about people suddenly leaving jobs, marriages or homes and acting out of character. Of course,' she clarified, 'not everyone does something extreme. Some will buy a sports car, get a tattoo or wish they were brave enough to step out of their own lives for an hour, a day or a year.' She softened her voice. 'It hits people in different ways, but does that sound familiar?'

'Are you sure my friends haven't set me up?' My giggle sounded high-pitched.

'No, Clem, they haven't. Another thing happening to you now which is exacerbating this is' —she frowned as if wondering what to tell me or how to explain a concept— 'your progressed sun is about to change signs, and that's something that only happens every thirty years.' Elbows on the table, she steepled her fingers under her chin. 'There are massive changes coming your way. You might want to push against them at first, but these transits are designed to help you become who you need to be – who you might've forgotten to be. That mightn't make much sense to you now, but it will soon. Plus, with Mercury about to turn retrograde through that part of your chart, you could find yourself revisiting people and places of the past. Let's pull a few cards.' She reached for a deck of cards on the edge of the table. 'Shuffle these for me.'

As I shuffled, Glenda rearranged the tumble of crystals on the table.

'Now, I'd like you to use your left hand to cut the deck three times before placing the piles back together in any order you like.'

I did as she asked.

'Sweep them in a fan shape across the table, face down and choose five cards.' She pointed to where she wanted me to put the cards. As I chose the last one, an extra card fell out. She moved it to the side.

I placed the cards, and she turned them over. As she did, a shiver ran through me, and if it hadn't been as dark as it was, Glenda would've seen the colour drain from my face. The Tower, Death, the Queen of Cups, the High Priestess and Ten of Pentacles – the same cards I'd seen in my dream last night. Finally, she turned over the two accidental cards: the Fool and the Emperor.

Glenda's eyes flicked to mine, and although I'd

attempted to keep my expression impassive, she must've seen something to concern her. 'Clients tend to be afraid when they see the Tower and Death cards,' she said. 'But it doesn't signify actual death – rather the death of something. These cards are about change – in the case of the Tower, unexpected sudden change – but with Death, it's more about the transformation that comes from an ending.' She looked up and smiled gently. 'Something needs to end or die so something else can begin or be born. Every new beginning comes from some other beginning's end.' At my slight nod, she continued. 'The Tower can sometimes be an Aries card because of the way Aries approaches change – as a challenge to be wilfully overcome rather than something to be frightened of, but I also think the High Priestess is you – someone whose subconscious mind and intuition is telling her something, but she's learnt over the years to ignore that.' I reached a finger out and traced the edge of the card, unable to explain the sudden pang deep in my stomach. 'The Queen of Cups is a woman too, a compassionate, caring, intuitive woman. Here she is sitting on her throne at the edge of the sea, her feet on the ground yet connected to the water. She's a woman in touch with her and other people's emotions, yet not overwhelmed by them. She's also at the centre of the situation this spread represents.' At my gasp, Glenda met my eyes again. 'Your aunt?'

The lump in my throat grew. 'I think so.'

'I do too. And as for the Ten of Pentacles, this one is

about financial security and wealth, but see the old man in the picture with the younger people? He's passing on what he's learnt. This card is also about legacy … inheritance, if you will. It could be money, or it could be knowledge or craft. I think the Emperor represents you too – see the rams on the throne?' I nodded. 'As for the Fool – have you heard about The Fool's Journey?'

'I think so.'

'The Fool signifies taking a step into the unknown – he has questions but no answers, and he's prepared to go on a journey to find them. Astrologically, it's like the new moon –when everything is as dark as it can be, but you trust there'll be light soon.' She peered at me in the dim light. 'For that reason, this is also quite an Aries card. It could be that you're being called on to go on a quest of some type … Pull another card.' I did as asked and turned over the Queen of Swords. 'Interesting. The Queen of Swords can also represent an Aries woman – someone who is independent, self-sufficient, intelligent and honest, yet is also blunt and able to get to the truth of a matter.'

The truth is important to you, Clemmy, and whatever you do, make sure you don't allow it to be covered up. Dig for the truth – even if it gets you into trouble …

'This spread is very much about you – almost as if it's a reminder of who you are.' She paused, 'Have you ever attempted to find your birth mother?'

I shook my head. 'No. It always seemed … disloyal …

to do it while my parents were alive.'

'Maybe that's your quest – to find your birth mother.' She straightened suddenly. 'Okay, that's our ten minutes. I'll get you to send one of your other friends over.' She passed me a business card. 'Take this and book in a reading with me if you'd like to know more and be kind to yourself.' She hesitated. 'Better yet, maybe you should give your aunt a call – before it's too late.'

I didn't tell her I hadn't spoken to my aunt in way too long, or that I hadn't spoken to her about astrology or the tarot or anything that used to be such a big part of my life in decades. I'd left that version of myself – along with a broken heart – in Whale Bay.

CHAPTER THREE

By the time I arrived home, it was still early enough in Singapore for me to catch Miles.

'Hello, darling.' The smile in his greeting lifted my spirits. 'To what do I owe this call? I'll be seeing you tomorrow.'

'I know, I just wanted to hear your voice.'

He must've heard the waver in mine as his tone changed to one of concern. 'Clem, is everything okay?'

'I think so … It's just Stephen called me in today and is forcing me to take extra leave.'

He delayed his response so long that I thought the connection had been cut. 'Did he say why?'

'Yes, apparently, they need to reduce accrued leave to twenty days – something about Fair Work and needing to tick boxes. He implied it's due to Helen Bouras' complaint about unreasonable hours.'

'Helen Bouras? Mark Pollock's junior? Really?'

'So Stephen said. I asked him if there had been any complaints about my work or any investigations involving me, and he said there wasn't, it's just …'

'It's got you wondering,' Miles finished.

'Yeah.' I paused and added caution to my voice. 'Have you heard anything?'

'Not a thing.' I pictured him in the hotel bar. He would've excused himself to his dinner companions and stepped into the lobby or somewhere quiet to take the call and would now be tapping his bottom lip in the way he did when he was thinking. 'I'm sure it's what Stephen says it is.'

Perhaps it really was a box-ticking exercise for finance and human resources – if it was anything more serious, if there was an investigation they needed to keep me away from, Miles, as a senior partner, would know.

'Have you thought about what you'll do? Maybe it's a good excuse to take yourself off somewhere else after we get back – a resort, perhaps. You've always said you wanted to go snorkelling on the reef, and you know it's something I'm not keen on – perhaps you should do that now?'

'Perhaps …' Again, that image of my aunt's front room came into focus. Maybe it was time to go back?

Before I could voice this, he said, 'Sorry darling, I have to run, but I'll see you tomorrow night. Don't forget we have dinner booked for your birthday.'

'How could I forget?'

'Oh, and Clem?'

'Yes?'

'Don't worry about it; I'm sure it is what Stephen said.'

His words should've reassured me, but they didn't.

I lay awake into the early hours of the morning, Glenda's words mingling with memories of Rose and her house by the beach at Whale Bay. Memories I thought I'd locked away forever.

Rose – she never liked being called Aunty Rose 'it makes me sound *so* old sweetie' – was my mother's sister, not that you'd ever guess it to look at them. Mum was tall, trim, gentle and long-suffering, the model of an army wife. Shorter and more comfortably built with an outlook on life that was the same as her name, Rose was exactly the opposite. Where Mum wore smartly tailored, practical separates, Rose was always bedecked in faded Bohemian-style dungarees, caftans or floaty beach dresses and was barefoot or wore rubber flip-flops. Even on the rare occasions she'd come to Melbourne for a New Age fair or conference, she'd dressed the same.

Despite their differences, Mum and Rose were close – which is why when Dad was posted overseas when I was twelve, Rose was the only person Mum trusted to look after me. The original posting had been for just a year, and it was quickly agreed that such a move would be disruptive at my stage of schooling. Mum, on one of the only occasions I recalled her stamping her foot, had declared boarding school out of the question, so for the five years my parents were in Asia, I stayed in Australia, living with my aunt in Whale Bay.

Despite initially feeling abandoned, I soon settled into life with Rose and school in Whale Bay. I made friends and ran wild, barefoot and free. I missed my parents, of course I did, but it was the best of times.

When Dad was posted to Melbourne the year I turned seventeen, it was agreed I'd stay in Whale Bay to finish high school but would come home for the holidays. While Mum was thrilled to have me back, Dad had no idea how to deal with a teenager full-time –especially not one who'd been left to form her own boundaries. He imposed rules, and I pushed against them. There was a constant battle between us, so when I left school, much to the horror of my parents, I stayed in Whale Bay and worked at New Moon with Rose.

When Mum suddenly passed away a couple of years later, Rose was the one to break the news to me, and when she held me close after my mother's funeral, it was as though she knew it was time I began my real life and time I left Whale Bay behind.

I turned over in bed and pummelled my pillow.

While I'd stayed in touch with Rose – although not as often as I should have these days – I hadn't been back to Whale Bay in the years since. It reminded me too much that my mother was gone and too much of everything else that had transpired on that terrible day and in the months after. As beautiful as it was, Whale Bay reminded me too much of events I'd worked hard to forget. Was it too late now to go back? It would give me something to do when we got back from Bali. Rose, I was sure, would be overjoyed, and after twenty-five years, maybe it was time I faced those memories head-on.

When I finally drifted to sleep, my dreams were filled with images of astrology charts and tarot cards whirling through the air so fast I had to duck to avoid them, and in the centre of the whirlwind was Miles.

I spent the following day transferring clients and files – temporarily at least – and accepting well wishes (and cake at morning tea) from my colleagues for my birthday and holiday. It was well into the afternoon before I managed to phone my father, and even then, he was unavailable, so I spoke with Prue, my stepmother.

'Happy birthday, Clementine; Phil will be sorry he missed you.' Prue's voice was warm. 'Are we going to see you this weekend? Fern and Troy will be around with the kids … it's been such a long time since we had a family lunch …' Her voice trailed away; she was missing her youngest daughter Willow who was living in London.

I grimaced. It wasn't Prue's fault that she inherited me less than a year after the death of my mother. She'd tried so hard to involve me in the family she and my father were creating, but what do you do with an almost nineteen-year-old who still misses her mother and resents her father for bringing a new wife and an eight-year-old stepsister into her life? And when baby Willow followed soon after …

Even now, all these years later, Prue was still trying to bring me into the family fold.

'I'll think about it, Prue, but Miles and I are flying to Bali on Monday, so we'll see.'

'You work so hard it will do you good to get away, but if you are here on Sunday, we'd love to see you.' The disappointment in her voice filled me with guilt. 'I know your father wanted to talk to you about an aunt of yours – your mother's sister?'

'Rose? Really?' Of late, everything seemed to point to Rose. First, the dream, then the memories of the house in Whale Bay, and last night, the tarot reader. 'That's so funny. I was thinking of visiting her when we get back.'

'Oh.' The silence that followed was awkward. 'Maybe you'd better speak to your father first.'

The same feeling of foreboding I'd had yesterday prickled across my neck. 'What is it, Prue?'

'I think it's best you speak with your father,' she said carefully 'I'll make sure he calls you back. Have a lovely birthday, and hopefully, we'll see you on the weekend.'

Long after Prue had rung off, I sat staring at the phone screen, dread filling my stomach.

Dad finally got hold of me as I was packing my bags for the early morning flight.

'Happy birthday, Clementine; you're a hard person to pin down.' Even though his words had a touch of scolding, there was pride in his voice. While my father and I had locked horns as I was growing up, he'd been proud I'd chosen a career in law and had climbed the ladder as far as I (so far) had. 'Is this a good time?'

'Thanks, Dad, and yes, it is. As of about now, I'm on leave for a month.' I injected a breezy tone into my response so he wouldn't worry.

'I'd almost forgotten you and Miles were off to Bali. Wasn't that only for a week?'

'We are. The firm is clamping down on excess leave, though, and I'm one of the worst offenders, so I'll take another few weeks when we get back.' I'd intended my laugh to sound light and nonchalant, but it came out uncomfortably, almost a giggle.

'I see. Is it anything you need to worry about?' Despite our battles, he'd always been able to see through me.

'I've been assured it's not. It's a good opportunity for me to take a break, though. Miles is still tied up with the acquisition he's working on, so I thought I might take a trip up to Whale Bay and see Rose.'

In the ensuing silence my heart skipped a beat. And then another.

'I'm afraid that won't be possible.' His words were slow and measured. 'It's why I was trying to ring you yesterday … I'm sorry to tell you, Clemmy, but Rose … Rose passed away last week.'

'Last week?' The words squeaked past the lump in my

throat, and I slumped back into my chair. 'How did I not know?' The image from the dream flashed through my brain.

'I'm so sorry,' he said again. 'I only found out yesterday when her solicitor tracked me down.'

'Her solicitor?' I seemed to be incapable of stringing a complete sentence together.

'Yes, she was trying to find you … Clem, Rose left everything to you.'

CHAPTER FOUR

'What do you think about the Chablis to begin, or are you happy to do the wine matching and maybe have some champagne to start?' Miles looked up at me from his examination of the wine list.

'Let's leave it up to them.' We'd wanted to eat here – a paddock-to-plate style restaurant with most of the produce coming from Victoria – for ages, and now we were here, my appetite had deserted me.

Although it had been a few years since I last saw Rose, we'd stayed in touch via the occasional email and the usual Christmas and birthday cards. Now, the place where I'd kept Rose in my heart felt empty. It wasn't just that she was my last link to Mum, but that she'd been such a big part of my teenage years. As well as sadness, the dry and bitter taste of guilt was on my tongue. How had she felt when I stayed away for so long? It was only now, when it was too late, that I realised I'd been her last link to Mum as well.

'You hardly ever mention your aunt, yet you're telling me she's left you her estate? Why have I never met her?'

Miles had asked this question – or a variation on it – at least three times since we'd left home.

'It's been a few years since she was last in Melbourne,' My stomach twisted with fresh guilt. 'She was down for the Mind, Body, Spirit Festival, and I saw her then. You were probably away.'

'Probably,' Miles conceded. 'But you say she's left you her house? Where exactly is Whale Bay?'

'A couple hours' drive north of Brisbane and an hour out of the Sunshine Coast, so not exactly the easiest place in the world to duck up to for a few days.' With my elbow on the table, I rested my head in my hand, no longer in this beautiful dining room but instead almost two thousand kilometres and twenty-five years away. 'It's one of those places that when you look back, it always seems to be summer – even though obviously it wasn't.'

'Although in Queensland, I doubt it would've been much of a winter.' Miles laughed at his joke.

I returned his laugh. 'No, it wasn't, but as soon as the temperature fell below twenty, we all rugged up. The tourists must've thought we'd gone mad dressed in our Ugg boots and jumpers while they were sunning themselves on the beach.' I chuckled at the memory. 'If I close my eyes now, I can still see it – the sweeping bay with a lighthouse at one end of The Spit guarding the entrance to the river and the fisheries, a row of houses that were probably built in the sixties or seventies – mostly fibro … you know the sort.

Rose's cottage was one of those – we'd cross the road and be on the beach. They're probably all gone now,' I mused, my mind still walking the path I'd wandered so often as a girl. 'If you kept walking, you'd reach the shops. There was the fish and chips shop on the corner, a bakery that did the best salad rolls and cream buns and a small grocer that sold the basics – for anything else, you'd need to drive down to the Sunshine Coast or up to Gympie – the New Age shop my aunt worked at, a hairdresser and a few others for the tourists selling hats, sunscreen and bait.'

I paused as a server delivered our drinks – champagne for me and a beer for Miles.

'Here's to you, Clem.' Miles held his glass up in a toast. 'Happy birthday, my darling girl.'

'Thanks.' I smiled as the bubbles danced along my tongue.

'Did you say your aunt's house is on the beach?' Miles asked. 'As in absolute beachfront?'

I knew what he was asking. 'Not absolute beachfront – there's a road in between. The posh houses at the other end of the bay have absolute beachfront, though – the road runs behind them. They'd be worth a fortune now – those and the ones in The Heights.' When he raised his eyebrows in a silent question, I elaborated. 'They're built on the side of the mountain – not that it's much of a mountain, more like a big hill – but from there, you have a view of the whole bay. We used to call it Nob Hill – on account of that's where the "nobs" lived.'

A speculative gleam came into Miles's eyes. 'Your aunt's place would have to be worth a pretty penny now, though, especially to a developer. How long has it been since you were there?' Miles had always stayed on top of the property market; his favourite weekend activity was to spread out with the real estate lift-outs in the newspaper.

'Not since Mum died.' I shrugged, the loneliness of those months after Mum's passing flooding back as if it were yesterday. 'The years I spent there were the best.' Until that last summer. That was the worst, and not just because of Mum. 'I hadn't even thought about any of it until yesterday … In fact, a funny thing happened last night—'

As I was about to tell Miles about the astrologer and how it had reminded me of my aunt, the server was there.

'To begin, we have oysters from the Mornington Peninsula and our house-made sourdough with whipped chicken fat butter. Enjoy.'

'Chicken fat butter?' I spread a slice of bread and took a bite, closing my eyes as the flavour filled my mouth. 'Oh my giddy aunt, that's good!'

Miles realised what I'd said before I did and tried briefly to keep a straight face before giving up and breaking into a chuckle. 'Rather ironic in the circumstances, darling.'

I clapped my hand over my mouth but quickly saw the funny side.

Once our laughter had died down, Miles said, 'What

were you saying before? You were about to tell me about something that happened last night …'

'Oh, it was nothing.' I waved my hand in dismissal. Miles would only laugh at me if I told him what the reader had said and especially if I told him I'd learnt astrology when I was young and had done readings for a living.

'It must've been something or you wouldn't have brought it up.'

Why was he being so persistent? 'It was just … when I was out with the girls last night, there was a woman there doing tarot readings—'

A short laugh burst from him. My assumption was correct. 'You're not going to tell me that a tarot card reader told you you'd be coming into money soon, are you?' His mouth curled into a disbelieving sneer.

'No, of course not, but it reminded me of Rose because that's what she did.'

'When you said she worked in a New Age shop, that's what I thought you meant – that she worked in the shop, not that she did that sort of thing.'

His frown was disapproving, and I bristled in response, unable to resist the impulse to defend her, even though she hadn't needed defending back then and certainly didn't need it now. 'Yes, that's what she used to do, and she was very good at it, too. I know you don't believe in it, and that's your right. All I'm saying is it reminded me of her … in fact, I'd decided last night to go and visit and then, well, this happened.'

His expression softened, and he reached across and patted my hand. 'I'm so sorry, Clem.'

The server cleared our plates before returning with a wooden board adorned with a generous mound of beetroot hummus and a variety of colourful vegetable sticks and chunks of baby turnips and radishes (which we were told came from a farm in the Yarra Valley).

'What are you going to do with it? The house, that is.' Miles smeared some of the scarlet puree onto the cut side of a halved chargrilled Dutch carrot.

I ran a radish through the small bowl that still held some of that amazing butter. 'I'll head up there when we get back from Bali and see the solicitor and make a decision then.'

'As to whether to sell? I thought that would be a no-brainer.' Miles appeared horrified that I could even be contemplating not putting the property on the market.

'I probably will sell it; I just need to work out what needs to be done to get it ready for sale.'

At this, he guffawed. 'If the property is as old as you say it is and it's beachfront—'

'Not quite – remember the road in between.' I picked up the butter dish and used my finger to capture the last of the fat.

'I doubt it's a busy road, is it?'

'No,' I conceded. 'It doesn't really go anywhere – the only traffic belongs to people visiting those houses.' I reached for my handbag and pulled out a pen, glancing ruefully at the tablecloth. 'It probably wouldn't do to draw a map on the tablecloth, would it?' He shook his head, a wry grin on his face. 'Lucky I have a notebook then.'

I proceeded to draw a crude map from memory. The road petered out two houses past my aunt's place and was replaced with a park through which wound a path that ran to and along the rock wall that lined the entrance to the river.

'That's the best I can do.' I passed across my drawing.

Miles let out a low whistle. 'A developer would pay good money for a house with that position.' He looked up. 'You could be sitting on a little gold mine there, darling.'

Was that an avaricious glint in his eye? Was he calculating what *he* could do with that money or what *we* could do?

The next course was delivered: a sharing platter consisting of a Thai-style octopus (from East Gippsland) on betel leaves, a mini inside-out spanakopita with whipped sheep's milk cheese on top, and little lamb meatballs with goat's cheese and a green olive in the centre. As the server was telling us the source of each ingredient and details about the accompanying wine, Miles was busy on his phone.

As soon as the server left, Miles pushed his phone across the table. 'Is this the place?'

He'd brought up the Google satellite photo of Beach Road, Whale Bay. Using my fingers to move the map, I followed the road until I came to Rose's cottage, a classic late sixties-early seventies fibro build – examples of which used to be found along every beach on the east coast once upon a time. 'This is it, although it's been painted since I was there last. I remember it being faded green, not yellow.' Using one finger, I pushed the phone back to him.

'How long has your aunt owned it?'

'No idea. My grandparents built it, and Mum and Rose grew up there.' I paused and took a sip of wine. 'Soon after my parents married, my grandparents left Rose in Whale Bay – she would've been about twenty, I suppose – and did the grey nomad thing long before it was a thing.' I chuckled. Rose must've got her free-spirited tendencies from my grandparents. 'They travelled around the country for a few years and eventually settled in Brisbane near where my parents were at the time. They both passed away when I was little.' I struggled to bring a picture of them to mind. 'From what I can understand, they left the house to Rose and Mum, and then when Mum died, her share reverted to Rose.'

'Presumably on the understanding it came to you,' he said. I shrugged in silent agreement. 'How many bedrooms?'

Sighing heavily, I reached for a betel leaf, folding the edges to form a little parcel around the seafood and popping it into my mouth. Realising I wasn't going to answer until I finished chewing, he did the same.

'Three, but there was always a sofa bed in the lounge room in case anyone needed to stay over. Does it matter? We can talk about this later … How about we enjoy this fabulous meal now. That octopus was lovely, and I thought the wine worked well.'

Seemingly oblivious to my growing annoyance, he said, 'All I'm saying is I think it's pointless to talk about making changes or sprucing it up for sale – not if it's going to be picked up by a developer and knocked down.' He popped a meatball into his mouth and chewed thoughtfully. 'It's the land and the position developers are interested in. If you like, I can make some enquiries.'

An image of that sun-filled room came into view again, Rose fluttering about in the kitchen making tea from the lemon balm and lemon verbena she grew in pots in the garden. 'The soil is hopeless here, Clemmie,' she'd say. 'I have to grow all my herbs in pots.' The picture was suddenly replaced by that of a bulldozer, and I shuddered involuntarily. Could I allow that to happen? If the house was still there, surely that meant she'd withstood offers to sell in the past. How would she feel if I sold to a developer now? I snuck a look across the table at Miles, who had his attention back on his phone screen – probably researching recent sales in Whale Bay to determine just how much I could get for the property.

'No need.' I wished Miles would get off his phone – and that we could get off this topic. 'I'll check it all out when we're back and go from there.'

'Actually, darling, I've been meaning to talk to you about that.' He grimaced, cleared his throat and grimaced again. I'd seen it before, and disappointment flooded through my body before he'd even said what he needed to say.

My fork clattered to the plate. 'We're not going to Bali, are we?' This, or something similar, had happened so often over the past few years I'd almost been expecting it, although that didn't make the news any easier to handle.

He seemed both oblivious to my anger and relieved that I'd guessed. 'No, darling, I'm sorry.'

'How is it I'm only hearing about this now? You must've known before this evening?' I almost spat the words out.

'Up until this afternoon, I thought we'd still be able to go, but we've reached a critical point in these negotiations, and I need to be back in Singapore on Monday so will fly out on Sunday morning. The Bali flights and accommodation are fully flexible, so we can get our money back, or you can go on your own if you like.' His smile was overly bright as if he was trying to turn this disappointment into something positive. 'Or why don't you go to Whale Bay instead? The sooner you're up there, the sooner you can wrap it all up. Did your aunt have any other relatives?'

'No, she never married.'

'That means probate will probably come through quickly. If you go now, you can get the lay of the land and an idea of the build quality associated with any developers up there. If they don't think you're in a hurry to sell, you'll be able to demand the best price too.' He crunched down on the spanakopita, little crumbs of flaky pastry falling onto the tablecloth.

Not sure I could answer him without losing my temper, I reached for my wine. It made sense to sell, but the idea of Rose's beach shack flattened by a developer was enough to turn my stomach. But if I didn't sell, what would I do with the house? Whale Bay wasn't exactly a convenient spot for a weekend getaway, and then there was Miles. There was no way he'd support that decision, not when there was a fortune to be made from selling.

As I sat silently seething over the beautiful meal, watching Miles respond to texts or emails or whatever it was that ranked higher than I did in his attentions, I wondered, not for the first time, whether I cared unduly for his support and again not for the first time, whether our relationship had run its course.

CHAPTER FIVE

The rain began almost the minute I left Brisbane Airport and hadn't let up for the entire trip, and by the time I arrived in Whale Bay, I felt as though I'd been on the road for much longer than the two hours it had taken me to drive here.

As I turned off the highway towards Whale Bay, the rain eased and stopped completely as I drove into town. At first glance, nothing had changed. Houses that lined the main road were (mostly) the same as I remembered – some new builds for sure, but mostly the same. Although that retirement village next to the bowling club looked new, as did the blocks of holiday flats on either side of the road closer to Beach Road and the town.

When the road hit the beach, if I turned left, I'd head towards the posh part of town, the houses with absolute beachfront and, rising behind them, The Heights. Instead, I turned right and, needing a bathroom and a coffee – in that order – pulled up in a vacant spot across the road from the strip of shops that lined Beach Road. Unfolding myself from behind the wheel, I stretched, reaching my hands to

the grey sky. After completing a few slow shoulder rolls, I
made my way to the toilet block in the park running along
the beachfront, the sea steely grey under the still leaden sky.

One pressing need taken care of, I crossed the road in
search of coffee, but a quick glance at my watch told me
that would need to wait until after I'd been to the solicitor's,
so with a regretful glance at Beach Brewz (new since I was
last here) and trying not to give into the temptation to walk
into New Moon (where someone other than Rose would
be behind the counter) I made my way to the end of the
block. Judging by the nameplates outside, the double-storey
red brick building was home to the professional services in
town: an accountant, a solicitor, a dentist and pathology lab
on the first floor, the ground floor being occupied by what
appeared to be a collective of allied health professionals.

After climbing the stairs to Margaret King's office, I
left my name with the receptionist, a girl who looked barely
out of her teenage years, settled back into a low blue two-
seater couch and picked up a magazine from the glass-
topped table.

'Mags will be with you in a sec.'

As the girl whose blue-streaked black hair was tied
back into two high pigtails spoke, I smiled, remembering
when I'd gone through the same phase. While Rose hadn't
batted an eyelid at my heavily-kohled eyes and emerald-
painted lips, it had horrified my father when I arrived
home, declaring to my mother that if Rose was going to let

me get around looking like that, he wouldn't be giving his permission for me to spend time with her again and I could spend my last year at school in Melbourne. Not that he would've needed much of an excuse – my father, with his disciplined army career, had never approved of his sister-in-law's free-spirited ways.

I thanked the receptionist and began leafing through the magazine produced by local businesses to showcase the region. Overall, it was the usual blend of real estate agents, homewares and beauticians – despite first appearances, Whale Bay must've expanded in the years I'd been away. Tucked back on page ten, though, a picture caught my eye.

Even though she was older than the last time I'd seen her, it was definitely Rose. Flanking her were two older men and another woman with pinched features who looked to be about my aunt's age. The caption read: "New Moon's Rose Lennox (centre) with Gordon Johnston (far left), Brian Walker (left) and Maureen Peterson (right)."

The headline: "Development not in the cards …" and the story seemed to be about how a group of Beach Road residents – whose spokesperson was my aunt – were standing in the way of development.

"Martin Cosgrove (45), from leading coast development company Cosgroves, had this to say:

'It's a sad day indeed when a group of short-sighted individuals stand in the way of progress. The proposed resort, Finz, will provide high-quality boutique accommodation, support local tourism and place Whale Bay as a luxury destination on the map. This part of the coast has so much natural beauty it should be shared. Their refusal to sell and blocking ofthis development opportunity is both selfish and narrow-minded.'"

I hadn't quite read to the end when my name was called. Reluctantly, I closed the magazine and sat it back on the pile. I was about to hold my hand out to the woman who stood before me, but she continued speaking. 'Clementine Russell … it really is you! You look so different, but I'd recognise those dimples anywhere.'

'It's Clementine Carter now.' I stood back; there was something about the other woman, something in her slight build, her blonde, slightly asymmetrical pixie cut, her green eyes, gamine features … 'Maggie Robson?'

A wide smile broke across her face. 'Maggie King now.'

'You married Justin?' I remembered Justin, tall and gangly and slightly shy. He and Maggie had begun dating in high school. 'What's he doing now?'

'He's an accountant – he has the office next door.'

'Wow.' For a second or two, I had no idea what to say. The last time I'd seen Maggie, she'd been back in town from uni for the long summer holiday. 'I thought you studied music or art or something like that.'

She chuckled. 'That was the intention, but I switched to law, and then a few years after we graduated, Justin and I decided to come back. The old solicitor – remember Dennis

Gillespie?' I nodded. 'He had a heart attack, and we decided that practising here would be our way of giving back to the town, so we did. Besides' —she grinned wryly— 'we couldn't afford a house in Brisbane.'

'Is there enough work here for you?' I still couldn't believe Maggie had ended up in the law, but she probably wouldn't have believed I had done it, too. When I'd walked away from Whale Bay, I'd also walked away from our friendship and now, not for the first time, regretted that. It wasn't her fault I'd ended up in such a mess.

'The town has grown since your day, although you wouldn't have noticed if you just came in from the highway. These days, there's not much space between where Whale Bay ends and Sunrise Point begins, plus the communities in the hinterland have grown, so there's plenty of work – almost too much work at times for one person.'

'And you had a family?'

If it was at all possible, her smile grew wider. 'Yes, we have two kids – one of each. Our eldest, Tyson, is a police constable here in town, and you met our daughter out there.'

'The receptionist?'

She nodded. 'Susie – she's nineteen and prefers to be known as Siouxsie these days – with an "x" like in Siouxsie and the Banshees. We go along with it even though Susie and Siouxsie sound the same. It's only the spelling that's different.' Maggie rolled her eyes.

'I can hear you, you know,' Siouxsie called.

Her mother ignored the interjection. 'She reminds me a bit of you – the last time I saw you, your hair was dyed as black as hers although yours was streaked green if I remember rightly. I used to think you had mermaid hair – in fact, we used to joke that you must be part mermaid with the amount of time you spent in the water.'

My breath hitched in my throat as I realised who the mermaid was in the dream I'd been having – it was me. No wonder she'd reminded me of someone. But what did that mean? Was the younger me beckoning the older me back to Whale Bay? And if so, why?

'Clem?' Maggie had an expectant look on her face.

'I'm sorry. What were you saying?'

'I was asking whether you still swim.'

'Not as much as I used to although I still do laps at least three times a week. I haven't swum in the ocean, though, for years.' Probably not since I was last here.

'Rose said you're a solicitor too?'

'Yes, I'm a family lawyer in Melbourne.' I still couldn't get over the fact that Maggie Robson had ended up back here. She'd always wanted to be in a rock band – and as a teenager, had the attitude to match – yet here she was, a lawyer married to her childhood sweetheart and back in her hometown with a couple of kids.

As if she knew the direction my thoughts had gone, Maggie smiled wryly. 'I know. I would've been the last person you expected to turn out so respectably.'

'I wouldn't have put it quite that way—' I began.

At the counter, Siouxsie scoffed. 'Well might you scoff, Siouxsie, but I'll have you know I used to be quite the rebel in my younger days, didn't I, Clem?'

The girl rolled her eyes in much the same way her mother had moments before.

'You should've seen her.' I chuckled. 'The spitting image of Stevie Nicks – all blonde hair, floaty white dresses and black Doc Martens.'

This time when Siouxsie's eyes rolled, Maggie reached for my elbow and led me into her office. 'Take a seat. Do you want a coffee?'

'Please.' My exaggerated slump illustrated just how badly I needed one.

'Siouxsie, can you please duck up and see Finn? What's your order?'

'A long black, please – double shot in a regular cup.'

Maggie's eyes widened at my order. 'You obviously need your caffeine!' To Siouxsie she said, 'I'll have one too. You can phone it through and get him to put it on my account; he knows my order.' Once Siouxsie had left, Maggie said, 'I'll leave the door open in case anyone comes in – not that I think they will.'

'Finn?' I asked.

'Finn Marella – he runs Beach Brewz – did you see it? It's next to New Moon. I don't know what the zed is about on Brewz, but it seems to be a thing now, putting zeds where they don't belong.'

As she chatted, the years fell away and we were sixteen again and listening to music in (usually) my bedroom, lolling about in beanbags or on cushions on the floor, talking about our dreams and plans. Maggie with Justin and me with … I pushed him back where he belonged – in the past.

'Did you ever hear from Nick? After, you left …' Maggie's eyes drifted away from mine to the paperwork on her desk.

I didn't pretend to misunderstand her. 'No, as you know, after Mum died, I didn't come back. Rose said he'd tried to contact me, but I asked her not to tell him where to find me. By the time I was ready to talk to him, he'd left town.' Determinedly, I pushed the memories back where they belonged. 'Do you know what he's doing these days?'

She shrugged an overly casual shrug that wasn't casual at all. 'He left not long after you did. Word was that his father sent him away to come to his senses once he found out about you two. It backfired on him, though. Nick was always supposed to take over the business but didn't want anything to do with it. Last I heard, he was up in Cairns – married, I think. He hasn't been back in years.'

I lifted a shoulder in the same casual way to let her know I didn't care what he was up to and that I'd noticed how she'd narrowed her gaze, looking for my reaction. 'I've barely given him a thought.'

She nodded as if she believed me. 'Obviously you married, though.' At my blank look, she added, 'Your surname is Carter now.'

I screwed my nose up. 'Briefly – a university romance that should never have gone any further. We were both too young and rebounding from relationships that had gone wrong, but by the time we'd worked that out, it was too late. He cheated on me with his ex, and it all got very messy – mainly because we were both to blame and knew it. They're married now and, from all accounts, happily.'

'I'm sorry to hear that.' The sincerity in her small nod and tight smile made my heart clench. 'Are you in a relationship now?'

'I am. His name is Miles, and he's a senior partner in the firm I work for. He's in corporate law, though, acquisitions, mergers, big-ticket stuff. We've been together for seven years, and before you ask, we've never married, and we don't have children.'

The front door opened, and Siouxsie was back with coffees.

'You're my saviour.' I gratefully inhaled the aroma. 'I've been hanging out for this.' Without taking the lid off, I took a sip, savouring the full-bodied brew. 'Your Finn knows his way around coffee beans.'

Siouxsie and Maggie exchanged a glance and a wicked grin. 'According to rumour, that's not all he knows his way around,' said Maggie.

As I raised my eyebrows at Siouxsie, she said, 'Don't look at me – he's way too old for me … he'd have to be at least forty.'

I coughed as the coffee met a surprised laugh.

'He's not too old for you, though,' Maggie said meaningfully.

'Except that I'm attached,' I reminded her with a laugh.

'I'll leave you to it.' Siouxsie chuckled and shut the door behind her.

'Yes, we probably should get onto business,' Maggie said, sobering instantly.

'What can you tell me about how Rose died? All Dad said was that she was found dead and that it was an accident.'

'Yes, a terrible accident. I'm sorry it took so long to let you know. Your father was listed as next of kin, and it took some time to track him down. Rose was very clear about her funeral arrangements – a private cremation with a separate memorial that she didn't want to be held until you could be present.' Her tone softened. 'She missed you, you know, and she was proud of you, but she also understood why you stayed away.'

I swallowed hard in the face of her scrutiny. 'The memories … I should have … it was selfish …' I blinked as hot tears threatened to escape.

Maggie reached out and placed her hand on mine. 'She understood, Clem. She really did. It's why she left it to you – the house and the shop – she knew she could trust you.'

I frowned. 'The house and the shop?'

'Yes, she'd bought New Moon … you didn't know?'
I shook my head. 'Sally – you remember Sally, of course?'
She didn't wait for my answer. 'Anyway, she had breast
cancer, and after she passed, Noel was ready to sell it to
Martin Cosgrove. Cosgroves had bought the bait shop and
turned it into a posh homewares store – sort of Hamptons
meets Noosa style … you'll see it later – and Martin wanted
to buy New Moon and Beach Brewz too. There was talk
he wanted to open a fine dining restaurant – Martin is all
about attracting the big money. Rose said she'd let the store
go to a Cosgrove over her dead body so she made an offer
to Noel, who was happy to accept it. She paid a lot less
than what Martin was prepared to pay, but Noel was happy
it would be staying in the family, so to speak. In any case, it
gave him enough to move down to the Sunny Coast and be
with his kids.' A wicked grin spread across her face. 'Martin
was furious.'

'Martin was always one of those boys born believing
they're entitled to whatever they see.' He'd learnt that from
his father. 'Is his father still on council?'

Maggie screwed up her button nose. 'Yes, Ray's the
mayor now, still struts around town like he owns the place
– although, to be honest, some would say they're certainly
heading that way – and he and Paula still live in the big
house on the beach. Martin took over Cosgroves from his
father about ten years or so ago, although old man Cosgrove

still pulls the strings. Martin and his wife – he married Kylie Lindsay …' Maggie laughed at the look on my face. Kylie Lindsay had been my nemesis – blonde, leggy, skirt up to her bum, and another one with an inflated sense of entitlement. A similar age to Maggie and me, she'd always seen me as competition, even though we moved in different circles.

'They have the biggest of the McMansions up on Nob Hill and consider themselves the Crown Prince and Princess of Whale Bay,' Maggie continued.

'I bet they do. Her father was on council too, wasn't he? He had a tourist boat, didn't he?'

She nodded. 'Bob was one of the first to jump on the whale tourism bandwagon when it began in the late eighties and early nineties. He still owns the biggest boat in the whale fleet, although he's pretty much retired these days, so Michael runs it now. He married Lauren Walker, you know. Anyway, Bob Lindsay and Ray Cosgrove are tighter than ever, so Michael and Martin are too … which is a pity as Michael was always one of the good guys.'

'According to the article I was just reading in the local magazine, Martin wanted to buy Rose's house?'

'Yes, and her neighbours' places as well. When you walk along Beach Road, you'll see how some houses have been sold up and replaced with the type of property that has always been at the posh end of Beach Road. There are also a couple of blocks of holiday units, although council has limited them to no more than two storeys. That's why

Martin wants Rose's place and the other ones between there and the park. They've recently managed to change the zoning, so Martin's plan is to build a massive resort – one of those built in a U-shape with the pool facilities at the centre and resort shops and a restaurant or pub on the street front. Finz they want to call it – with another zed on the end.' She grimaced at the thought. 'I know it's progress, but you can't tell me there's nothing dodgy going on when the councillors lobbying for the zoning change happen to be the same ones who bought the vacant block in Wharf Road backing onto the Walker place and stand to make a fortune from developing it.' She shook her head in disgust. 'Justin and I cheered when Rose and the others held firm even though we all knew it was just a matter of time before one of them died and their beneficiaries sold it off. It would only take one and they'd all fold.' She lowered her eyes to the paperwork on her desk as if she just realised the implications of what she'd said. 'And now Rose has died, and you'll probably sell.' She lifted her eyes and met mine, the accusation hanging between us.

'I don't know.' She didn't need to know that was what Miles thought I'd do or what my father also had assumed I'd do when I'd spoken to him about it over lunch yesterday.

'I wish a long-lost relative would die and leave me a house by the beach,' my stepsister Fern had said, casting a mournful look at her husband. 'It's unfair that you've got it when you don't even need the money. After all, it's not as though you have children to educate and you and Miles are raking it in.'

Knowing how Fern always thought other people had easier lives than hers, I'd gritted my teeth and counted to ten. 'I haven't decided whether I'll sell.'

Dad had given me a strange, indecipherable look. 'I'm sure you'll do what you think is best.'

Despite telling Miles and my father I wasn't sure what I'd do with the property, the truth was, I couldn't see an option other than selling. That was, however, before Maggie had mentioned that Rose had been determined not to sell to Cosgroves. How could I, in all conscience, go against her wishes?

'I'll see what offers are on the table and weigh them up against all the information once I have it.' Hope fell from Maggie's face, and I cringed.

'Of course,' she said. 'That makes sense.' She thumbed through the paperwork.

'Besides, what would I do with a house and a shop in Whale Bay?' Even as I asked, I wondered why her opinion still mattered.

'Absolutely. Good decision. Good decision …' She rifled through the documents. 'I'll just need a few signatures from you …' All the friendliness had gone from her manner, and Maggie was now strictly business.

'Maggie … I'm sorry.'

She nodded briefly and passed me a document. When it became clear she wasn't saying more, I picked up a pen and skimmed through the will. It was straightforward – whatever Rose had would come to me. Somehow, that only made me feel worse. When she'd written this, had she thought I'd come back? Would I be letting her down if I sold? Miles would tell me it didn't matter. He'd probably point out that she was dead so wouldn't know one way or the other. I signed where Maggie indicated and completed my account details.

'The transfer documents need to be lodged, but we don't need to go through probate, so I'll begin all of that. Your name has always been listed on the paperwork for the shop, so there's nothing we need to do there.'

My mouth fell open. 'What?'

She looked up, her expression softening again. 'Rose insisted your name be on the paperwork for the shop – said that way, if anything happened to her, there'd be nothing to stop you from immediately taking it over … if you wanted to, of course.'

'But…' Shaking my head, I closed my mouth. What could I say? That I already had a career? What would I do with a shop? How could I manage it from Melbourne? Rather than contemplate any of that, I brought the focus back to Rose. 'How did she die?' I asked. 'No one has told me how she died.'

Maggie sat upright, a slight frown creasing her

forehead. 'They haven't?' I shook my head. 'Well, it was a tragic accident. Her neighbour, Gordon, found her lying on the grass in the backyard.' The final image in my dream flashed before my eyes, and I gripped the arms of my chair. Maggie didn't seem to notice. 'They think she'd been up a ladder – probably cleaning out the gutters – and fell … The ladder was lying nearby. She wasn't found until the next morning, so she'd been lying there overnight. Martin Cosgrove, of course, said that was why she shouldn't have been living there alone … Clem, are you alright?'

It was the thought of Rose, who had cared so much about other people, being alone when she died that brought me undone, and once the first tear had snuck out, no amount of blinking would keep the others at bay.

Maggie was quickly out from behind her desk and crouched by my side, her hand stroking my arm. 'I'm so sorry, Clem. If it's any comfort, the pathologist said she died quickly and hadn't been conscious and waiting for help.'

Sniffing, I reached for the box of tissues on the desk and ineffectually dabbed at my streaming eyes. 'Sorry about this. It seems silly to be so upset when we'd drifted apart as we had. It's just … the shock and … the memories.'

'It's not at all silly. You loved her,' Maggie said simply.

'I did.' I forced a tight smile. 'She'll be missed around here.'

Maggie nodded, her own eyes full of unshed tears. 'She certainly will be.' With one last rub of my arm, she stood and walked back to sit behind her desk. 'The house keys are here, and these are the keys to the shop.' She passed across a ziplock bag. 'You're welcome to stay at the house – unless you don't want to, of course.'

The keys felt cold in my hand. 'No, that's fine, I'll stay there. What's happening with the shop?'

'It was shut the day after her death – out of respect – but Nina has been opening it as usual ever since.' At my blank look, she clarified. 'Nina Hart. She's new in town. Blew in about a year ago in her Kombi van, absolutely nothing else to her name, and Rose gave her a job working at New Moon – you know Rose, always a door open for anyone who needs it. She began helping out and doing a few tarot readings, but Rose brought her out of her shell, and she's now a different woman – and the customers love her. She was devastated when Rose died.' Maggie cast me a sly glance. 'I don't know what she'll do if the store closes.'

If her words were designed to inspire guilt, it worked, although I didn't let on. 'I'll drop in and see her after here. After all, it's not as if I can do anything quickly anyway – we still have to wait for the paperwork on the house to be finalised.'

'And plenty can happen in that time. Who knows' — that sly smile was back— 'you might fall back in love with the charms of Whale Bay and decide to stay. If you do, I could always do with a partner. At the moment, if you want a divorce, you have to travel for it.'

Maggie laughed as if it was a joke, but the speculative gleam in her eyes held a different message, one I didn't want to think about. I stood and walked across to the window. The rain had cleared, the sky now a clear blue and the sea almost turquoise. A woman and two children scurried across the street, towels over their shoulders, both children carrying brightly coloured buckets and spades. I could certainly think of worse places to be for the next couple of weeks.

'I don't suppose Justin was my aunt's accountant …' I began.

'He was.' Her voice had brightened. 'Do you want me to arrange for you to see the shop accounts?'

'If you could, yes, please.'

The children had dropped their buckets on the sand and were running down to the water. Yes, there were worse places I could be.

CHAPTER SIX

On the pavement in front of Maggie's, I paused for a second, not so much to get my bearings but to adjust to the light and consider my next move. Seeing Maggie had been a surprise – it hadn't occurred to me that any of my old school friends would still be in town, although perhaps it should have. Just because I'd moved away was no reason to assume they had too.

Before I left the office, Maggie had made me promise to come to dinner at their house that night. 'After all,' she'd said, 'We have twenty-five years to catch up on.' At the time, I'd agreed reluctantly, but now conceded it would be good to catch up with her and her family.

First, though, I had to check in with Nina at New Moon, and only after I'd done that would I go to the house. I told myself that I needed to tell Nina what my immediate intentions were regarding the shop – put her mind at rest for the time being, at least – but deep down, I was avoiding having to walk into Rose's house and see the spot where she'd died. Again, the final image from my dream flashed before my eyes. I blinked to remove it and turned right.

While the town might've looked almost the same as I'd driven in, the shops were completely different. Before I got to New Moon, I'd walked past a homeware store that appeared to be aiming at the upper end of the market, a clothing store that, with its fine Italian linen separates, wanted the same cache of clientele, a hairdresser (Split Enz) and Sundaze which sold hats, towels and swimwear. Making a mental note to drop in later, I continued to Beach Brewz. What was it with the random 'zeds' in this town?

'What can I get for you?' With his unruly curly salt and pepper hair and wearing a well-worn T-shirt sporting the name of a popular surfing brand and a pair of floral board shorts, the man behind the counter looked as though he'd ducked into the café on his way back from the beach and had decided to help out.

'I'll have a regular long black with a double shot, please.' I glanced around the café set up as if it was a beach shack that just happened to be open for coffee. On one wall was a mural with swirls of turquoise and blue, and propped up against another timber-clad wall were brightly painted surfboards.

'You'd be Maggie's visitor?' I returned my focus to him, my heart skipping a beat as I met his eyes, as rich and dark as the beverage he purveyed. 'With an order like that, you must be serious about your coffee.'

'I am … and you must be Finn.' I found myself responding to his flirtatious smile. 'And yes, I am serious about my coffee.'

'Melbourne?' He looked me up and down in a way that from anyone else would feel pervy, but from him, it felt like something else entirely – something I shouldn't be feeling with a boyfriend at home.

'How did you guess?' I countered.

'A combo of your coffee order and the designer pants suit gave it away. But tell me' —I held my breath as he leant forward— 'your name? After all, you know mine, so it's only fair … plus, I need it to write on the cup.'

A laugh escaped me. Those eyes would be lethal on an unsuspecting female; fortunately, my job had made me immune.

'I'm Clem.' I held out my hand, and when he took it, a fizz of sensation ran through my nerves straight to where our hands were joined. Perhaps I wasn't *that* immune.

He dropped my hand immediately, the twinkle in his coffee eyes subdued. 'Rose's niece? The lawyer? You'd be here to sell up, I suppose.'

Yet another wave of guilt washed through me. 'You knew my aunt well?'

'Everyone in town knew your aunt well. I also know that in the years I've been here, you haven't been once to see her.'

'It's complicated,' I mumbled.

'I bet it is,' he almost growled, all flirtation gone.

At his judgemental tone, my guilt turned into something more defensive. 'Obviously you have opinions on things other than almond milk, so come on, let's hear them.' My hands found their way to my hips.

'Alright, seeing as how you've asked … Your aunt spoke about you a lot, about how you were a hot-shot lawyer in Melbourne. Mostly she said she could trust you to do the right thing, yet here you are more than a week after she passed and presumably only in town to sell the house and shop she fought so hard to hold on to.' His eyes blazed into mine, and the heat that suddenly infused my body wasn't only the heat of battle.

'Not that it's any of your business' —my hands remained firmly planted on my hips, my chin jutting forward— 'but the relationship between me and my aunt *was* complicated. She understood why I didn't come back, and I don't give a flying … fig … about whether you do or not.' His eyes widened, and a small smile played around his lips at the flying fig comment. It only riled me more. 'As for why I'm here now? I only found out Rose had passed the other day, so I came as soon as I could. And, for your information, I don't know whether I'll sell up or not, but I'm sick to death of everyone presuming they know more about what I will or won't do than I do. So there.' I cringed inwardly at the immature 'so there', but if I'd expected him to be cowed by my reaction, I was disappointed. Instead, his scowl was replaced by a grin, a wicked grin that went all the way to his eyes so it seemed as though his whole face was grinning. It also felt as though he knew about my reaction to him, which made me say, 'You know what? Forget about the coffee,' and spin on my heels to stalk out, his low, throaty chuckle following me.

Outside, I leant against the dividing wall between Beach Brewz and New Moon and put my hand to my forehead, surprised to feel I wasn't burning up. What had that been about? One thing was certain, I'd need to find somewhere else to get my coffee fix – I couldn't show my face in there again. I didn't need that complication … but oh, his eyes … and the way I felt when they met mine. I almost groaned aloud at the memory. No, this wasn't happening; it was just that my emotions were heightened because I was back in Whale Bay. That's all. Besides, I *was* tired of people presuming they knew best – okay, mainly Miles . How dare a random barista I'd just met (regardless of how cute he was) do the same. It was, however, a pity I'd need to find somewhere else for coffee – his really was excellent.

Sucking in another deep breath, I straightened the white shirt that sat over my black trousers, walked into New Moon and was immediately met with a different kind of assault. The tinkling of the bell as I opened the door and the scent of incense – patchouli and something else … sandalwood? – taking me back twenty-five years. I paused inside the door, my hand to my stomach as if I'd taken a physical blow, memories clouding my brain, blocking my throat, holding me to where I stood.

'Are you alright?'

Unaware I'd closed them, I opened my eyes. The gentle voice and the woman standing before me looked and sounded so like my aunt that I whispered, 'Rose?'

She gently put an arm around my waist and led me to a tattered armchair at the back of the shop. 'You must be Clem.' She handed me a ceramic cup of tea.

I sniffed the yellow liquid in it suspiciously. 'Rose's lemon balm?' I took a sip, the citrus freshness taking me back to her sun-filled room. My eyes filled with tears for the second time that morning, but this time, I didn't try and stop them. I was crying for Rose, for the girl I used to be, the one I left behind here, for the years where I'd allowed my pride and my hurt to separate us.

She let me cry, seeming to understand all the reasons why I cried. Once I finished, she said, 'You called me Rose – why was that?'

I wiped at my eyes with the back of my hand and accepted the tissue she offered, blowing loudly into it. 'You looked so much like Rose did when I first moved here to stay with her.' I sipped at my tea. 'It was in this shop, and she was wearing faded denim dungarees and a little T-shirt under them, just like you are. Even the rubber thongs and your long, brown, curly hair are the same. The shop smells the same as it did then, and the bell on the door … I'm sorry, it sounds silly … and you'll ask why I haven't been to visit if she meant so much to me …'

'Hey,' she said gently, 'I understand. Rose told me all about it.' After a brief break, she added, 'I'm Nina, and I cared very much about your aunt too.'

I smiled tentatively. 'You must be wondering …'

'Whether you'll sell the shop?' I nodded. 'Rose always said if the time came, you'd do what you felt was right.' Her gentle smile managed to simultaneously incorporate understanding, sympathy and patience. 'I trusted Rose, so I trust you to do what you feel is right.' My eyes flicked to hers, looking for a hidden meaning and finding none. 'In the meantime, I'll continue to open the shop as Rose would have – if that's okay with you.'

'Of course.'

I cast my eyes around the shop. Over the years, it had grown into an Aladdin's Cave. Against the back wall between the heavy crimson velvet curtains I assumed led to the reading rooms, still hung a wooden Wheel of Fortune, a little wooden shelf below it containing the readings and affirmations associated with the numbers spun. The ceiling had been painted a dark navy, with pinpricks of gold representing stars in the night sky, while the walls were filled with shelves: one for all things Wiccan – tools, books, amulets – another was devoted to astrology books, and yet another to tarot. Then there were the display cases holding jewellery, crystal balls, pendulums, incense holders and candles.

I stood and pulled the curtains aside. 'Sometimes, I would find myself in here doing my homework.' I let out a short laugh. 'Once, I asked Rose why it was that I could ask the pendulum anything, but it couldn't help me with my maths test.' I shook my head slightly to dislodge the memories and bring me back to the here and now. 'I don't know what I'm going to do with the shop yet,' I said. 'But I'll tell you when I do decide.'

'That's all I can ask for.'

The quiet sincerity in her expression strengthened her resemblance to Rose and made the twin weights of guilt and responsibility sit even heavier on my shoulders.

CHAPTER SEVEN

I retrieved the hire car and drove the short distance up Beach Road to Rose's place. As Maggie had warned me, most of the other properties in the street had been either replaced by larger, more modern houses or now held blocks of holiday units. Nina had told me that Wharf Road, which ran behind and parallel to Beach Road, had gone the same way. 'Although there are shops there now too – behind this strip – a Thai restaurant, another hairdresser, beautician … You'll have to go for a look – you won't believe what they've done to the wharf itself in the last couple of years. Everyone says it's unrecognisable from what it was.'

The only houses that hadn't been developed were the last three in the street – Rose's being the first of them. Gordon Johnston lived in the house next door, and the Walkers had lived in the one closest to the park. Their son Chris was a couple of years ahead of me at school, in the same class as Martin Cosgrove and Michael Lindsay; their daughter Lauren used to be friends with Maggie and me – until she got in with Kylie Lindsay and her crowd. After that, she'd sneer at us. Maureen Peterson – the woman in the photo with Rose – was, Maggie had told me, Brian Walker's sister who had moved up from Brisbane to live with him after his wife had passed.

I pulled up outside Rose's house and sat in the car for a few minutes. The last time I'd seen this house had been through a blur of tears. 'I'm so sorry, sweetie,' Rose had said. 'It's your mother.'

I squeezed my eyes shut against the memory, and when I opened them again, the house looked different. Instead of being painted a faded light green, it was now sunshine lemon, the gutters a contrasting mint, the wooden door and window frames white. The same mint had been painted on the fence posts, although the fencing wire and wrought iron gate had been left unpainted. The detached garage was also painted mint, with white wood trimmings. Someone, though, had had fun painting the wooden garage doors as each paling was a different colour. I imagined Rose would've had her friends around for a barbecue and paint session. 'Pick up a brush and there'll be a sausage sanger in it for you.'

Finally, I managed to get out of the car and swung open the wrought iron gate, smiling as it squeaked the way it always used to. Rose never seemed to get around to oiling it. 'That gate is better than a doorbell,' she'd say.

The concrete path hadn't escaped the paint brush either, although restraint had been exercised and rather than the rainbow I'd expected to see, a line of terracotta led me to the front door. I almost laughed aloud when I saw Rose had never changed the white-painted wrought iron screen door, a very unbeachy reindeer greeting me.

Using the key Maggie had given me, I opened the front door, stepping straight into the hall. To the left was Rose's bedroom – I couldn't face that yet – and to the right was the front room, a large sitting room that ran into the kitchen diner. Tomorrow morning, the sun would fill this room the way it was in my memory; now, though, it seemed old and tired. The multicolour striped jute rug that lay on the floorboards was faded, a few loose bits at either end threatening to unravel; the once charcoal grey sofa bed covered with an assortment of batik throws presumably, I grimaced, to hide stains. In the corner still sat the old rattan papasan chair I used to curl up in with a book. If Rose could afford to buy New Moon, why hadn't she updated her furniture? Even as I asked myself the question, I knew the answer: she wouldn't have noticed it needed updating.

On the old oak dining table were scattered astrology charts, a foolscap-sized notepad and the coloured pens Rose always used when analysing transits. There was also a laptop, and I grinned, realising she must've joined the twenty-first century at some point, even though I'd been asking her to get a Facebook account so I could keep up with her life – and she with mine. 'As far as I can tell, social media isn't very social,' she'd said. 'No matter how long it takes, we catch up eventually. I can wait.'

Balancing on top of her tattered ephemeris was a mug filled with herbal tea. I took a sniff – chamomile – and took it into the kitchen and tipped it down the sink. I did the same with the milk I found in the fridge and tossed the yoghurts, cheeses and the crisper full of vegetables, which were now well past their best, into the kitchen bin, screwing my nose up as I opened that receptacle.

Removing the bag from the bin, I tied the corners and took it out through the back door to the council garbage bin Rose always used to keep behind the garage, breathing a sigh of relief that she was such a creature of habit. Only after I'd dealt with it did I step back and survey the back of the house. Where had she been found?

No one had mown the lawn since she'd died, and weeds were springing up in the raised corrugated garden beds in which Rose grew her vegetables. An assortment of pots near the house contained her herbs: lemon balm, rosemary, thyme, lemon verbena, sage, basil and parsley – the latter of which had bolted to seed.

As I contemplated whether Rose would've captured the seed for next year, the squeaking of the front gate alerted me to a visitor, so I walked around to greet whoever it was.

'It's you then, is it? I'd heard you'd arrived. You've changed your hair colour.'

The white-haired man holding out his hand tentatively to me was Gordon Johnston. He and his wife (until she passed) had been great friends of Rose's.

'It's good to see you, Mr Johnston.' I shook his hand.

He chuckled at my formality. 'I think you're a bit old to be bothering with the Mr these days, Clem. It's Gordon … and it's good to see you.' His welcoming smile fell away. 'It's just a shame it's under these circumstances.'

There it was again, the twinge of guilt. 'I know, and I'm sorry, it's just …'

He smiled his understanding. 'I know, love, Rosie explained how she would always remind you of your mother and this place of that other business with … But I'm sure you don't want to discuss that. She never stopped missing you, though, and wouldn't have a bad word spoken about you.'

I blinked away my tears. 'Can I offer you a cuppa, Gordon? I'm not sure what's in the kitchen, but I'm sure I can find something.'

'Rosie always kept a tin of coffee in for me – I can't be doing with that herbal rubbish she drank – but no thanks. I just dropped by to say hello and see if there's anything you need.' His eyes lingered on the lawn at the side of the house, the lines on his forehead deepening.

'Is that where she was?' I asked.

He nodded again. 'Lying just there she was, on her back, her eyes open.' The final scene in the dream flashed before my eyes again. 'I don't know how I missed seeing her the previous day when I walked past. At this time of the year, I walk most afternoons around four and often call in afterwards if she's in the garden. We'd sit in the swing chair and have a beer together' —he nodded towards the swing chair underneath the old fig tree— 'but I'm sure I didn't see her that day.' His eyes moistened. 'I only went looking for her that morning because she hadn't been out to bring the bins in and she always brought the bins in as soon as the truck had been. Maybe if I'd had a closer look …'

I reached for his arm. 'Don't, Gordon … don't beat yourself up like that. You had no cause to look for her on the ground.'

He smiled gratefully. 'What I don't understand is what she was doing up there. Young Harry had only done the gutters a week or so earlier.' He pursed his lips and shook his head. 'Maybe she was checking them …' As his voice trailed off, I knew he was picturing Rose lying there, her eyes open, gazing sightlessly at the blue sky. He shook his head once. 'I'll leave you to it, but if you need anything, you know where I am.'

'Thanks, Gordon.' I kissed his whiskered cheek, and he left the way he'd come, his hand held up in a wave.

I stood looking at the roof near where Rose had died for a bit longer. If Harry had cleaned her gutters shortly before, what was she doing out here and up a ladder? Nothing I'd learnt about Rose in the few hours I'd been back told me she'd changed markedly, and yet she never used to be the type to check up on someone's work. If they said they'd done it, she'd believe them, and strangely enough when it came to Rose, her faith in human nature was usually rewarded.

As I stood there, a magpie flew down from the fig tree and hopped along the rock border. 'Hello, maggie. Did Rose used to feed you?' The magpie paused and considered me; its head tilted, its beady eye meeting mine before resuming its pecking.

After retrieving my suitcase from the car, I returned to the house and opened the door to the second bedroom off the hall. Back in my day, it had held a single bed, and Rose had used it as a box room, keeping boxes of books and other items that no longer fit in her wardrobe. Having confirmed the room's use was unchanged, smiling wryly, I shut the door again and made my way down the hall to my old bedroom, a lump in my throat as I opened the door to find very little had changed in there either. The surfaces of the white bookcases, which still held the books from my teenage years, some astrology reference books and the old Nancy Drew, Hardy Boys and Trixie Belden mysteries Rose had given me, had only a week or so worth of dust on them. The double bed was made up, a brightly coloured patchwork throw over the top. Sitting on it, I smiled at the mural Rose and I had painted together on the far wall. It had been a cool autumn Saturday afternoon not long after I'd arrived, and I'd been missing my parents.

'You know what we need?' Rose had announced. 'We need some paints and brushes, and we need to paint something beautiful on this wall.'

I'd giggled nervously at the thought of what would've happened if I'd suggested painting a wall at home and said, 'What if it's really bad?'

'If it is, we paint over it again – and again if needed – until we love it.'

So we painted the wall with a giant sun in a light blue sky with a few fluffy clouds looking down at the ocean, a swirl of turquoise and shades of deep blue. Swimming through the waves of green seaweed were rainbow fish – their scales bright silver, pink, purple, blue and green. Rose had drawn an octopus and laughed at how it made it into an octopus's garden – although I didn't get the reference until she played me The Beatles' song of the same name, and we mucked about singing the bit where they gurgle the words. She'd also painted a mermaid with long emerald-streaked black hair, her tail the same colours as the rainbow fish. The mermaid from my dream. Me. When I'd dyed my hair, I must've looked just like her and wondered now whether Rose had thought the same, whether she'd come in here during the years I'd been away and missed the girl I was back then.

I pulled out one of the Nancy Drews: *The Secret in the Old Attic*. Maggie and I used to read these and dream of our own investigations. Rose only needed to say she'd misplaced something before we'd built a case and a vision board around it. I leant forward to sniff at the pillowcase –

either Rose had regular guests staying in here or she'd kept the room visitor-ready.

My stomach rumbled, reminding me I'd not eaten since having a snack in the airport lounge in Melbourne this morning. I glanced at my watch – it was now almost two, so my best hope would be finding a sushi roll or something that would tide me over until dinner at Maggie's. Plus, I needed groceries. Picking up my car keys from the kitchen counter, I headed back out. Once my belly and pantry were satisfied, I could think about my next move – which would include a swim. I was, after all, here on holiday.

CHAPTER EIGHT

The calendar might've said we were in autumn, but the ocean was warm and welcoming as I strode into it later that afternoon. I walked out until I was thigh-high before adjusting my goggles, sinking in and stroking out.

While I hadn't swum in the ocean for years, my body quickly remembered what it needed to do, and my rhythm soon caught up. It helped that the bay – usually protected from waves by the offshore islands and sandbars – was today glassy, the water clear. It was still some time before the top of the tide, and the current was in my favour.

I swam from one end of the beach to the other before flipping myself onto my back and floating, tasting the salt on my tongue, the water gently supporting and soothing my muscles, my breathing slowing.

Turning over, I began swimming back. What was it Gordon had said? Something about how he couldn't believe he hadn't seen Rose's body lying there on the afternoon before he found her. Gordon was as much a creature of habit as Rose had been. He would've walked past at the same time as he did every day, peering into the garden to see if Rose was there pottering about. If she'd been lying on the lawn, Gordon would've seen her – I was sure of that. He also would've noticed if the ladder had been there – either propped against the house or lying on the ground. Gordon didn't see her because she wasn't there when he walked by just before five. And if she wasn't there just before five, what was she doing out there later than that?

Of course! The thought occurred so suddenly that I mixed my in-breath with my out-breath and swallowed a mouthful of water. Sputtering, I stopped, the water here shallow enough to stand while I choked.

Rose always made herself a mug of chamomile tea before she went to bed each night; it had always been the last thing she'd do before turning in. She even did it when I'd visited her in Melbourne hotels. The mug of tea on the ephemeris was almost full, which meant she hadn't long made it, and as Rose always turned in by nine, she must've made the tea close to that time. Plus, she would never use her ephemeris as a coaster for hot tea – I remembered her uncharacteristic glare the one and only time I dared do such a thing. The only reason Rose would leave her tea on her book would be if she'd been interrupted on her way to bed.

I'd assumed, as had Gordon, that she must've fallen from the ladder sometime late in the afternoon and lain there overnight – after all, why would she be up a ladder at nine at night? The simple answer, the logical answer, is that she wouldn't be.

A splash interrupted my musings. First one and then a second golden retriever bounded into the water after a stick. Stick retrieved, they were out just as quickly and over to me for a soggy doggy pat – and a good, drenching shake.

Laughing, I bent down for the stick and threw it up the sand towards the walker I assumed was their owner, both dogs chasing it. As I caught up with them, I groaned; it was Finn from Beach Brewz, and as he was standing right next to where I'd left my towel and beach bag, there was no avoiding him. While I hadn't been at all self-conscious walking up the beach with only my bathers on, now his eyes were on me – and I could *feel* them on me – I felt exposed.

'It's you,' I muttered in greeting, picking my towel up and shaking it out before tying it around my waist in what I hoped was a casual way.

'Hello to you, too.' Finn pushed his sunglasses on top of his head, his eyes dancing with restrained laughter at my discomfort. 'Sorry 'bout my dogs,' he added as they jumped around me, eager for me to throw the stick again. I obliged, taking the opportunity to hide my blushes. Finn pointed to the dog on the right. 'That's Cosmo' —he tousled the other dog behind its ears— 'and this is Beans.'

'Hopefully not with a zed,' I said under my breath.

'What did you say?' His smile told me he'd both heard my comment and hadn't taken offence to it.

'Just that everything in this town has an unnecessary zed at the end of the name, and I wondered whether Beans was the same.' As my towel began to slip down my hips, I tightened it, cursing the warmth that coursed through my veins as his eyes followed the movement.

'Look, Clem, I'm glad I ran into you—' He threw the stick for Cosmo or was it Beans? 'I'm sorry for assuming the worst when we met earlier. Regardless of whether you've been in regular contact – and I'm not judging you either way – you must still be grieving, and I had no right to assume you'd already made up your mind to sell. Nor have I any right to make judgement if you choose to.'

My mouth fell open as he finished. 'Wow, that's quite the apology.'

His smile faltered. 'Now I suppose you're going to say something about how you didn't think men could apologise.' His toes dug into the soft sand, and he reached down to ruffle one of the wet dogs.

I shook my head. 'Not at all. I was going to apologise for the "so there" comment. I'm normally more mature than that.'

'You probably normally don't get judged by random guys in coffee shops either, though.' He'd pulled his sunglasses back down to protect against the late afternoon glare off the water, but I could still see the crinkles at the side of his eyes.

'Or come back to towns I haven't been to for way

too long and have it rightly pointed out that I shouldn't have stayed away so long.' I put my hand to my eyes in a makeshift visor.

'Okay, we can go back and forth with this all afternoon. I've apologised, you've apologised, so let's start over again. What do you say?' He held his hand out for me to shake. 'Hi, I'm Finley Marella, but you can call me Finn. I run Beach Brewz – the coffee shop just down Beach Road. Have you heard of it?'

I wiped my salty, dog-dribble hand on my towel before taking his, again surprised by the jolt of electricity that fizzed where we touched. I pulled my hand from his. Something in the slight quirk to his lips told me he'd felt it too. 'It's nice to meet you, Finn; I'm Clementine Carter, but you can call me Clem. I've heard of Beach Brewz; in fact, I had an excellent coffee from there earlier today.'

'Clementine? Like the orange? Or like the darling Clementine song?' His laughter broke the awareness between us, and I fell in step beside him as he whistled for the dogs and began walking back to the beach entrance.

'My grandfather sang it to my mother when she was a child. He loved the movie, so my parents named me after a song in which the subject drowned in, if I'm not mistaken, a horse trough … It might've been a river, who knows.'

He laughed at the rueful grimace on my face. 'Whereas my name means fair warrior in Scottish Gaelic.' He gave a little so-there head wobble. 'I know, it's quite the combination – my mother is Scottish and my dad Italian. Seriously though, can I buy you a drink tonight?' As I hesitated, he added, 'Not because I fancy you or anything—'

'Oh, I wasn't thinking that you … Umm. I have a … a Miles back in Melbourne, so I can't … I shouldn't …'

'A Miles? Is that like a boyfriend or a partner or, God forbid, a husband?' He seemed to be trying very hard not to laugh.

'He's my partner.' My voice was small, my face on fire.

Finn, however, didn't miss a beat. 'Well, Miles is safe; this would just be a welcome to Whale Bay drink or a get to know you drink or … okay, yes, I fancy you, but I also want to get to know you better.'

I laughed again at the comical expression on his face, the banter – and Finn's admission – warming me.

'Not that I know how long you'll be in town …' His eyes flitted about as he dug himself into a deeper hole.

'In that case, how could I say no? Not tonight, though; Maggie King has invited me for dinner – we used to be friends at school.' We'd reached the park and headed for the beach showers. He ran his feet under the lower tap to clear them of sand, but I held back, not wanting to get under the shower in front of him. Even though I was wearing a swimsuit, it felt too … I didn't want to dwell on how it felt. 'I'm here for a couple of weeks.'

He lifted his sunglasses and his eyes met mine, and

while his were twinkling, I could've fallen into their coffee-coloured depths and quite happily drowned. 'Excellent. Let's make it tomorrow night, then. Come by in the morning; coffee is on me.'

Once he and his dogs had walked off, I stepped under the shower, tipping my head back to rinse the saltwater out of my hair. Finn's banter had distracted me from thinking about Rose and what might've happened to her, but now he was gone, the thoughts came pouring back – and wouldn't go away.

They were with me as I returned to the house and showered, dressing in a knee-length cotton skirt, T-shirt and sandals; they were with me on the walk to Maggie and Justin's – at the other end of the bay. I'd hoped the twenty-minute walk would shift the conclusion I'd come to while swimming, but instead, it had solidified it. No matter which way I thought about it the official explanation of Rose's death made no sense.

Justin King had been a tall, gangly, pimply teenager and had grown into a tall, gangly man. Other than losing the pimples, he'd barely aged; I would've known him anywhere. Back in the day, no one had understood what the rock chick saw in the nerd, but to me, they'd seemed perfect together from the start. Over the years, they'd obviously grown the way long-term couples do – she'd moderated a tad, he'd relaxed a tad, and now they'd met somewhere in the middle.

'It's good to see you, Clem.' Justin kissed me on the cheek, a warm smile echoing his words. 'Just a pity it's under these circumstances.'

'It's good to be back.' I wanted to say how I wished I'd come back sooner, but that would only bring the guilt that I hadn't rushed back again. Instead, I followed him down a hall to a kitchen that opened up through a series of bifold doors to a wraparound timber deck. 'This is nice.'

'Thanks, we love it.' Maggie handed me a glass of white wine. 'We built it about five years ago, didn't we, darl?'

Justin put his arm around his wife's waist and kissed the top of her head. 'About that.'

'Well, it's lovely.' I took a sip of wine, flavours of pear and peach nectar on my tongue. 'As is this wine. Thank you for having me; I know it can be a hassle midweek.'

'We're glad to have you. I couldn't let you spend your first night back in Whale Bay alone, especially after what's happened.' Maggie clinked her glass against mine. 'To old friends – and absent ones …'

I swallowed away the tightness in my throat with another sip of wine. 'Something smells good.'

'It's just a barbecue.' Maggie walked out onto the deck where Justin was now back on tong duty. 'But I hope you're hungry. I wasn't sure whether you'd be vegetarian or gluten-free or anything but figured you'd have told me if you were, so I've done a whipped feta dip, and Justin is chargrilling some cauliflower for us to dunk in that. And you couldn't come back to Whale Bay without having prawns. Then there's some grilled chicken, sausages and a salad.'

'It all sounds lovely. I'm glad I only had a couple of sushi rolls for lunch and went for a swim this afternoon.' I walked over to the edge of the deck and gazed across a clear, blue pool with sun lounges around it. 'This really is perfect; I don't know how you can bear to leave it to go to work.'

'Have a seat and tell us about what you've been doing,' urged Maggie.

Siouxsie came home from the gym just as Justin took the cauliflower off the barbie. Maggie arranged it on top of the feta dip, added some chargrilled lemon and scattered across some pine nuts.

'This is delicious!' The barbecue had given the cauliflower a smoky nuttiness that I hadn't known cauliflower was capable of.

'How long are you staying?' Siouxsie poured herself a wine and settled back into a rattan chair, one long leg nonchalantly thrown over the armrest.

I sucked some feta off my thumb. 'About two weeks, but I'm on leave from work for four so might stay longer. It's been years since I had a proper holiday and being back is … it's nice.' I inwardly winced at how lame that sounded.

'Won't your partner miss you? Miles, wasn't it?' Maggie reached for a prawn Justin had just taken off the barbie. 'This is hot!'

'That would be because it's just come off the grill,' Justin said drolly.

Grinning at their exchange, I said, 'To be honest, I'm not sure he'll notice. He's away a lot.' I lifted my shoulders to let them know it didn't matter, but Maggie wanted to take it further.

'You said you've been together for seven years?' I nodded. 'Have you grown closer over that time or drifted?'

'The latter, I'm afraid.' I began gingerly peeling one of the prawns, licking the juices from my fingers. 'This could be a good thing, me being away. The space will help me decide whether our time is done.'

'It sounds to me as though it is.' Siouxsie unpropped her leg and sat properly. 'If he's away that often and you don't miss him, that is.' She glanced around the table. 'Sorry, was I too blunt?'

'Not at all. Your attitude is quite refreshing.' I popped the peeled prawn into my mouth, closing my eyes against the firm sweetness.

When I opened them again, Justin was smiling. 'They're good, aren't they?'

'Best prawns in Australia.' Maggie reached for another. 'There's a place down at the wharf where you can buy them fresh from the fisherman's co-op downstairs and take them upstairs to eat. With a bottle of white, it's perfect on a sunny day.'

'It sounds it.' I began peeling another. 'I walked past

the wharf on my way here tonight – it's unrecognisable. It used to be just the fish co-op and dive stores, and now there's a pub and a couple of restaurants.'

'That's down to Bob Lindsay.' Justin wiped his fingers of prawn juices on a serviette, picked up his tongs and gave the sausages a turn. 'He bought the wharf a few years back.'

'There was talk that he wanted to get it rezoned for tourist accommodation—' began Maggie.

'What she means to say is that Bob, and Ray Cosgrove, had plans for a posh hotel there – one of those where the accommodation is wrapped around the wharf – but your aunt mustered enough local support to turn up to council and successfully blocked it.' Siouxsie grabbed the plate the feta dip had been on and used a prawn to scrape out the last of it. 'Bob and Ray were furious with her.' She chuckled at the memory. 'You should've seen Ray's face. He went so purple that Mum thought he was going to have a heart attack, didn't you, Mags?'

'I did. Finn Marella – the cute barista we were telling you about earlier—' At the barbecue, Justin smiled wryly. 'Don't look like that, Justin; a girl can window shop, you know. Anyway, Finn handed out leaflets at the café and spoke to pretty much everyone who came in about it. He and Rose organised a town meeting and Finn stood up and said that even though he'd only been in Whale Bay for five minutes, he'd fallen in love with the beauty of it and felt that it was something everyone could enjoy, not just the people rich enough to fork out for high-end accommodation.'

'Wow. No wonder he was so judgemental regarding my intentions.' I grimaced as I recalled the sneer in his voice before heat swept through my body at the remembrance of the blaze in his dark eyes.

'When was this?' Siouxsie leant over and topped up our glasses.

'After I left your office. I called in to get another coffee, and we started talking.' Maggie and Siouxsie exchanged knowing glances; my cheeks were on fire. 'Once he knew who I was, he had a go at me for never visiting. Then he had something to say about how my aunt had trusted me, yet I was obviously here to sell up and move on.'

Siouxsie chuckled. 'I bet he was hot when he was riled.'

'Siouxsie!' chided Maggie.

Siouxsie was undaunted. 'Come on, Mags, you were thinking it too – and check out how red Clem's cheeks are.'

Over at the barbecue, Justin chortled. 'Isn't it fortunate the lighting is so good out here?'

'What did you tell him?' Maggie leant forward, her face wearing an avid expression.

'I told him I didn't know whether I'd be selling up or not. I know people assume I will – I think Miles has already decided what we'll spend the proceeds on—'

'You signed a prenup before moving in together, of course?' Maggie interrupted to ask. 'I only ask because you're thinking of dumping him.'

'Hello, we're both lawyers, and he's a senior partner; of course there was a prenup,' I scoffed. 'But seriously, everyone assumes I'll sell, and it would be easier to do that, but now I'm here? I'm honestly not sure …'

As my voice trailed away, Maggie's gaze narrowed. 'What's happened? Something has happened. You might've cut your hair and changed the colour, but I still know that face.'

I hesitated as I debated whether to talk about my suspicions. Would they think it was ridiculous, or was I projecting my guilt for my lengthy absence onto a far-fetched theory? Besides, it made no sense to me, so it would be unlikely to make sense to anyone else.

Justin placed a tray of meat on the table. 'You might as well tell them, you know. You think Mags is bad, you haven't contended with Siouxsie yet. She'll keep going until she gets it out of you, so my advice is to capitulate and move on.'

Maggie removed the covers from the salads. 'Go on, just tell us.'

'No, it's nothing. It's just that hearing how Rose had actively fought to keep both her house and New Moon out of the clutches of the Cosgroves, I don't know how I can sell either.' I forced a smile. 'It would feel as though I'd betrayed her, but nor do I know how I can hold on to them. I guess I just have a lot to think about, is all.' I shrugged one shoulder. 'I know she's gone, but she feels so close still.'

Maggie smiled gently. 'Of course she does. You take your time, Clem. Rose trusted you to make the right decision – for you.'

I smiled gratefully at her and raised my glass to the sky. 'To Rose.'

With solemn faces, the others did the same. 'To Rose.'

CHAPTER NINE

Although it had been strange being back in my teenage bed, I'd slept surprisingly well. As if the dream world was satisfied I'd gotten the message, neither the mermaid nor the tarot cards visited via my dreams, although this time, my dreams were full of magpies and ladders. What was it the dream was trying to tell me? Despite this, for the first time in weeks, I'd woken refreshed and with the sun and the birds.

The light had filled the front room the way I'd remembered, and over the road, the sun cast a golden beam across the ocean as it said good morning, beckoning me in. I didn't need to be asked twice and quickly donned my bathers, a long T-shirt I'd found in my bedroom, a pair of rubber thongs, and shoved my phone, goggles, and keys into a hand-sewn tote hanging off the back of a chair, slung a towel over my shoulders and was out the door.

An hour later, I sipped my post-swim coffee and grimaced as the burnt bitterness hit my tongue. Ugh. No matter how good the sourdough I'd just purchased, coffee from the baker's wouldn't cut it. Maybe I should swallow my pride and venture back into Beach Brewz? After all, we'd both apologised for our respective behaviour, and he had said coffee was on him, but would me turning up in my swimmers (again) be construed as ... well, inviting more of that heat-filled eye action? At least this time, I'd covered my bathers, although the T-shirt was damp and my legs bare.

Shaking away the thoughts and with more confidence than I felt, I strode into Brewz.

'Morning, Clem, good swim?' Finn called from behind the coffee machine.

My face flamed as I realised that from that position, he would've seen me toss the rejected coffee in the bin. 'Excellent, thank you.'

'It's okay, Lainey.' He smiled at the girl behind the counter. 'I've got this one – it's on the house. She'll need something to take away the taste of Bron's coffee.' He gave me his full attention. 'Bron's an incredible baker, but her coffees —' He shook his head. 'Let's just say even she comes here for coffee.' He inclined his head towards one of the round tables on the deck overlooking the beach. 'Take a seat, and I'll bring it over.'

'No need.' I waved his offer away. 'I'll take it away. I've ... ummm ... I've got a lot to get through this morning.'

'Really?' He raised an eyebrow, not fooled by my performance.

'I need to tackle the house.' The defensive tone

creeping into my voice was not pleasant. What was it about this man that made me feel so uncomfortable? 'I wasn't able to face going into Rose's room yesterday, so I guess that needs to be done. And the lawn needs mowing, although I haven't yet worked out where Rose kept her lawnmower. Then there's—'

Finn must've picked up on the growing overwhelm in my tone and gently shook his head. 'Don't take on too much before you're ready,' he warned. 'As for the lawns, Harry Glover did them for Rose – he's the person people call if they want odd jobs done. He's a chippie, sorry, carpenter, by trade, but his priority is fitting his work around surfing, not fitting surfing around work, if you get my drift. In fact, if you hadn't wasted time getting coffee from Bron this morning, you would've seen him.' His grin was cheeky. 'He's in every morning.'

'Okay,' I conceded. 'You've made your point. I'll be getting my coffee from here each morning.'

'Excellent decision.' When he winked, it brought that stupid smile to my face.

When I strolled back from the beach with my second coffee, it was to see a young man with over-long bleached blond hair, a deep tan and wearing a faded T-shirt and board shorts at work in the garden with a whipper-snipper. At my approach, he turned the machine off and removed his headphones. 'You must be Clem; I've heard a lot about you

– all good – from Rose.' He gave a sunny smile I imagined would make any female heart under the age of about thirty swoon. 'I'm Harry,' he added as an afterthought. 'I do odd jobs for Rose – lawns and gardening mostly.'

He didn't look to be the handshaking type, so I smiled and said tentatively, 'Hi Harry.'

The grin faded. 'I'm sorry about what happened to Rose – she was one of the good ones, you know? She gave me a go when no one else in town trusted me – I got into a bit of trouble at school – but she saw the good in me.' He shook his head sadly. 'As Gordon said, they broke the mould when they made Rose. There's not many like her out there.'

'No.' The word squeezed past the now-familiar lump in my throat. Would I ever learn to live with the guilt of my absence? Somehow, it only made the loss so much worse. 'There's not.'

'I used to do Rose's lawns for her and thought it would be getting a bit ratty here by now so figured I'd just tidy it up a bit and run the lawnmower over.' Uncertainty clouded his face. 'If that's okay, of course.'

'Absolutely. I'm happy for you to continue with the same arrangement you had with Rose for the time being. You'll just need to let me know how much she used to pay you.'

With a thumbs up, he popped his ear protection back on and resumed his work.

Taking my coffee to the swing chair under the fig

tree, I slumped into it and tipped my head back to look up into the labyrinth of branches, the early morning sun snaking through, sending shafts of gentle light along its path. Sipping at my coffee, my gaze wandered, as I knew it would, to the piece of lawn where Gordon found Rose. It was overly long, yet I imagined I could still see the indent left from her body. The night she died, the grass would've been short, drops of dew clinging to the tips.

'What happened to you, Rose?' The words slipped out in a whisper. I was unsure whether I was hoping for some sign, even though, logically, that wasn't how these things normally worked. Rose had always believed in signs, though.

Over near the rock-lined border, a magpie pecked in the grass. Pausing, it raised its head and warbled its song. What was that old rhyme Rose used to say whenever she saw a magpie?

One for sorrow, two for joy, three for a girl, four for a boy, five for silver, six for gold, seven for secrets to never be told, eight for a wish, nine for a kiss, ten a surprise you should be careful not to miss.

A second bird flew down and landed on one of the rocks. Sorrow then joy? I laughed out loud at my fancy and watched the birds peck around the lawn for their breakfast until the sound of the whipper-snipper drew closer and frightened them off.

Taking that as my cue to move too, I gave Harry a wave and headed inside.

After a change of clothes and breakfast of fruit, yoghurt and a handful of locally made muesli I found in the pantry, it was time. My hand paused on the doorknob, the metal cold and hard against my palm. Inhaling deeply, I turned it and flung the door open before I could change my mind.

Rose's bedroom was almost exactly as I remembered it although she had freshened up the walls, which were now an almost jacaranda blue, the wooden trims around the filmy, white-curtained windows and the door the same mint that had been used outside. I sat on the bed's edge and cast my eyes around the room. Dust motes played in the stripes of light that filled the space, and on hooks behind the door were her batik dressing gown and several scarves. It was as if she'd come back through the door with her mug of tea any minute.

On the wall behind the wrought iron bed, the frame of which had been painted blue, hung a macrame mandala-style dreamcatcher. Peeking out from under the pillow was the faded T-shirt that had habitually been her night attire, and on the white-washed bedside table sat three paperbacks – all mysteries from the council library and all with folded corners marking the spot. Rose always had a few books on the go simultaneously. 'That way, I can decide what I'm in the mood for reading,' she'd say. 'I can always pick up where I'm up to within a page or two. Although,' she'd say with a laugh, 'sometimes I don't even pretend to keep up – a bit from this, a bit from that makes for a rather lovely, chaotic story.' Smiling at the memory, I made a mental note to find out what day the library bus came through Whale Bay so I could return them.

I pulled the once-pink T-shirt out from under the pillow and buried my head into it, my throat closing and my eyes burning as Rose's favourite essential oil mix – a combination of neroli, orange and coriander – filled my senses. She always blended her own and used to add it to everything – body wash, shampoo, even the water she used as an ironing spray. It was warm, upbeat, cheerful and a little spicy all at once – all characteristics I associated with Rose. I folded the T-shirt neatly and replaced it under her pillow, straightening the rose-red and sage patchwork throw she used over her sheets in the summer months.

On the room's far wall stood the antique oak wardrobe and a dressing table I'd helped her to 'upcycle' that last summer. I ran my hand over the surface, feeling the bumps and chips that had occurred in the intervening years.

I opened each drawer without knowing why and did the same with the wardrobe; while I'd need to address the contents of both before I headed home to Melbourne, I wasn't yet ready and wondered whether I ever would be.

Shutting the door behind me, I walked back into the sitting room. Outside, the lawn mower had finished, so I took a jug of cold water and a glass out to Harry, who had removed his T-shirt and tucked it into the back of his board shorts.

'This looks so much better,' I said, pouring him a glass while trying not to notice his admirably flat stomach. 'Thank you.'

'No probs, Clem. Rose always liked her lawn to be looking good.' He sculled the water in one go, so I poured him another. 'Thanks for this. I reckon this is the last of the heat for the year – it starts to cool down a bit after Easter, but it's always ANZAC Day before it's proper cool at night.' He wiped his brow with the back of his hand. 'You'll be gone by then, I suppose.'

'I'm not sure … Probably.' Against the clear blue sky, the grass looked impossibly green. After the grey of Melbourne, it was the colour I noticed most about being back – how everything seemed saturated in colour.

As if he knew the direction of my thoughts, Harry said, 'I bet you don't get skies as blue as this where you're from.'

'Sometimes we do, but Port Phillip Bay certainly bears no resemblance to Whale Bay.' Across the road, the water shimmered blue as if someone had scattered a bag of diamonds across the top. 'I'd forgotten how beautiful it is here.'

'Maybe you should stay then.' Harry poured himself another glass of water.

'Perhaps,' I said noncommittally, my gaze drawn again to the patch of grass where Rose was found.

His eyes followed mine. 'I felt so bad when I heard

she'd fallen off the ladder,' he said. 'Especially if it was something I should've done for her. I'm surprised she managed to move it, though …'

I turned to face him, the hair at the back of my neck standing up. 'What do you mean?'

'The last time I used it was to clean the gutters, and I'm positive I left it leaning against the garage wall. You could never get it into the garage while the car was in there, and Rose couldn't remember where she left the keys.' He drained his glass and poured another. 'I was due to return the day after it happened and finish the garage. I would've finished that day, but the surf was up – king tide, Rose said, because of the super moon – she always knew that sort of stuff. Anyway, like I said, I made sure she wouldn't need it before I left it there.'

'You said you were surprised she managed to move it,' I urged, hoping he didn't hear my impatience.

'Yeah … she broke her right arm a couple of years ago and never recovered full strength in it. She was alright with light stuff, but no way would she have been able to move the ladder on her own.' He pulled his T-shirt out of his shorts and used it to rub the sweat from his brow. 'Someone must've helped her move it, but I still wish she'd rung me, and I would've done it for her. Poor Rose.' He seemed lost in thought for a few seconds, but then the sunny smile was back on his face. 'Anyway, I'll be off – places to be, you know how it is.' He pulled his shirt on.

'Thanks, Harry, and please don't blame yourself. What happened to Rose had nothing to do with you not finishing the garage.'

With a wave, he was off, completely unaware of the havoc his words had created. Rose wasn't alone when she died. That's when the awful alternative hit me. What if what happened to Rose wasn't an accident? What if she didn't fall off that ladder, but somebody wanted to make it look like she did? What if Rose was murdered? My hand pressed into my forehead, but still, the thoughts and what-ifs chased each other around my brain. Heart racing, I paced the lawn, trying to make something that made no sense make sense.

The magpie was back down, pecking about in the rock border, seemingly oblivious to my presence. It lifted its head and stared at me, its beady eye maintaining contact with mine briefly before flying away.

Of course! I pulled my phone from the back pocket of my shorts and selected a number. 'Maggie? It's me, Clem. I'm going to need your help and probably Justin and Siouxsie's. Are you free?'

'Sure, but are you okay? Because you certainly don't sound it.'

'I can't explain now, but I can be there in fifteen minutes.'

CHAPTER TEN

Maggie, Justin and Siouxsie were waiting for me when I burst through the door to Maggie's office.

'It sounded serious, so we ordered coffee.' Maggie indicated the cups lined up on the counter.

'Thanks.' I placed my hands on my hips and caught my breath. While I hadn't exactly run down here – running was impossible in thongs – I'd certainly walked very quickly.

Maggie placed a cup in my hand. 'You look like you need this … my office?'

I nodded and allowed her to lead me through, but when Maggie offered a chair, I shook my head and paced the floor instead.

'Clem, you're starting to worry me.'

Hearing the concern in Maggie's voice, I took a breath and forced myself to stop moving, leaning against the edge of her desk.

'Well …' My gaze went to each of them, then to the coffee in my hand and back again. 'I don't believe Rose was alone when she died.'

Siouxsie's mouth dropped open, and Maggie sputtered on her coffee. Only Justin remained impassive. 'Why do you say that?' he asked.

I let out the breath I hadn't realised I'd been holding. 'The theory is that she fell from a ladder while inspecting gutters, isn't that right?'

Maggie nodded. 'Yes, the ladder was found on the ground near her body, and the wound to the back of her head was in line with a fall of that nature. Why do you think that isn't what happened?'

I began ticking the reasons off on my fingers. 'Because a) Gordon Johnston told me Harry had only cleaned the gutters for her the previous week and Rose was never the type to follow up on people's work. And before you ask, I wondered whether there had been a storm and that's why she needed to check, but I've researched it and the weather had been fine. Secondly, Gordon had called by that afternoon on his usual afternoon walk; he always looks for her and she wasn't on the ground then. Apparently, they often have a beer together in the afternoons.'

Maggie and Siouxsie shared a look, and Siouxsie raised her eyebrows. 'Really? Rose and Gordon? How long has that been going on for?'

'Years,' said Maggie. 'It's more of a friends-with-benefits thing and suits them both.'

I lifted a shoulder. 'Good luck to them, but no wonder Gordon was so upset. Also, while tidying up, I found a full cup of chamomile tea sitting on the ephemeris.' When all three looked at me blankly, I clarified, 'It's a book with all the planetary positions in it for one hundred years. The thing is, Rose only drank chamomile tea at bedtime, and bedtime for her was always around nine. Plus, she'd never put a cup of tea on any of her books unless she was interrupted.'

Maggie chortled. 'I can vouch for that!'

'Go on,' urged Justin.

'So what I want to know is, what was Rose doing up a ladder at nine at night, especially when there was no outside light at that part of the house?' I looked around at the others. 'The answer is, she wouldn't have been. At least not alone … Which leads me to my final point.' I inhaled raggedly. 'I spoke to Harry Glover this morning when he dropped around and did the lawns. He told me he'd left the ladder leaning against the garage wall and that Rose wouldn't have been able to move it herself.'

'Crap.' Siouxsie broke the ensuing silence. 'And if she wasn't alone, why wasn't her body discovered until the next day?'

Maggie reached for her phone and punched in a number, placing the phone on speaker. 'Tyson, we need your help.'

A heavy sigh came through the phone. 'I'm on duty, Mum. Can it wait?'

'I know you're busy, but can you check one thing for me, please?'

'It depends on what it is,' Tyler said slowly.

Maggie looked at me as she spoke. 'Can you please check what the pathologist had to say about Rose's time of death?'

'Seriously? You rang me about that? What does it matter?' Tyson's exasperation came through loud and clear. 'Besides, I don't think I should be telling you this.'

'Please, Ty, it's important. Rose's niece, Clem, is here, and as family, she has a right to know.' Maggie crossed her fingers. 'Clem, tell him you're here.'

'Hi Tyson, it's me, Clementine Carter. Rose was my aunt.' Then, because it all sounded weird, I added, 'It's nice to meet you.'

'It's nice to meet you too, but how do I know it's you?' Another sigh. 'Okay, if it means I can get back to work, I'll look it up. Hang on a tick.' The phone went silent for a few seconds. 'Alright, here we are … The coroner ruled it an accidental death, but you already know that, and the time of death was between eight and ten pm.'

My head tipped forward, and I let out a little breath of relief that my theory wasn't so ridiculous, that I hadn't let my fancy fly away with me. But in that exhalation was also trepidation. What now? The police weren't likely to reopen a closed case with no firm evidence other than a full cup of tea and faith in the work people did for you.

When I lifted my head, Maggie's eyes met mine as she spoke to her son. 'I know it's been listed as an accidental death, but riddle me this: what would a sixty-something-year-old woman be doing up a ladder alone at nine at night? Hmm?'

'Tyson' —I leant forward so he could hear me clearly— 'was a torch found beside her body?'

'Hold on … There's no record of one in the deceased's – sorry, your aunt's – personal possessions … But there was a phone.'

Maggie scoffed. 'A phone? No one in their right mind would climb a ladder in the middle of the night with only a phone torch for light.'

'It was hardly the middle of the night, Mags,' her son retorted.

'Thank you, Tyson,' I said. 'If I came by the station, would I be able to talk to someone? I'd like to know how my aunt died. After all, if the case has been closed, surely I can collect her possessions?'

He hesitated, his voice no longer sounding so sure, but all frustration was gone. 'I'll see what I can do,' he finally said. 'But please don't mention I've told you what I have.'

I sat back in my chair and exhaled. 'Thank you, and yes, it's between us.'

Maggie took back control of the phone and switched it off speaker. 'Thanks, Ty … I know I shouldn't have asked you that stuff, but it was an isolated incident and important … Yes, well, thank you anyway.'

'You shouldn't have compromised him like that,' added

Justin when she hung up.

Maggie waved his words away. 'Don't worry about it; he'll be fine.'

Siouxsie grinned. 'Besides Dad, you know old Ted's always had a soft spot for Mum.'

'Don't tell me Ted Winters is still there?' He'd been a junior policeman when I was a girl.

'He certainly is, in fact I think they'll need to carry him out of that station.' Maggie rolled her eyes good naturedly. 'And that's a good thing. He had a lot of respect for your aunt, so he'll want to know what happened to her.'

'Is now the right time to be reminding you that the file has been closed and they deemed her death an accident?' If Justin was exasperated, he certainly didn't show it, but then he'd had a lifetime to get used to Maggie, and I suspected Siouxsie was cut from the same cloth.

Drawing a deep breath, I got my thoughts in order. 'I'm not saying it wasn't an accident; I'm just saying I don't think it happened the way they say it did. If the file is closed, maybe we need to find out what happened to Rose ourselves.'

'Yes.' Maggie's little chin pushed forward determinedly. 'We'll conduct our own investigation.'

Justin rubbed his hand across his eyes. 'That's what I was afraid of.'

A speculative gleam came into Maggie's eye. 'Are you thinking what I'm thinking?'

Despite the seriousness of the subject, I couldn't help the grin that spread across my face at the memory of our teenage investigations. 'I think I might be thinking what you're thinking …'

She nodded once, decisively. 'What we need is a murder board.'

'Hold on,' said Justin hesitantly. 'Are we now saying Rose was murdered?'

'Heavens no,' exclaimed his wife. 'But whoever had a "suspicious death board"—'

'—or a "doesn't make sense but needs investigating board"?' finished Siouxsie.

'Fair enough,' he said with the resigned tone of a man who knows when he's beaten.

'Whatever we're calling the board, that's what we need.' I stood and slid my phone back into the pocket of my shorts. 'My place tonight?'

'You're on.' Maggie held up her coffee cup and knocked it against mine before raising it to the ceiling. 'Don't worry, Rose. We've got this!'

As I dabbed at the corner of my eyes, I said more softly, 'We'll find out what happened to you, Rose. I promise.'

CHAPTER ELEVEN

The last time I'd been in this police station had been the one and only time I'd attempted shoplifting.

As I was shown into Senior Sergeant Ted Winter's office by a young constable who introduced himself as Maggie's son, Tyson, I couldn't help wondering whether he remembered the incident as well as I did.

He stood and held out his hand for me to shake. 'Clementine Russell! It's good to see you all grown up.' He softened his voice. 'I'm sorry about your aunt – Rose Lennox was one in a million.'

'Thank you, she was.' My throat tightened as he expressed his sympathy.

'I still remember that day she marched you and young Maggie Robson in here over some nicked nail polishes.' He sat back in his chair and laughed, his hands on his expansive belly. 'I must've been the same age as young Tyson is now, and let me tell you, it was a struggle not to laugh. I bet you never did it again, though.'

'We certainly didn't! I've always remembered how you

told us that to us, it was just cheap nail polish, but to the owners, it might've been the day's profits, and someone who'd been saving for it would be disappointed to find it gone. It certainly taught us about consequences – and working for what we wanted.'

'Well, there you go, that's my job done,' he said with a double pat on his stomach. His smile fell. 'Tyson tells me you want to see the file on Rose.' He hesitated. 'He seems to think you're worried it wasn't an accident.'

I drew in my breath and recounted my reasoning. 'If Rose had intended to go up that ladder for any reason, she would've taken a torch with her.' I paused. 'Then there's her tea. The way she left that indicates she'd been interrupted on her way to bed; it's as if she'd just set it down on a surface on her way out the front door.'

'What makes you think it was the front door and not a disturbance out the back?' Ted had picked up a pen and tapped it against the folder on his desk with Rose's name on it.

Relieved that he seemed to be taking me seriously, I warmed to my subject. 'Because she'd left the tea on a book on the dining table. If she'd been on her way out the back door, she would've left it on the kitchen counter. Besides, that front gate has always squeaked louder than any doorbell. Rose was a creature of habit; somewhere between eight-thirty and nine, she'd make her tea, take it to her room, get changed and go to bed. I'm not sure what clothes she was wearing when she was found, but her night clothes were still under her pillow. But there's more—' I hesitated, knowing exactly how far-fetched this would sound. 'Harry Glover says he left the ladder against the garage and not against the house, and he doesn't think Rose could've moved it on her own.'

Ted nodded slowly, his frown deep. 'Someone else could've moved it for her.'

'Perhaps,' I conceded. 'But who?' My eyes strayed to the folder on the desk. 'Who signed it off as accidental? Was there any investigation?'

Ted cleared his throat and flipped open the folder. 'Because it was an unexplained death, one of the detectives from the Sunny Coast came up. It was pretty straightforward though – Gordon found Rose with the ladder lying beside her, a head wound commensurate with a fall like that …'

'I understand. Can I see the scene photos?'

The furrows in his brow deepened. 'Are you sure you want to?'

I swallowed hard. 'Yes, I am.'

He nodded reluctantly and passed over three photos. The first was a close-up of Rose lying on her back on the lawn, her eyes gazing sightlessly at the sky. It was so like the final image in my dream that I had to squeeze my eyes shut for a second, willing my heart to slow. The second showed the ladder lying beside her, and the third was a close-up of her head wound, something I quickly passed back to Ted.

Tyson knocked on the door. 'Senior … excuse me, sir, but can I borrow you for a second?'

'Excuse me, Clem. Will you be right here?' He pushed the folder across to me with a wink.

As soon as he was gone, I whipped out my phone and took photos of the scene images and the pathologist's report. By the time he was back in the office ten minutes later, I'd flicked through the file and pushed it back to his side of the desk.

With a wry smile, he closed the folder. 'Sorry about that. Do you have any more questions for me?'

'No, thank you. I'm good. Tyson mentioned there were some personal items?'

'Yes, I have them here.' He passed me an evidence bag containing a phone and a tarot card. At my raised eyebrows, he added, 'The card was found in her dress pocket.'

'Hang on, so she was up a ladder with her phone for a torch wearing a dress and' —I consulted the notes I'd made from the file— 'rubber thongs?'

'It would seem that way.' He leant forward, his forearms on the table, a serious look on his face. 'Look, I'm not saying that mistakes might've been made here, but I can't reopen a closed investigation based on a hunch, a cup of tea and the word of a handyman who's had his own brushes with the law' —he held up his hand as I would've opened my mouth— 'no matter how much sense it's making to me. Get me more than that, and I'll look into it, okay?

Your aunt did a lot of good for this town, so if her niece wants to make sure all boxes have been ticked, I don't have a problem with that.' My throat tightened in gratitude as he continued speaking. 'Not, of course, that we ever had this conversation. Just do me a favour and tread carefully, eh?'

'Understood.' I stood to leave. 'And thank you.'

'No problems, Clem.' He stood and shook my hand before seeing me out. 'Has Martin Cosgrove been in touch yet?' I shook my head. 'He will be, and my advice is to watch that one – he's learnt too well from his father and is slippery as a snake.'

'I'll bear that in mind.'

Miles called when I was walking to get lunch in one of the cafés at the wharf. 'Hello, darling; I can't talk for long, but just checking that everything is going as well as can be expected up there. Have you found out yet whether probate is required?'

I held the phone away from my ear so he wouldn't hear my scoff of disbelief as he jumped straight into the subject of the money. 'Hi yourself. Yes, it's good to be back. I've even caught up with some old friends already.'

'Well, don't get too comfortable – you're only there to sell up, after all. I know you can't settle until the legals have been completed, but there's nothing stopping you from doing the deal.'

'Actually, Miles' —my shoulders stiffened with anger— 'I'm not sure I will be selling.'

In the buzz at the other end of the phone, I thought I heard a woman's voice and then Miles's muffled. 'You can't be serious. That's all you're there for.'

'I'm deadly serious. I'll listen to any offers, but as it stands, I haven't decided what I want to do. The idea of staying here for the entire four weeks I'm off work is starting to appeal to me.'

Silence again. 'But what about me?'

'What about you? You're never home, so it won't make any difference. Besides' —I forced moderation into my tone— 'I think this is a good opportunity for us to take some space and decide what we each want.' I'd reached the wharf and wandered over to where the tourist boats left from, silvery school fish darting here and there around the pier as the sun's beam lit the green water. 'You have to admit we've drifted apart over the last few years, and honestly, I can't remember why we're together.'

'Are you saying what I think you're saying? If so, you could've chosen a more appropriate time to discuss it.' I wasn't sure whether he sounded upset or annoyed or simply inconvenienced.

'I'm saying exactly that, and given you're never home, there is no appropriate time. Anyway, I'm sure you're busy, so let's leave it for now, but that's where my mindset is.' At the next pier, a dive boat was preparing to go out, the occupants settling into their seats with much excited chatter.

'And I don't get a say in it?' His tone softened. 'Listen,

darling, I know you're unsettled being away from work and with your aunt and all that, so I'll overlook this little blip and talk to you in a few days.'

Without letting me get another word in, he hung up, leaving me seething. Deciding I'd deal with Miles later, I chose the pub at the far end of the wharf and ordered a Vietnamese-style salad and a beer.

As I sipped at my beer and waited for my salad, I pulled out the plastic bag Ted had given me with Rose's phone and the tarot card enclosed. Turning the card over in my hand, I pondered the significance. The Fool. Rose always said the Fool card was like the new moon in astrology – a time when there's no light, but also a time for new beginnings, when you need to take a step and trust it. What else had she said? That the Fool could symbolise a young person, someone starting a journey, doing something rash. But why did she have the card in her pocket when she went outside? Or was it in her hand? Had she been completing a reading when she was interrupted? She'd often create a spread of cards and let it sit while contemplating the meaning. There had been cards on the dining table, but I hadn't noticed if they were in a spread.

Pulling her phone from the bag, I tried to turn it on, but the battery was dead – no surprises there. Making a mental note to charge it when I got home, I was about to open the photos I'd taken of the police file when a shadow loomed over my table. Standing there holding a beer and wearing a million-dollar smile and the latest in Queensland business-casual wear was Martin Cosgrove.

'Clem, I heard you were back in town.' Without waiting for an invitation, he pulled out the chair opposite me and sat down. 'I'm glad I ran into you; I wanted an opportunity to give you my condolences for your aunt. She'll be missed.' His words might've been of sympathy, but his mouth wore a smug half smile.

'Thank you.' Wariness tinged my voice.

'You'd be here to wind up her estate, I imagine,' he said, overly casually. 'If you need any help, let me know. In fact,' he added as if the thought had just occurred to him, 'you're probably not aware that your aunt was about to agree on a price to sell me the cottage before she passed away …' The lie tripped off his tongue easily, and if I hadn't heard the background story, I would've believed him. 'I was happy to pay above market to help Rose out, and because of the circumstances, I'll stick to that deal when you're ready to sell.'

My blood started to simmer as it had when I was speaking to Miles earlier. 'Thank you, Martin, but I need to consider all my options before I sell.'

His mouth curled at the end like it used to do when he was talking down to one of the lesser beings in the schoolyard. 'Sensible decision; you always were one of the smart ones at school. Take your time, but when you're ready, we can talk.' The server placed my salad on the table, and Martin stood to go. 'I won't interrupt your lunch, but Kylie was saying last night – you know I married Kylie Lindsay, right?' I nodded. 'Anyway, Kyles was saying how great it would be to get you over for a barbecue – how does tomorrow night sound?'

'That sounds fabulous,' I said, not meaning a word of it. The last thing I felt like was socialising with Martin and Kylie Cosgrove, but if it helped fill in some background, it could be valuable. 'But I was meant to be meeting a friend tomorrow night for a drink …'

'No problems, bring them along – the more the merrier. Six-ish fine with you?' He took his wallet out from his back pocket and removed a business card, handing it to me. 'What's your number? I'll text you the details, or rather, I'll get Kylie to.' I recited my mobile number, and he entered it into his phone. 'We'll see you then – no need to dress up, we're pretty casual around here.' He drained his beer and set it on the table next to mine. 'Kyles can't wait to see you.'

Even if Ted hadn't warned me not to trust Martin, I still wouldn't have believed a word he said.

Finn and the dogs were standing by my towel when I emerged from the water later that afternoon. While he greeted me with a smile, it didn't reach his eyes.

'Siouxsie was in to see me this afternoon,' he began tentatively as I slipped a T-shirt over my swimmers. 'She mentioned you don't think Rose's death was an accident,

and then she said something about a murder board?'
I groaned inwardly at the thought of how quickly that
rumour would spread if Siouxsie was talking about it.
'Don't worry,' he said, correctly deciphering my expression.
'She told me because she thought I'd want to be involved; I
don't think she intends to tell anyone else.' He paused and
said, 'And she thought right. I do want to be involved, so
how about you tell me your theory?'

Searching his face for any sign that he was making fun
of me – and finding none – I went through my thought
processes.

At the end of the telling, Finn's shoulders fell, his eyes
narrowed, frowning. 'If you're right, it means …' His hand
swept from his forehead to cover his mouth as if he was
stopping himself from saying the words aloud.

I bent and picked up and threw the ball Cosmo (or
was it Beans?) had been hopefully looking at. 'Yes,' I said
quietly. 'I know.'

His eyes flicked to mine. 'What happens now?'

'I've spoken to Ted, and there's not enough evidence
to warrant reopening the case. I've had a quick look at the
accounts but need to dive deeper into those – not that I
think I'll find anything there, but I need to see what's going
on with New Moon anyway. And then—'

'According to Siouxsie, we'll meet at yours this evening
for a council of war and a murder board.' His frown
deepened. 'Just what is a murder board?'

I tried to hide my embarrassment with a half smile. 'It's like a vision board, but you connect suspects and theories and clues—'

'Let me guess: with red string?'

'Something like that,' I conceded. 'It's something Maggie and I used to do when—'

'Good God, don't tell me you two investigated murders when you were young?'

I almost laughed aloud at the expression of disbelief on his face. 'No, nothing like that, but we'd examine real cases like who'd been spreading rumours about so and so behind the bike shed – for the record, it was usually Kylie Lindsay – and who was behind the theft of the maths tests from the common room.'

'Who was behind the theft of the maths tests?' That twinkle was back in his eyes.

'We could never prove it, but Martin Cosgrove passed that term, so I think we know the answer.'

When he chuckled, his curls bobbed, the setting sun highlighting the greys, and I wondered how it would feel to run my hands through those curls. 'Anyway' —I stood and swung the towel over my shoulder— 'I'd better be off …'

After taking a few steps away, he caught up with me. 'You forgot your bag.' Confusion at my sudden departure crossed his face.

'Thanks,' I muttered awkwardly. 'I'll see you later, then.'

When I couldn't resist looking back, he was still

standing there. As if I'd done exactly what he'd been hoping I'd do he grinned and waved. Telling myself to get a grip, I walked as briskly as it was possible to walk in rubber thongs back to the cottage.

CHAPTER TWELVE

To prepare for tonight's meeting, I purchased a notebook with a pretty Bohemian-style floral cover from New Moon (heaven knows we needed the business – I'd seen the accounts), two cork notice boards and a couple of balls of red wool from the discount shop, and some Post-it stickers, noticeboard pins and marker pens from the newsagent.

Siouxsie had uploaded the photos I'd taken of the scene images and printed me some larger copies; I'd stocked the fridge with beer and wine and had cheese and biscuit platters ready to go.

It was as I was tidying up the dining table that I remembered the tarot card found with Rose. Scattered across the tabletop were, as there always used to be, an assortment of charts. Instead of hand-drawn charts, though, these were produced by a software application that must be on her laptop. While some were birth charts, others were questions or electional charts – who, what, why and when – with Rose's distinctive scribbles and scrawl covering them all. While I didn't think any of them related to her death, I couldn't discount that she hadn't cast any with the purpose of finding out the identities of what she used to refer to as secret enemies. 'Twelfth house people, darling,' she'd say. 'The ones who smile to your face but plot behind your back.'

Under one chart labelled 'who?' was the tarot spread I'd been looking for. My heart beat faster as I recognised the same cards featured in my dream. Had the Fool been part of that spread? I took a photo of the cards and placed them back with the rest of the deck, adding a reminder in my phone to ask Nina tomorrow what she made of the spread.

Maggie, Siouxsie and Finn (with Cosmo and Beans) all arrived together. 'I hope you don't mind I brought the dogs,' Finn said, an apologetic look on his face. 'Rose never did, and I didn't think …'

'Of course I don't mind.' I ruffled the head of first one and then the other before they took off to reacquaint themselves with the cottage.

'You know it's a test.' Siouxsie's eyebrows arched. 'Love him, love his dogs.'

Heat rushed to my face, but Finn laughed and said, 'You know it, but luckily, she passed the wet dog test at the beach yesterday.'

Maggie shot me a 'you didn't tell us about *that*' look.

'No Justin tonight?' Siouxsie smirked at my obvious change of subject.

'He has a meeting – Chamber of Commerce.' Maggie

had a gleam in her eye as she took in my embarrassment. 'He said he'd spoken to you about the accounts this afternoon and thought he'd be better placed attending that in case any of our suspects mentioned Rose or this house.'

'Any of our suspects?' Finn chuckled, picking up the red wool. 'You already have suspects?' When the dogs jumped onto the sofa, he moved to shoo them off.

'They're fine.' I waved away his concerns. 'As for suspects, we certainly do.' I held my hand out for the wool. 'But let's get drinks before we put them on the board, eh?'

Once the platters were on the table and everyone had a drink, I called us to attention.

'Thanks for coming tonight and for not laughing at me when I told you of my suspicions. I like to think Rose would be happy we're standing up for her.' I raised my glass towards the ceiling. 'To Rose.'

The others did the same. 'To Rose.'

'Who never shied away from a fight,' added Finn. 'Even if it was unpopular.' He met my eyes, the message in his clear: Rose trusts you to see this through. I nodded once to let him know I understood.

'I spoke to Ted Winters this morning, and while he didn't dismiss me, he did tell me he'd need actual hard evidence before they could reopen the case.' I paused and smiled. 'He did, however, accidentally leave me with the police file while he attended to something else in the office, so I've managed to get the scene photos. Siouxsie, do you mind pinning these up?' I passed the images across to her.

'Not at all.'

'So, here's what we know for sure. According to the pathologist, Rose died sometime between eight and ten pm, although knowing her habits as we do, that window is narrowed to, say, eight-thirty and nine-thirty. Cause of death was head wounds commensurate with a fall from a ladder, and as we can see from the second photo, the ladder is lying by her side.' Finn stepped forward to examine the photo, a deep frown marring his brow. 'Found with her was her phone – which I'm currently charging – and this tarot card.' I handed the card to Siouxsie, who pinned it beside the scene photos. 'I'll ask Nina about that tomorrow – and a five-card spread she'd been working on.' When Siouxsie had written that onto a Post-it sticker, I continued. 'When she died, she was wearing a cotton beach-style dress and a pair of rubber flip-flops.'

'Neither of which are conducive to ladder climbing at night,' commented Maggie.

'Did she have a torch?' The question came from Finn, who was peering closely at the second photo.

'No, just the torch on her phone.'

'Well, looking at this, unless someone has moved the ladder, there's no way that ladder and Rose fell together.' He turned to face us. 'Look at how it's lying almost exactly parallel to the body. If you were up a ladder and it fell backwards, your instinct would be to hold on to it for as long as possible.' He demonstrated this by gripping the rails of an imaginary ladder. 'You'd let go at the end, but the ladder would likely fall on top of you or bounce out to the side. It certainly wouldn't be straight as it is in this picture.'

'I see what you mean.' Maggie leant in to look more closely. 'That does look strange.'

Siouxsie wrote 'ladder?' on a sticker and stuck it onto the board.

'As you know,' —I inclined my head in Finn's direction— 'I spoke to Harry this morning, and he categorically told me Rose could not have moved it on her own. I'll see if I can catch him tomorrow morning and get him to tell me exactly where he left it.'

Finn grinned. 'If you don't waste time getting coffee from Bron's like you did this morning—'

Siouxsie shot me an appalled look. 'You didn't buy coffee from Bron?'

'Really, Clem?' Maggie's expression was almost one of disgust. 'I'm surprised at you. Bron's a great baker, but her coffee is shit.'

'Is that because you and Finn had that little spat yesterday morning, or was there another reason you wanted to avoid him?' That speculative gleam was back in Siouxsie's eyes.

'You told them about that?' Judging from Finn's grin, one of us was enjoying themselves.

I took a sip of my wine in a vain effort to hide my

blushes, which seemed to be all too frequent when it came to this man. 'I wasn't avoiding Finn; I was just there to buy sourdough and thought I should spread around some coffee love.'

'Don't worry, she's learnt her lesson, but as I was saying, if you come straight to my place in the morning, you'll catch him.'

'Okay, I'll bear that in mind for tomorrow.' I picked up the notebook, pretending I couldn't feel the zip of electricity between us. 'I saw nothing in the police file that indicated they'd taken fingerprints from the ladder—'

'There'd be no need to. They'd obviously had it pegged as an accident from the start.' Maggie's mouth had turned into a disdainful sneer. 'But I'll check with Ty anyway.'

Finn headed towards the fridge. 'Anyone for another drink?'

Once Finn topped up the drinks, I stood back and looked at the board. Siouxsie had captured all our facts, questions and assumptions on different coloured stickers so we could tell the difference between each at a glance. 'Right, let's talk suspects; who would want Rose dead? Maggie, you mentioned Rose successfully campaigned to stop Bob Lindsay's wharf development from happening ...'

'True, but Bob, and Ray Cosgrove, pivoted quickly and no one can deny the outcome has been a favourable one ... Have you had a look there yet?'

'I have – I had lunch at the pub today.'

'And I bet it was busy. For all we say about Bob and Ray, that redevelopment has brought life into the town. I don't, however, think they deserve to be listed as suspects, even though if there's ever anything dodgy going down, their names are usually all over it.' Maggie shook her head. 'But the business about the wharf was too long ago to be a motive for a murder now.'

'I agree,' said Finn. 'I think it's more likely to be the son rather than the father; Martin was pretty pissed when Rose bought New Moon. He had plans to pick up that and Brewz and open the space into a beach bar slash fine diner. I'm almost positive he'd already put out feelers with the council over approval. Mags, it might be worth asking Justin about that.'

'On it.'

'I think the main motive, though,' —I tapped at my bottom lip— 'has to be Finz – and that means Martin. Can you guys find out what plans were submitted for that? Maggie told me the Cosgroves had been waiting for zoning to change on these blocks.'

'Martin snapped up the house behind this one when it came on the market a few years back and has been running it as an Airbnb ever since,' added Maggie. 'That's why he wants these three houses. He's the one who came up with the concept for Finz. I think he wants to show his father and father-in-law that he can deliver on something of this magnitude.'

'I think you're right.' Tapping at the board with a marker I added, 'He's always had daddy issues.'

'Exactly. But is that reason enough to kill Rose?' Maggie screwed up her nose as she thought. 'I suppose it could be. There's certainly a lot of money at stake, and if Rose wasn't there, the other two would sell. She was the one who talked them into holding out on the basis that they should be allowed to stay in their family homes for as long as possible. Not that it will be that long, I don't imagine. Brian's mobility isn't great, so that's just a matter of time, but that's why Rose didn't think it was fair to cause him more confusion.'

'Don't forget,' said Siouxsie, 'she hated the thought of the resort Martin was planning.'

'But surely holiday accommodation is a good thing …?' I struggled to understand what Rose so vehemently objected to.

'It's not the accommodation itself as much as the nature of it,' explained Finn. 'It was pitched at the top-end of the market, whereas what we need is something more family friendly. Her argument was they could build something perfectly nice that would cater for children as well – and might not even need her house to do so. Martin, being Martin, is hell-bent on doing it his way and won't even consider a compromise. In fact, I'm surprised he hasn't been in touch with you already.'

The way he raised his eyebrows made me think he knew we'd spoken; I'd forgotten how fast news spread.

'He has, sort of … I went to the pub for lunch, and he happened to be there and plonked himself down to talk as though we were long-lost friends.' I hesitated before telling them the rest. 'My … ummm … partner Miles—'

'The one you were thinking about dumping?' Siouxsie asked, her halo positively beaming.

Ignoring Finn's raised eyebrows, I nodded. 'Yes, that one. Let me say, if I was undecided before … anyway, he really wants me to sell.'

'And you're not?' Hope was in Maggie's question.

'At this point, no.' My teeth caught my lower lip. 'Rose trusted me to do the right thing. Now, that doesn't necessarily mean not selling just because *she* didn't want to, but doing it for the right reason when that time comes.' I ducked my head, not sure whether I should completely trust them, but simultaneously knowing that these people in this room were probably the only people I *could* trust. 'The thing is – and I know this is going to sound weird – even before I came here, before I knew Rose was dead, I was having these nightmares where I was being beckoned back to Whale Bay.'

'It doesn't sound like much of a nightmare to me,' said Maggie with a slightly uncomfortable laugh. Siouxsie and Finn, however, were watching my face closely.

'Maybe not, but at the end of the dream, there were five tarot cards lined up on the beach – the same cards in the spread I found on the table.' I didn't know if the gasp came from Maggie or Siouxsie. 'Rose's face was on the

Queen of Cups, and she was lying on the lawn exactly like that.' I pointed to the photo on the murder board. 'So even before I knew she was dead, I was coming back here.'

'I remember as a teenager you used to have dreams that came true,' Maggie said softly. 'I wondered whether you'd grown out of them.'

'I learnt to ignore them,' I conceded. 'At home, talk like that was certainly not encouraged. With Rose, though, it was okay, so even though I know it makes no logical sense, it feels as though she wanted me to come back to investigate what happened to her.' I ducked my head not wanting to see disbelief on their faces.

'It sounds like she *trusted* you to find out what happened to her.' Maggie took my arm.

Siouxsie took my other arm. 'It's not weird at all. Rose used to tell us how you were a natural reader – you just had to trust what you felt and knew.'

Finn still hadn't said anything, and I wasn't brave enough to look at him.

'Rose knew exactly what she was doing when she trusted you with her cottage and her shop,' he finally said. 'I can only apologise again for what I said to you yesterday.'

I lifted my head to meet his eyes, and what I saw in them took my breath away. Maybe Rose was matchmaking from beyond the grave – I wouldn't have put it past her.

Forcing myself to bring the conversation back onto practical grounds, I turned back to the others. 'I have an invite to dinner at the Cosgroves tomorrow night' —I grinned at Finn— 'and so do you.'

'Me? I hardly think so. The likes of the Cosgroves don't mix with the likes of me.' If he'd had a forelock, I was sure he would've tugged at it.

'Maybe not you per se, but when I said I was meeting a friend for a drink, he told me to bring them … the more, the merrier, he said.'

'Perhaps it wasn't what I had in mind for our first date, but yeah, why not?' Maggie and Siouxsie exchanged knowing glances. 'It'll be worth it to see the look on Martin Cosgrove's face when I walk in.'

'Hey.' The light and playful punch to his arm was intended to hide the way my heart had skipped at his words 'first date'. 'We'll be there to suss out our suspects, not socialise.'

'Right, you are.' His cheeky smile did nothing to calm my traitorous heartbeat.

CHAPTER THIRTEEN

Finn was leaning against the counter, nursing a coffee and chatting to Harry when I arrived at Brewz the next morning.

'Good to see you've learnt your lesson,' Finn said by way of greeting.

'Hey, Clem, what lesson would that be?' Harry's smile was almost blinding.

'I bought my coffee at the bakery yesterday,' I admitted, adding a dramatic shrug and swinging around when a couple of other customers giggled.

Harry shook his head sadly. 'Bron's a great baker,' he said, echoing Finn's words from yesterday, 'but man, her coffee's shit. I don't know what she does to it.'

'Burns it, I think,' said one of the customers who had giggled at me. 'See you tomorrow, Finn.'

Finn held up a hand to wave. 'I'm looking forward to it already, ladies.'

'Do you ever turn it off?' I asked, chuckling.

'Turn off what?' Finn asked with a completely straight face.

'The flirting.'

This prompted a spurt of laughter from Harry. 'No, he doesn't, but on that note, I'm off. See ya.' Harry continued laughing as he waved and stepped onto the footpath.

Finn clutched his chest dramatically. 'I'm wounded.' Still grinning, he said, 'Take a seat, Clem, and I'll bring your coffee over.' When I rummaged in my bag for my phone to pay him, he waved it away. 'It's on me.'

'Thank you, but you can't keep buying me coffee. It's not a successful business model.'

'Is that where I've been going wrong?' His expression was so crestfallen that I couldn't help but laugh as I headed onto the deck.

Hanging my towel on the back of a chair, I placed my bag on another and sat facing the beach, my legs stretched out in front of me, my sunglasses protecting my eyes from the sun. A drip from my still-wet hair landed on the table, so I reached around and ran my fingers through the back of it so it wouldn't dry in clumps.

Finn placed two coffees and a couple of ANZAC biscuits on the table and slid into the chair opposite me.

'Thank you.' Taking the lid off the coffee, I inhaled and sipped, my gratitude escaping in a little sigh. 'Oh, that's good.'

Realising how that must've sounded to him, I risked a glance and grinned when his cheeky smile told me he knew the direction my mind had gone in. I broke one of the cookies into four and popped a piece into my mouth, savouring the oaty, buttery crunch.

'How are you today?' Finn asked, raising his hand to wave at a customer.

Touched at the genuine concern in his voice, I replied honestly. 'I'm actually okay. The last couple of days have been a whirl of activity, but now my suspicions have been confirmed, I just want to get to the bottom of it, whatever "it" is.' I took another sip. 'I know we were talking about suspects and referring to Rose's death as if it were murder, but I'm still not convinced it was. All I know is, she didn't fall off that ladder.'

He nodded soberly. 'I hear you, but all we can do is gather the evidence to convince the police to reopen the case.'

'Or figure out what happened to her on our own.'

'Or that,' he agreed.

Brian Walker was sitting on a chair on his sun-filled verandah when I walked past on my way back from the rock wall later that afternoon. I waved as I passed, but he beckoned me in.

'Young Clem,' he said. 'I wondered when you'd be around to say hello.' As he struggled to get out of his chair, I waved him back.

'No need to stand, Mr Walker. Stay where you're comfortable.'

'No one has called me Mr Walker for years, and you're

too old to do so.' He chuckled. 'I'll let my sister know you're here; she moved in when my wife passed.' A flicker of sadness crossed his face. 'Maureen,' he called. 'Come here, we have a visitor.'

His sister appeared in the doorway. Although Maureen must've been the same age as my aunt – in her mid-sixties – thanks to her almost-gaunt build, pursed lips and narrow-eyed suspicious stare she seemed so much older.

'Maureen, this is Clem, Rose's niece.' To me, he said, 'I was sorry to hear about your aunt.' He shook his head, his lips pressed together. 'She's the last person I would have thought to have ended up like that. She was always doing things for other people. I said to Maureen that I was surprised she hadn't got that young Harry to help her although he was probably out surfing or something.'

'It was certainly a bad business,' added Maureen. 'Particularly as she didn't have family here to help her.' Her gaze narrowed on me, the implication clear – I should've been here and wasn't. While I'd shouldered plenty of self-guilt over my absence, Maureen Peterson was the first to voice it. 'I suppose you're here to sell up.'

Holding her stare, I refused to let her see she'd rattled me. 'I haven't decided what I'll be doing yet,' I said.

'Well, you haven't wasted any time talking to Martin Cosgrove. I heard you had lunch with him yesterday.' She turned to Brian. 'Maybe now Rose is gone, you'll reconsider selling. You'll have enough to get yourself settled somewhere nice and still have some left over. I'm surprised you don't want to help your children out financially while you're still around. Lauren is fine, she married Bob Lindsay's eldest, Michael, you know' —I assumed that comment had been meant for me— 'but heaven knows poor Chris could do with the money now, not when you're gone. If Rose hadn't talked you out of it, you'd be sitting pretty in one of those lovely units near the bowling club Martin Cosgrove offered to help you into – at a substantial discount too, mind you.'

As she spoke, I fought the temptation to defend my aunt. 'But I thought you didn't want to sell.' Wasn't that what the magazine article had said?

'*I* don't.' Brian directed a glare towards his sister. 'I want to stay here as long as I can. This is the house I built with my wife and the house we brought our kids up in. Rose understood that.'

Maureen shook her head. 'She pandered to it more like, took it as an excuse to go off on another of her crusades.' Okay, so Maureen wasn't a fan. 'Like that ridiculous business about the wharf. The mayor and Bob Lindsay have done a lot for this town, and Rose and that coffee-making friend of hers had no right to think they knew what the town needed better than what our elected councillors know.' She sniffed haughtily and continued, warming to her subject. 'Have you seen that girl she's got running that ridiculous shop? She blew into town without a cent to her name and lives out of a van, so what does Rose do? Trust her with a shop; that's what she does. She's probably got no idea how much money that girl is skimming off the top. If I were you, I'd be checking those accounts carefully. I know she always worked there with her cards and stars – hocus pocus it is in my book – but' —she sniffed again— 'some people believe all that rubbish, I suppose. You know, of course, she only bought it so Martin Cosgrove couldn't. I don't know what she's got against that poor man, but she seemed to do whatever she could to stop him from getting ahead. A good, honest worker, he is. Not like that brother of his who let the family down … When Nick walked away from the business, it broke his father's heart, it did.'

I blanched at the direction her diatribe had taken.

'I might not know the full story there – something about an unsuitable woman who probably had her claws into him – but it's a good thing Martin was there to pick up the pieces.'

She finally paused to draw breath, and although my fists were clenched by my side, I took the opportunity to glance across at Brian, who simply raised his eyebrows in exasperation.

'Then there's that thing that was going on between her and Gordon.' Maureen screwed her nose up in disdain. 'You would've heard about that, of course. Carrying on, they were – at that age. I never saw the like. I heard he wanted to make an honest woman of her and she wasn't having it. Poor Gordon, I'm sure he was heartbroken, but it didn't stop him. I wouldn't be surprised if she used her hocus pocus whatever to cast some sort of a spell on him – and everyone else in this town. I was never taken in, though. I always saw Rose clearly; even when she was at school, she was the same. Trouble. That's what she was. So different to her sister; now Grace knew when to leave well enough alone.'

Did she even realise that the sister she was talking about was my mother?

'As for that Harry, now, he's another one I wouldn't trust as far as I could throw. You know he was in strife even in school, but Rose, she didn't listen to anyone's warnings about him and look where that's landed her.' Maureen raised her eyebrows meaningfully. 'Not that I want to speak ill of the dead, of course.'

'Why stop now?' I said wryly, digging my nails into my palms as I fought to suppress the rising anger. 'I hope you're not implying that Harry's the reason she died.'

Under my stare, her chin jutted defensively. 'That's not what I said.'

'It's what you implied, and let me say this: Harry was a massive help to my aunt and has done nothing wrong, and for you to say what you're saying – and I don't believe for one second you haven't bandied your opinion around town now Rose is gone – is cruel, and it's wrong. Rose believed in giving people second chances, and nine out of ten times, her faith in humanity was rewarded. I'd like to believe she probably even gave you a second chance, but' —I shrugged dismissively— 'there are some people even Rose can't help, I suppose.'

Maureen turned to scowl at Brian when a laugh burst from him.

'I'm sorry, Brian, I'll go now. If you need anything, you know where I am. I'd like to say it was a pleasure to meet you, Maureen, but I'm not as generous of spirit as my aunt was and this was anything but.'

Fuming with anger, I stormed back to Rose's cottage, unable to fully process what Maureen had said about Rose. The vitriol that had come out of her mouth was decades of dislike dating back to their school days. My mother, Gordon and Brian had all gone to school together, along with Bob and Carmen Lindsay and Ray and Paula Cosgrove. Rose and Maureen were a few years younger than the others. What had Rose done to her back then? Or was it, as most problems between teenage girls tended to be, simply a case of jealousy? Whatever it was, was it enough to wish Rose dead?

CHAPTER FOURTEEN

Even though Martin had said the evening would be casual and Kylie had followed his invitation up with a text and the instruction 'don't dress up, any old thing will do', the Kylie I'd known would be anything but casual. At school, she had to be the Queen Bee, and I doubted anything had changed in that regard. It would be just like her to use her outfit to try and put me on the back foot. While my khaki jersey halterneck maxi dress and flat spangly sandals might've looked casual, Kylie would recognise the cost of each and know it was anything but. I'd also made an effort with my make-up, slicking some gold across my eyelids to bring out the green-gold tones in my hazel eyes and taking the sort of time barely there she's-not-wearing-any-make-up takes to apply.

Finn's eyes widened when they took in my appearance. 'Wow, you look great. I thought you said it was casual.'

Although the appreciation in his eyes made my heart beat faster, I patted his cheek. 'Finn, my dear, in Kylie Cosgrove's world, I suspect this is casual.' I looked him up and down; he'd swapped his board shorts for a pair of dress shorts and his surf T-shirt for a navy polo that made his eyes look almost black. 'You look pretty good yourself.'

'Good enough for the nobs on Nob Hill?' A wicked grin played across his lips.

'Way too good for the nobs on Nob Hill.' I picked up the car keys. 'Do you want me to drive?'

'If you like, although I'm happy to drive home.'

'Deal.' I picked up my handbag and a light cashmere throw I'd tossed into my suitcase as a just-in-case, and we were on our way.

'How was your day?' Finn asked once we were on the road.

'Well, we might have another suspect to add to the murder board.' I told him about Maureen Peterson and what she'd said about Rose.

'She did realise who she was talking to?' Finn's eyebrows had shot up in surprise as I spoke.

'I think that was probably her point. In fact, I wouldn't be surprised if she's transferred her dislike for Rose to me.' I shrugged it off.

'But you think she could be a suspect?'

'I don't know, no, not seriously.' I turned up the street that led to the Cosgrove house. 'She's the first person who's spoken openly about her dislike for Rose, so …' I shrugged again and pulled up out the front of an imposing rendered concrete and glass house. 'Welcome to Nob Hill.'

Finn peered up at the house, his eyebrows raised.

'Indeed.' He turned to me. 'Are you ready?'

I slid out of the car and squared my shoulders. 'As I'll ever be.'

Martin had opened the double timber doors before we'd had a chance to ring the bell and greeted me as a long-missed friend. 'Clem!' He kissed my cheek. His welcome for Finn wasn't quite as effusive. 'And Finn too.' He smiled a tight smile and held out his hand.

If Finn noticed Martin's lack of enthusiasm at his presence, he didn't show it. Shaking our host's hand, he said, 'Thanks for inviting me, Martin. I've often wondered what this house was like on the inside.'

Suppressing a grin, I added. 'Finn was the friend I said I was meeting tonight, and you did say the more, the merrier.'

'I did, didn't I? Well, come on through.' He led us down a wide marble-tiled hall into a sleek open-plan kitchen and expansive deck overlooking Whale Bay. He turned to face me, a cocky smile on his face. 'Impressive, isn't it?'

'Whale Bay?' I deliberately misunderstood him. 'Indeed, it is. I'd forgotten quite how impressive it is.'

If he was disappointed by my reaction, he hid it well. 'Kylie, Clem's here. And Finn Marella too.'

Kylie didn't skip a beat, a wide smile on her smooth features that went nowhere near her eyes. 'Clem, lovely to see you again.' She performed a double air kiss. 'And you too, Finn. Come through and meet the others.'

The 'others' turned out to be the senior Cosgroves and Lindsays, Kylie's brother Michael and his wife Lauren, and Lauren's brother, Chris. 'I'm sorry our children aren't here – our eldest, Beau, is at university in Brisbane, and our daughter Sophie is in Europe on her gap year.' Her tinkling laugh had a practised sound. 'So it's just Martin and me rattling around this place most of the time.'

'Well, Kylie, it's a lovely house to be rattling round in,' said Finn, turning the full throttle of those espresso eyes on her. When Kylie flicked smooth, expertly styled waves of blonde hair across one shoulder and giggled, I had to stop myself rolling my eyes.

'That dress is lovely, Clem. Ted Baker?' Kylie had dragged her gaze away from Finn and was back on me.

'Thank you. It's actually Armani – from a few years ago, but Martin did say tonight was casual.' I felt Finn shake with suppressed laughter. 'You look lovely too.' Kylie wore a green tiered and gathered dress that finished high enough to show off her slim, tanned legs and strappy gold heels.

'This old thing?' She laughed again and twirled, a performance intended for Finn.

'Really? I'm sure I saw something similar in the new season drop for Country Road, but there you go.'

Kylie's smile stayed in place and her brow remained smooth, but her gaze narrowed. I smiled back, but the gauntlet had been thrown down; we each knew where we stood. She might've been able to intimidate me once upon a time, but I'd grown up.

'Well, I'd best be getting you both a drink,' she said, adding another of those tinkly laughs.

Once she'd left us, Finn laughed. 'You and Kylie obviously have a history.'

'You could say that,' I replied, my gaze taking in the other members of the party. 'Now, I think we need to separate and mingle – see if anyone says anything they shouldn't.'

'You want me to leave your side? Chris Walker has been eyeing you off since we came in. I can't say I blame him, though.'

Our eyes met, and what I saw in his flooded me with warmth.

'Remember, this isn't a date,' I muttered, cursing my traitorous body. 'I have a boyfriend at home.'

'The one you're planning on dumping?' That wicked grin of his was back.

Damn you, Siouxsie, for letting that piece of information be known. 'Maybe, but I haven't done it yet, and until I do, well, I have a boyfriend at home.'

He reached out and tucked a lock of hair behind my ear, and it was all I could do not to sway towards him.

Martin was back and grabbed my elbow. 'Let me introduce you to my father.' My eyebrows raised at his blatant snub of Finn, who merely grinned and walked off to help Kylie with the drinks.

Over the next few hours, I was the subject of a subtle sales job with the men telling me about the changes that had occurred in the town since I'd been gone and the impending boom on its way to Whale Bay – the implication being that Ray and Bob had been responsible for all past progress, with the future now safely in the hands of their offspring – Martin and Michael respectively. There was no mention of Nick; it was as though he'd never existed, and I was certainly not going to be the one to bring him up.

While Martin was full of talk, Michael was more circumspect, and while his greeting was friendly enough, he seemed happier listening to what the other men had to say rather than joining in the conversation. Even though it was hinted that their proposed resort, Finz, was central to that boom, the sale of Rose's cottage was never explicitly mentioned.

The women, however, were less subtle. Their conversation was about my job in Melbourne, how fortunate I had been to climb the corporate law ladder (hard work obviously had nothing to do with it) and how I was doing so much good for society.

'I'm not sure about that, Paula,' I said. 'Essentially, my job is about helping rich people uncouple at the least possible expense to themselves while getting as much as possible from the person they once loved. While there are some exceptions, most of the time, there's nothing noble in what I do, and most of the time, it's not pretty. It does, however, pay well, so that makes it easier to overlook the ugliness.'

We talked about real estate prices and fashion and how I must notice the absence of any sort of decent society and taste since I'd arrived. Paula went so far as to cast a contemptuous look in Finn's direction.

'I bet you can't wait to get home,' she said. 'To your job and' —with another meaningful glance towards Finn, who had just said something that made Lauren laugh (and Michael frown)— 'and to your husband.'

'My husband? I'm not married.' I deliberately misunderstood her.

'But Martin said he'd been talking to your partner—'

A prickle of unease ran up my spine. 'Really? Miles didn't mention it.'

'Yes,' Paula continued. 'Martin said how your husband or partner, whatever he is' —her laugh sounded false— 'had called him and mentioned you were in the market to sell your aunt's property.'

Carmen was watching me keenly for a reaction.

My jaw ached from the effort of holding a neutral expression. 'Miles didn't mention that to me when I spoke to him.' I added a short laugh, one of those exasperated laughs women laugh when their partner has failed to communicate. 'That's so like him – to smooth the way for me. It's just a pity he's jumped the gun a little this time.'

Carmen's eyes were beady. 'You're not selling?'

My smile remained fixed in place, but inwardly, my mind was racing. Why would Miles have contacted Martin? 'I didn't say that; I said he's jumped the gun a little.' I shook my head and laughed ruefully. 'Miles has been busy so probably thought we'd had a conversation we hadn't had. You must know what that's like – you and Paula, both married to important men? While we can spread our energies in multiple directions, they tend to compartmentalise and focus completely on what they're working on, sometimes forgetting we exist.'

Paula visibly preened, but Carmen was less easily distracted. 'Husband or partner, does he know you're seeing another man while you're here? The town rake no less. I'm sure you wouldn't want that information getting back to him.'

Suppressing my laughter at the term 'rake', I played dumb. 'You mean Finn? We're just good friends.'

'Yet he's here with you tonight.' Carmen was formidable and, I was beginning to suspect, the real power behind Bob Lindsay.

'Yes, we'd planned to go out tonight, and when I told Martin I'd committed to seeing a friend, he insisted I bring him.' Adopting a look I saved for difficult husbands on the witness stand, I said bluntly, 'Is there something I'm missing here because that sounded awfully like a threat?'

Carmen and Paula exchanged glances. 'Let's just say Finn was a central figure in some problems Bob had a few years ago, and as a result, he's not one of our favourite people … No one has mentioned that to you?'

I shook my head.

'They wouldn't have because – and I don't like to speak ill of the dead, you know – but Rose was involved too.' Paula sighed heavily and shook her head. 'It was ridiculous, really, but I think Rose convinced herself that she knew best about what the town needed. Mind you' —she leant closer— 'I don't blame Rose.'

She inclined her head towards Finn. I looked over to see Kylie had now joined Lauren – almost elbowing the other woman aside to get closer to Finn. Something that could've been anger flicked across Chris's face. Now, what was that about?

'Come on, Paula,' said Carmen. 'You and I both know what a troublemaker Rose has been over the years; even at school she'd jump on any and every cause, and she's never changed. While Ray and Bob were smart enough to pivot, and there's no denying the wharf redevelopment has been a success, she cost us a lot of money. Then there's that shop of hers. You know she only bought it because she knew Martin had offered to buy it.'

Paula laughed cruelly. 'Ah yes, the shop. The kind of people we want to attract to Whale Bay aren't interested in that sort of tat.'

'I understand it's fashionable these days, especially amongst your generation, to play with crystals and fortune-telling,' Carmen said. 'I know my daughter-in-law is into it, but please do it in a tasteful way.' She paused and frowned as Lauren laughed loudly, indicating with a single glance at Michael that he should control his wife. Michael, however, turned his back on his mother. 'You're a lawyer, so I imagine you're too smart for all that.' She smiled tightly. 'When you're ready, chat with Michael; I'm sure he'll give you a good price to take the shop and all its worries off your hands.'

I knew Martin originally had plans to turn New Moon and Brewz into a fine dining restaurant, but what could Michael Lindsay possibly want with it?

'What do you mean when you say "all its worries"?' I asked.

'You wouldn't have had a chance to go through the books yet, but I've heard it's running at a loss, and I wouldn't trust that Nina girl Rose has had working there.' Carmen screwed her nose up at the mention of Nina's name. 'The way I see it, that shop is one disaster away from closing its doors for good, and when that happens, Michael will be happy to take it off your hands.'

I pushed my nails so hard into my palms that I was sure the indentations would show for days. 'I see. Thanks for the heads-up. I'll certainly bear it in mind, but I thought it was Martin who was interested in buying the shop from Rose?'

'Oh, he is.' Paula rushed to clarify.

I smiled beatifically. 'Well, if that's the case, I'll certainly be able to get a good price, especially if both Michael and

Martin are interested. A little healthy competition to force the price up and all that. Now, if you'll excuse me, ladies, I must catch up with Chris Walker.'

'I thought I might need to jump in and rescue you,' Chris said when I joined him at the edge of the deck. 'Can I top up your wine?'

'Please.' I sighed in exaggerated relief, holding my glass out. He laughed and reached for a bottle at an adjacent table. 'Thank you.' I leant on the balcony.

'Even at night, it's beautiful from up here,' Chris said wistfully. 'But then, not many people can afford a view like this.'

'True, that.' I turned to face him, my back against the railing. 'So what brings you back here or are you just visiting?'

'Just visiting. I can only take my aunt's ministrations for so long.' He chuckled, and I resisted the urge to agree. 'It's okay, I know what she said to you earlier. Dad was full of it; he thought it was hilarious. He said no one had stood up to Maureen in decades. Rose mostly ignored what she had to say, but you, he said, took her on.' He clinked his glass against mine. 'So here's cheers to you, Clem.'

While I couldn't see his face clearly, there was admiration in his voice. 'Thanks, I think. I can't abide bullies, and I'm sorry, Chris, but that's how your aunt sounded this afternoon – like a bully.'

'You're right, of course. She's always been like it. She

treated my mother appallingly, and Dad never really stood up for her; he says he didn't notice, but I think it was easier for him not to.' He took a sip of his drink and changed the subject. 'They tell me you're a lawyer these days?'

'Yes, family law … In Melbourne.'

'Is that the same as being a divorce lawyer?' He'd moved slightly, just enough so the overhead light caught his face, his eyes interested, his smooth jaw taut.

'Yes, although it's about more than that. Why? Are you in the market for a divorce?' My gaze strayed to his bare left hand.

'Me? No – been there done that, have the custody agreement, crippling child support and debt to show for it.' He laughed as if it was nothing, or rather something everyone did. 'One of my … friends could be, though.'

'Well, unless they're in Melbourne, I can't help them, but if you need it, I can get you the number of someone good in Brisbane.' I ran a finger through the condensation on my glass. 'You never said, what are you up to these days?'

'I live in Brisbane but have my own business. I'm an accountant.'

'Yet you're here midweek? Business must be good.'

'It's okay, but being here? This is business.' He nodded towards Ray, Bob, Martin and Michael, still huddling near the barbecue.

'Aaaah, *they* are your business,' I guessed.

'Quite a bit of it, yes. They certainly keep me busy.'

'Let me guess … When they're doing well, you're doing well?'

'Something like that, but they've always got some deal in the pipeline.' He drained his glass and reached again for the bottle. 'Another?'

'No, thank you. I think I'm driving home.' I hadn't kept track of how many beers Finn had consumed, but it was better to be safe than sorry.

'So,' he began. 'You and Finn Marella … You've only been in town a few days …'

'I'm a fast worker, is that it?' I grinned so he wouldn't think I'd taken his comment as a slight.

'No, it's just that Martin said you had a boyfriend back home. I think he thought you were probably bringing Maggie King tonight.' When my eyebrows raised in silent question, he clarified. 'When you said you were supposed to be meeting a friend tonight.'

'Aaaah, I see. Finn and I are friends – and that's all.' At the other end of the deck, Finn was still holding court with Kylie and Lauren.

'Are you sure? The way he's been looking at you isn't exactly friend-like.' Kylie's tinkly laugh floated through the night air, and Chris turned briefly towards the group. 'Although he seems busy in other directions at the moment.'

The same expression I thought I'd seen earlier flitted across his face. Anger? Concern? Or something else? It was, however, gone before I could figure it out.

'I wouldn't worry about her … with Finn. It's just the way he is; he can't turn the flirt off.'

'Worry about who?'

'Lauren, of course. I saw Michael's face before, but it's all just a bit of fun with Finn.' I narrowed my eyes, watching him closely for a reaction. 'I'm sure your sister is perfectly safe.'

'Right. Of course.' He laughed, and this time, the laugh had a touch of relief in it. Was it Kylie he was concerned about? Surely not. Although, if there was trouble in the Cosgrove marriage, that could have a bearing on the Cosgrove finances and, by extension, his own.

'Tell me about this boyfriend of yours,' he said. 'Is he a lawyer too?'

'He is, but corporate law. He's in Singapore at the moment.' Chris's mention of Miles reminded me about what Paula had said earlier, and again, annoyance burned at the pit of my stomach.

'I see. If he doesn't mind you being friends with other men, perhaps you might like to have dinner with me tomorrow night.'

Michael was now beside his wife, a proprietorial arm around her waist. Finn had made his excuses to the two women and was approaching us.

'Thank you, I'd like that.'

A smile spread across Chris's face. He really was quite attractive, just not showily so, as Martin and Michael were.

Chris's charm was more subdued, his light dimmer than the other two as if he'd always been second tier to them – and Nick. 'Excellent. If you like Asian food, there's a fabulous new restaurant on the wharf I think you'll love.'

'Sounds good to me.'

'I'll pick you up at six-thirty?' At my grin, he added, 'I know it's probably early by Melbourne standards, but, well, this is regional Queensland, and the kitchen closes on a Thursday night at eight.'

'It's fine,' I said. 'I'll see you then.'

He touched my hand and kissed my cheek lightly, and my heartbeat didn't change at all.

'What was that about?' Finn had joined me, but his attention was on the other man now with his sister, brother-in-law and Kylie.

'I'm having dinner with Chris tomorrow night.'

'Are you now?' Finn frowned slightly. 'Be careful of that one. He mightn't be as obvious as Martin Cosgrove, but there's something about him I don't trust.'

'I'll bear that in mind.' I sat my half-empty glass on a table. 'Are you ready to go?'

'I sure am. I can drive if you like; I've only had a couple of beers.'

'Oh, but I thought …'

'That I'd been knocking them back with Lauren and Kylie?' I nodded. 'That's what you were supposed to think.'

'And presumably, that's what Martin and Michael were

supposed to think. If it was, it worked – Kylie couldn't keep her eyes off you.'

Was that tinge of bitterness on my tongue jealousy? Maybe just a smidge. After all, it wasn't the first time someone I fancied had preferred Kylie. This begged a new question … Did I fancy Finn?

As if he knew what I was thinking, he grinned, the reflection of the lights dancing in his eyes. 'Aah but Clem, we both know I've only got eyes for you.'

My heartbeat quickened, but I managed to scoff lightly. 'You really can't turn the flirt off, can you?' Without waiting to see how he'd reacted to my comment, I turned away. 'Let's say our goodbyes and get out of here.' I spied Martin in a huddle with Michael. I touched Finn's arm lightly. 'Can you give me a quick minute?'

'Sure.' There was a quizzical expression on his face.

I felt his eyes on my back as I covered the short distance to where the two men stood. 'We're off now, but thank you for a lovely evening,' I said.

'You're welcome,' said Martin. 'It's not every day the prodigal daughter returns home.'

'Actually,' I said as if it were an afterthought. 'Can I have a quick word with you?'

Martin looked at Michael and grinned, a smugness to his smile that irritated me the way it always had done. 'Anything you need to say, you can say in front of Mick.'

Michael shrugged, the casual movement at odds with

the wariness that had come into his eyes.

'Alright then. The thing is…' I paused and held a finger to my lips as I gathered my words into their best possible arrangement. 'The thing is, if I choose to sell my aunt's cottage, my partner will have nothing to do with either that decision or any negotiations that are entered into.' Martin's smile stayed in place but had begun to lose its smugness. 'Just so we're clear. Anyway' —I kissed the air above his cheek— 'thanks for this evening, it's been … illuminating.'

Martin frowned. Before he could say anything in response, I turned to Michael. 'I know we didn't get a chance to talk properly, but it was nice seeing you.' I kissed his cheek lightly and left.

Back in the car, a combination of the dark and the silence made the space feel smaller, as though Finn was taking up all the room and all the air, my every nerve aware of his presence even as my brain was full of Miles and his interference.

When he pulled up outside Rose's place he handed me back the keys. 'You were quiet on the drive home; are you alright? What was that business between you and Martin just then?'

My stomach dropped as I turned to look into the fathomless depths of his eyes, and for a beat, I was lost for words, wishing he'd close the gap between us and kiss me already. I couldn't remember wanting anything more. It would be so easy to push all thoughts of Miles aside and reach for Finn. It wouldn't, however, be fair to either of us.

'Clem?'

'Yes, sorry, I'm fine. Just a bit tired, I think.' I forced a smile. Opening the car door, I got out and walked towards the gate. Behind me, I heard his door shut and the click of the lock.

I turned to face him. 'We've both got early mornings, so how about we debrief then?'

If he was disappointed I didn't invite him in, he didn't show it. 'Sure, sounds good. I'll see you in the morning.'

Handing me the keys, he leant in and kissed my cheek, just as Chris had done, but unlike Chris's kiss, Finn's touch made my heart race. I watched, my palm against my cheek where his lips had been, until he'd disappeared into the darkness. He didn't turn back. Finn Marella was turning into a complication I didn't need.

CHAPTER FIFTEEN

A new tarot card appeared in my dreams last night – Strength – a woman subduing a lion. I vaguely recalled Rose teaching me this card represented Leo in the tarot, but it was a vague recollection. Regardless, it was a reminder I needed to see Nina about the meanings of this card and the others.

More troubling than the tarot cards were the dreams featuring Finn that left me so hot and sweaty that I wondered whether I was going through perimenopause. Consequently, I found myself down at the beach earlier than usual, walking until the sun came up.

Cosmo and Beans saw me before Finn did, jumping over me in a pleased but soggy doggy welcome.

'You're early this morning,' Finn said when he drew level with me. 'Trouble sleeping?'

I looked sideways at him; his words didn't seem to carry any hidden meaning. 'Yes, I'm not used to these warm evenings and don't like to swim until the sun is up.'

'Thus avoiding shark feeding time. Sensible.' He fell into step beside me.

'What's your excuse?'

He looked across at me and grinned. 'This is normal time for us. I bring the dogs down for a run before returning to Brewz. Hey' —he hesitated briefly— 'I'm glad I ran into you ... Last night ... there was a moment in the car ...'

'Was there?' I walked closer to the water's edge so the next wave caught my knees.

'Yes, Clem, there was.' He sounded amused. 'It's okay; I know you have a Miles at home, and I know you need a friend, so I just wanted to let you know you don't need to worry about me trying anything on with you. I don't want things to be awkward with us.'

'Oh.' I bent down to pick up a pipi shell and tossed it back.

'You sound disappointed.' He stepped into the water and placed a finger under my chin to lift my head to meet his eyes. 'Did you want me to try something on?'

I shook my head and tried to laugh it off, but the laugh came out more like a nervous giggle. 'Of course not. As you said, I have a Miles at home.'

'If you didn't have a Miles at home?' Finn asked softly, the question swirling around like the water.

My toes sank into the sand as the water receded. 'Then yes,' I said bluntly. 'I'd want you to try something on. But there is a Miles, so you can't, we can't. This ... this eye thing that you've got going, this can't happen anymore.' I formed two fingers into a 'watching you' sign. 'It's distracting and not helpful.'

'Eye thing?' He almost spluttered with restrained laughter.

'Don't play dumb with me, mister. You know exactly what you're doing. You with those coffee-coloured eyes I could drown in.' On the horizon, the sky was colouring with first light. My face was so hot it had to be almost fluorescent in the pale light as he laughed at me. 'Oh, you…' I stalked further into the water and bent down to scoop some in his direction.

If anything, he only laughed louder. 'Really, Clem? Really?' And then he was in there with me and we were larking about, splashing each other like teenagers, the dogs jumping around us to join in the splashy fun.

Eventually, when we were both soaked through, I held up my hands in surrender. 'Enough!'

'Is that you giving up?'

'Yes,' I said, still laughing.

He flung a wet arm around my shoulders and guided me out of the water. 'We good?'

'Yeah, we're good.'

'So tell me then, how did you go last night? Uncover anything?'

'None of the men said anything about Rose, not overtly. I felt as though I was being sold on the town's prospects and how I could be part of that progress if only I sold Rose's house although it was always implied, not spoken. The women, though, that was another story. Paula is the perfect wife for a dodgy mayor, just dumb enough not to know what he's up to but ready to jump on board and support whatever he's pushing. As for Carmen, she's different and, I suspect, the real brains behind Bob Lindsay. She also resented Rose – and you, actually – for the impact on their finances at overturning the wharf proposal. If any of those four were involved, she'd be the one behind it for sure. She controls Michael in much the same way as she does Bob. You should've seen her face when you were flirting with Lauren and Kylie last night. She was basically ordering Michael to go in and control his wife. She also made a veiled threat regarding Miles, potentially letting him know I'd been seen out and about with the town rake.'

Finn's laugh came from his belly. 'The town rake? I'll take that … But how does she know Miles?'

'Yes, well, here's the thing. Apparently, Miles contacted Martin to let him know I was in the market to sell Rose's cottage, but until I speak with Miles, I'm not sure how much truth is in that.' My jaw tightened, and I was surprised to see my right fist balled. 'Carmen also was on about the shop – how it wasn't making any money and was one disaster away from being in trouble and that when that happened, her son would be happy to take it off my hands.'

'I thought Martin was after it?'

'So did I, but it seems Michael is too, and I don't believe their visions are the same. I wouldn't be surprised if this is a test for Michael and Martin set by their fathers.'

'To see which is better placed to become the senior partner when their fathers eventually step away? I know Ray and Bob have said they've handed over to their sons, but the way I hear it, they're as involved as ever. There was another brother – Martin's twin, Nick. I never met him, but apparently, he was being groomed to take over until he suddenly declared he wanted nothing to do with the business and left town. Martin has been trying to prove himself ever since.' He turned to me. 'Did you ever meet him?'

I paused and bent down to trail my hand through the water, effectively dislodging Finn's arm and hiding my face. 'Yes, I knew him. He was a better man than Martin but perhaps not a better businessman – he used to be too nice. He and Michael were close back then, and Martin was more on the outer.' I straightened, and we began walking again. 'The impression I got is Carmen is pushing for her son to win the race for senior partner. The fascinating thing is, though, I think Martin and Kylie's marriage might be in trouble, and I don't think Carmen's aware of that.'

'Really? What makes you think that?'

'It was something Chris said. He mentioned that one of his friends might be in the market for a divorce lawyer soon, and he also told me he manages the finances for the Cosgroves and the Lindsays and, I imagine, their spider's web of companies and accounts. The implication being that if things are going well for them, they're going well for

Chris, and a divorce could see a realignment of funds. Also, I saw him watching Kylie when she was flirting with you, and he didn't look happy.'

'Interesting ... I got the impression that Kylie was only flirting with me because I was there with you.' He turned to face me. 'Have you and Kylie got a history in that regard?'

We'd reached the spot where he'd normally head home and I'd head into the water. 'You could say that. But that's a story for another time.'

'I'll hold you to that. Enjoy your swim, and I'll see you shortly for coffee ... and will fill you in on what the young wives had to say.'

'Did they have much to say?' I dropped my swimming bag to the ground and pulled out my goggles.

'Let's just say it'll be a quick conversation.'

With a grin and a wave, he was off. I watched him for a moment and then pulled my soggy cover-all over my head and ran towards the water, my stroke faster than usual until I could no longer feel the scar tissue around my heart throbbing.

Finn had been right – it was a brief conversation, which was fortunate as he was short-staffed and needed on the counter. Kylie and Lauren, it seemed, took very little interest in their husband's business ventures other than how it affected them. 'As long as they have the money for their shopping and lunch trips to Noosa, they're happy,' he said. 'Lauren, I think, would do whatever Kylie told her to do.'

'She always did at school too,' I reflected. 'Kylie was Queen Bee and Lauren her faithful assistant.'

'If that's the case, I don't think things have changed … although I got the impression that while I was trying to get information about her husband, Kylie was trying to get information about you. Hang on a sec, I'll just get these coffees.'

As he worked, I hung back at the edge of the counter. Finn had a grin and a word for everyone, seemed to know the regulars' orders without being prompted and could charm a smile out of even the grumpiest early morning visitor. He flirted with them all, but it was light and playful and, as I watched, it occurred to me that the way he flirted with them and the way he flirted with me was different. Even though I'd told him it had to stop, knowing he was different with me filled me with a warmth I had no right to feel, and when he caught me watching him and flashed one of those grins that twinkled all the way to his eyes, that warmth set a chaos of butterflies free in my stomach.

'Sorry about that,' he said when he finally had a break. 'One thing Lauren did ask me was what your intentions are regarding the shop. I hadn't thought much about it until you said that Michael's interested in buying it, and now I'm wondering whether he's interested in buying it for Lauren to run.'

I contemplated that for a second. 'It could make sense.

Carmen was very interested in telling me what was wrong with it and mentioned Lauren was into crystals and the like. She probably wants to turn it into one of those designer wellness-type places.' There was a queue forming again. 'I'll let you go.'

He passed me across a fresh coffee. 'Have fun tonight, but be careful, eh?'

'I will.' I held up my cup. 'Thanks for this; I'll see you tomorrow.'

After trying (and failing) to reach Miles, I left a message for him to call me and spent most of the day at New Moon with Nina, going through the accounts and getting an idea of how the shop operated. While Nina resisted asking me outright what my plans were for the shop, it was apparent from the way she over-explained the sales figures – almost as if she was justifying them and herself – that it was top of mind for her.

'Even though you haven't asked, I know this is important to you,' I said. 'And while I don't know what I intend to do yet, I promise I'll give all options full consideration before I do decide.'

'Thank you, that's all I can hope for.' Although she smiled her understanding, the tightness in her shoulders showed her apprehension.

The space, filled to the brim with all things esoteric, took me back to those teenage days with Rose. 'Rose loved this shop, and I remember the thrill of turning the wheel and reading my fortune before curling up in a corner with a book on astrology or tarot. It was a special shop then, and it's a special shop now. I owe it to Rose to make the right call.'

She impulsively clasped my hands in hers. 'She knew what she was doing when she entrusted its future to you. Whatever decision you make will be the right one.' Narrowing her gaze, she searched my face. 'How are you sleeping?'

'Not well,' I admitted.

'Bad dreams?'

'Amongst other things.' The last thing I wanted was for her to know I was investigating Rose's death. It would be, I feared, one worry too many for her gentle soul to bear.

'I have a full list of customers this afternoon, but come in tomorrow for a reading,' she suggested.

'A full list – does that mean you need help on the counter? I'm happy to if you need me.'

'Bless you, but no, Bella will be in soon … in fact, here she is now.'

As I walked home my mind was on New Moon's future. The accounts had confirmed what Carmen had told me the previous night – New Moon was barely breaking even. Justin had told me Rose had been propping it up with the small amount of money she had left from when my grandfather died, but that was gone, and any unexpected event would see the shop dip into the red. If I kept it, unless there were major changes, I'd be throwing good money after bad, but I couldn't shake the feeling that keeping the shop going was exactly what I should be doing.

Gordon walked by when I was on my way home after my afternoon swim. 'I was hoping to see you. I heard you had a bit of a set-to with Maureen Peterson yesterday.' He inclined his head towards the house at the end of the street.

'I certainly did, and I had to bite my tongue from saying more too – very unpleasant, she was.' I adjusted the towel over my shoulder.

'She always has been. I always felt sorry for that fella she married – Malcolm he was – I reckon she nagged him to death.' He chuckled at the thought.

'I've been meaning to ask you why she disliked Rose so much.'

'Now, there's a story that dates back to high school.'

'Come in, Gordon, and have a seat. I need to dry off some more before I go inside anyway.' I led the way to the swing chair.

He sat down with a sigh. 'Even though I know I can see where she fell from here, this seat will always remind me of Rose.' He sniffed but quickly recovered. 'You know they were in the same year at school? Maureen and Rose?' I nodded, and he continued. 'And your mother was in the same year as Brian and me; a lovely woman your mother was. So different to Rose, so gentle. Where Rose would charge off after everything – she was a ball of fearless energy, one of life's truly free spirits even back then – your mother was made of more practical stuff. Where Rose would be spontaneous and impulsive, your mother was graceful and measured; like chalk and cheese, they were, but two closer sisters I never did see.

'When your mother married your father and moved away, I thought Rose's heart would break; when your mother passed away, I think it did. Even though Maureen was Rose's age, she idolised your mother – thought she was the bee's knees. I think she was only ever friends with Rose because it brought her into your mother's orbit and, through that, to the rest of us.

'When they were about seventeen, Maureen developed what you'd probably call a crush on Bob Lindsay. The problem was Bob had taken a shine to Rose and didn't know Maureen existed. When Bob asked Rose out and she accepted, Maureen got nasty and started sprouting all these stories about Rose and her morals. Once Rose realised what was behind it, she backed away from Bob, but as far as Maureen was concerned, the damage was done – especially since Bob moved straight onto Carmen. Maureen never forgave Rose for what she saw as a betrayal.'

'Seriously? She's held onto it for all those years?' It all sounded so petty.

'Brian once said Maureen is so tight she won't let go of anything – including a grudge.' Again, he chuckled. 'To be honest, I think Maureen knows how ridiculous it all was so now jumps onto anything she can to justify her dislike.'

'She mentioned a few things ...'

'Let me guess – cheating Bob and Ray out of that posh tower they wanted to build at the wharf; then there'd be the relationship between Rose and me – I'm sure she told you about that?' I nodded, grinning when his ears turned pink. He cleared his throat and continued. 'Her current beef is she thinks Rose has talked Brian out of selling to young Cosgrove even though she knows the reason Brian won't sell is because if he does, he'll be under pressure to give some of the proceeds to that waster of a son of his.'

'Chris? Really? I met him last night. He seemed more charming than I remember him being.'

'Of course he would be. If you sell, he knows his father will too. He fancies himself a player, that one, but always seems to have his hand out for a loan. Maureen thinks the sun shines out of him – always has done – and he knows it and plays up to it.'

'Interesting.' I decided not to mention I was meeting Chris for dinner that night. 'What about Ray? Maureen seems to still have a soft spot for Ray and Bob.'

Gordon nodded. 'She did back then too – very quickly moved her affections from Bob to Ray, but Ray wanted your mother – not that she was interested in him. I think he carried a flame for her long after she met your father. At the time, the word was he married Paula on the rebound.

Because Maureen had always idolised your mother, she didn't blame her in the way she did Rose. In fact, it was as if she blamed Rose for that too.'

Mum and Ray Cosgrove? I couldn't imagine it. Mum was gentle and quiet and preferred life in the background. She was happiest when she was bustling about looking after Dad and me. Paula Cosgrove, however, was the perfect wife for a mover and shaker like Ray Cosgrove.

'If Maureen blamed Rose for taking Bob and Ray away from her, how was she when they married Carmen and Paula?'

'Most of the time, I think she pretends Carmen and Paula don't exist, but she's never disliked them as much as Rose. By the time they were married, she'd been married too and had left Whale Bay. She stepped out a bit with Malcolm Peterson; I've always thought it was to make Bob or Ray jealous, not that either of them noticed. The joke was on her, though, as next thing you know, she's pregnant, and they're getting married in a hurry. Sadly, she lost the baby and could never have another one, and soon after that, Malcolm got a job down in Brissie, so they moved away. It's why she's doted on Brian's children even though she never had any time for their mother – criticised her no end, Maureen did. She probably thought she could do a better job raising them. Anyway, the minute poor Marion passed away, Maureen moved in with Brian – supposedly to look after him.'

'It sounds to me like she doesn't like women.' The

magpie was back and hopping about the rock border again.

'You could be right, Clem. I'd never thought about it that way. You know she even set her cap at me for a time after my wife passed – God rest her soul. When she found out about me and Rose, well …' He turned his head away, and I reached out to lightly touch his arm in comfort. 'Aaah, Clem, I miss her.'

'I know you do, Gordon,' I said softly. 'I know you do.'

The magpie's mate flew down and landed close to where we sat, looking at me intently with its beady eye before hopping across to the rock border.

'One for sorrow, two for joy …' Gordon whispered. 'Rose always used to say that. She loved the maggies, and they never swooped her.' He chuckled. 'But they always used to swoop Maureen Peterson. Good judges of character, these birds.'

'I remember her telling me once how they grieve for their fallen friends and sometimes make little grass wreaths. I don't know if that's true, but I like to think it could be,' I mused. 'She also told me how they know where to peck by listening for insects moving underground.' I let out a short laugh. 'I haven't thought about any of this in years.'

'You know, Clem, it's okay to miss her too. She knew that just because you didn't come back didn't mean you stopped loving her.' As he said it, Gordon continued looking straight ahead as if he knew how his words would affect me.

'Thank you.' We sat watching the magpies for a few minutes longer, neither mentioning the tears running down my face.

CHAPTER SIXTEEN

Chris hadn't been exaggerating when he'd talked up the food in the restaurant. We had a lovely meal, and I enjoyed his company. While we'd barely spoken at school (or, rather, he barely spoke to me), we found plenty to chat about over dinner. In fact, it wasn't until we'd finished eating that the conversation went in the direction I'd been hoping.

'This is fantastic. I know it sounds patronising, but I hadn't expected this in Whale Bay. I'd queue for food like this in Melbourne, and given that I hate queueing, that's saying something.' I reached for another eggplant chip. 'What is in this? It's savoury but sweet and spicy and sticky all at the same time.'

He beamed as I complimented his choice of restaurant. 'I know it's disloyal, but Rose and Finn were on the right track when they opposed the resort proposed for here. This development with its restaurants, bars and shops has been exactly what Whale Bay needed, and all credit has to go to Bob for talking Ray around to that.'

'The way I see it, he was going to win either way. This

sort of development supports his tour boats and provides a longer income stream, I'd imagine. The accommodation option might've struggled without the restaurants and bars to support it.' Regardless of what Chris had said, I sensed Carmen's influence behind the pivot.

'True, and the infrastructure here will support Finz when they can get that through.' As if he'd just realised what he said, he put his hand to his mouth. 'Sorry, that was out of line.'

I lifted one shoulder. 'That's okay; it's best to be open about these things. Is it generally assumed that now that Rose is gone, I'll sell?'

Taken aback, he wrinkled his nose and straightened in his chair. 'Why wouldn't you sell? Your life is in Melbourne, and there's no reason to hang on to the house here.' He paused, then added, 'You are going to sell, aren't you?'

I carefully placed my knife and fork back on the plate and, with one elbow on the table, rested my cheek against my forefinger. 'To be honest, Chris, I don't know. Everyone is talking as though my selling the house to the Cosgroves is a done deal, but as no one has made me a firm offer yet, as far as I'm concerned, all my options remain open. I have friends in Melbourne who'd love this place as a holiday house or even an Airbnb.'

He seemed lost for words. 'But I thought … without your land … Have you told Martin this?'

I shrugged my other shoulder. 'Why would I need to?

It's not like we have an agreement. As I said, he hasn't even made me an offer and until he does …'

'Will you sell to him if he does give you a good price?' There was desperation in his voice, panic in his eyes and a little pulse beat in his jaw. Why was he so invested in this? Was it just that without me selling, his father would be unlikely to as well? Did he need the money that badly?

'That depends on how good the price is,' I drawled, observing his reaction carefully.

He reached over and grabbed my wrist, his grip tight. 'You don't understand; if you don't sell, my father won't either.'

I yanked my hand from his grasp and rubbed at my wrist, glaring at him.

'Oh God, I'm so sorry.' He rubbed at his forehead. 'I don't know what came over me. I have no excuse other than to say I've been under a lot of pressure … Martin … he's invested a lot in this deal, and when he doesn't get his own way, it makes life difficult for everyone in his orbit.'

'By everyone, do you mean Kylie?' My wrist was still burning, and I was in no mood to accept his apology.

'What do you mean by that?' His eyes suddenly became wary.

'I saw how you looked at her last night when she was flirting with Finn. You seemed worried.' I paused. 'Does Martin take it out on Kylie when he's upset?'

Was that a flicker of surprise? 'He can do …' he said

slowly. 'How did you guess?'

'And I take it Kylie is the "friend" who might be in the market for a divorce?'

He exhaled, his shoulders slumping, and nodded slowly. 'But you can't say anything. Martin keeps such a tight control on everything, and he's worse when things aren't going well.'

'I see. And you're interested because …' Suddenly, it all made sense. 'Oh. My. God!' I leant closer so the tables around wouldn't be able to hear me. 'You're having an affair with Kylie? Are you mad?' I sat back in my chair, my hands over my face as I thought this new development through. Removing my hands, I hissed, 'Has no one told you not to shit where you sleep?' His expression was a combination of glum and resigned. 'I'm guessing no one knows?'

He shook his head. 'God, no. I'd be dead if Martin knew – not literally, of course, but professionally and that's just as bad.'

'And,' I spoke slowly, giving him the option to interject, 'you want to help her get a divorce because you love her?' He shook his head. 'You want them to stay married because you don't love her?' He nodded. 'Yet you say he's not the nicest of husbands.'

Chris shrugged. 'She likes the life he gives her. Here in Whale Bay, she's got the best house and the most money, and everyone knows Martin will be mayor someday. I can't give her any of that.'

'So you do love her?' I shook my head in exasperation. 'I can't keep up, Chris. You either love her or you don't – which is it?'

'The first,' he said miserably. 'But I know I can't give her what she likes, and while she says she loves me now, I think she loves the excitement of the affair more.'

'No doubt,' I muttered. 'What I don't understand is how this has anything to do with whether I sell the house to Martin or not?'

'He's told Kylie that he'll shout her and Lauren a trip to Paris for fashion week to celebrate when he gets the deal for Finz over the line, and when Kylie's happy, she's not looking to rock the boat. If there's a divorce, it will cause all sorts of problems within the company and the way we've set up the trusts, and there's no way Finz will get done. Martin won't be able to engage in any financial transactions until it's sorted. Believe me, Martin and Kylie need to stay married, or everything will come tumbling down, including my professional future.'

'Hmmm.' As convincing as Chris sounded, I refused to allow the state of Martin and Kylie Cosgrove's marriage to influence my decision-making. 'I'll bear it in mind.'

'Thank you, Clem, I appreciate that.' He looked sheepish. 'And I'm really sorry about the wrist – that's not who I am; I don't know what got into me. It won't happen again.'

'It had better not,' I warned. I bent to pick up my bag.

'I think we'd better be going.'

'Yes.' He called for the bill. 'I really am sorry; it's not how I wanted the evening to end.'

I raised my eyebrows. 'Just how did you want it to end?'

He laughed awkwardly. 'Not like *that*, obviously. You told me you have someone back in Melbourne, but …'

'It's okay, Chris, let's forget it.'

'I'll walk you home.' He sounded as weary as I felt.

'Thanks.'

We covered the short distance in silence, and at my gate, he shook my hand instead of kissing my cheek. 'You'll think about what I said?'

'Yes, Chris, I will. I won't promise you anything, but I'll bear it in mind.'

'That's all I can ask.' As he walked away, his shoulders were slumped, and he seemed somehow beaten.

Once inside, I texted Maggie.

Me: Hiya, can you please get Justin to find out if Michael Lindsay has lodged any plans with council for any of the shops on Beach Road?

Her reply came back quickly.

Maggie: Sure. How's it going? Any new suspects? Anything to report? How was last night?

Me: Plenty to report. I've just had dinner with Chris Walker. Gathering around the murder board tomorrow night?

Maggie: Sounds good. I'll round up the troops and arrange the takeaway.

Another thought struck me.

Me: Are you able to do a title search that tells me what property interests Kylie Cosgrove has?

Maggie: Sure. Any reason?

Me: Just an idea – I'll explain tomorrow.

I was just settling down to sleep when I woke with a start. Was that the gate? With my bedroom at the back of the house, I couldn't be sure. Jumping out of bed, I grabbed my phone and thrust my arms into the old kimono-style wrap I'd found in my wardrobe.

Barefoot, my heart pounding, I ran through the house, switching on the lights as I went, and flung open the front door in time to see a shadow pass through the gate. I heard it squeak shut, and the pounding of feet growing fainter as they ran towards the shops.

Lying on the mat was a large yellow envelope. Ignoring it, I stepped onto the path and swung my phone's torch in a wide arc, holding my breath, my ears on alert for any sound that didn't belong. A sudden rustling followed by a dull thud made my heart skip. My torch followed the sound, only to land on a possum running along the front fence.

Whoever was here had now gone. Still on alert, I retraced my steps to the front door and picked up the envelope by its corner.

Back inside, I slid on a pair of silicon gloves from the box under the kitchen sink – beetroot gloves Rose had always called them, given they were primarily used for cutting beetroot – grabbed a kitchen knife and gingerly lifted the flap on the envelope, pulling out the sheet of paper that lay within.

Do you want to end up like Rose? Stop asking questions.

My hand sprang to my chest as if it could stop my heart from beating out of it. Breathing heavily, I carefully replaced the message in its envelope and checked the locks on both the front and back doors. Leaving the kitchen and sitting room lights on, I went back to bed. I lay there, my eyelids snapping open at every noise, finally dropping off sometime after three.

CHAPTER SEVENTEEN

After my disturbed night, I struggled through my swim the next morning, replaying the events of the previous evening: the dinner with Chris, his revelations about the Cosgrove marriage and the part he was playing in that, and my late-night visitor and the message they'd left. Should I take it to the police? Even though I'd told Ted of my suspicions, taking a single note in was, by any standard, dramatic. If, however, it was something, it would be better to be safe than sorry.

Finn was busy when I called by, so beyond a 'How was your night?' and my 'Interesting – I'll tell you about it later', we didn't chat.

Ted Winters wasn't in when I called by the police station, so I left the envelope (in the plastic sleeve I'd slipped it into) and a note for Ted with Constable Selina Gupta.

I spent the remainder of the morning working through the random charts Rose had left on the dining table – the ones I'd put aside for later. While I needed to refer to some of the astrology books still in my bookcase the principles came back to me quickly. It was like another language, just one I hadn't spoken in a long time.

As free-spirited as she was, Rose had always been a proponent of what she referred to as traditional astrology – practical, commonsense astrology. Her clients came to her for 'what do I need to know' advice rather than 'when will this end' or 'why is life so unfair' readings. She also specialised in question-and-answer astrology – the type that had been practised for centuries, and it was those charts I was keen to examine.

Some were straightforward and clearly labelled: best day to get married and will I get the job? – which I assumed were client files – while others were more obscure. It was the latter I was interested in.

The chart titled 'keys' seemed a good place to start. Harry had said she'd lost her car keys, and it would've been so like Rose to have made a cursory search and then consulted a chart.

The chart was dated the day she died and set at half past eight that night. Goosebumps ran through my body at the thought I was now looking at what was probably the last chart she ever worked on. Less than thirty minutes after casting this, she made a cup of herbal tea and was interrupted by a sound outside, and soon after, she was dead.

Consulting the exercise book I'd written all my scrawled teenage notes in, I quickly worked out that in the chart, the keys were signified by Saturn, although the

Moon could also be a general signifier for things that roam or are lost. In this case, Saturn was in the part of the chart representing home, and the Moon was in a water sign in the segment of the chart ruled by Scorpio. Somewhere wet, and … Didn't Rose once tell me that Scorpio was about plumbing life's shadows and depths?

Heading into the bathroom, I checked the cabinet to no avail. Standing back, I cast my eyes around the small room with the same avocado green bath and shower combo (with matching avocado toilet) that remained unchanged since my youth. Was that something on the floor behind the toilet? Bending down, I reached into the narrow gap and pulled out a set of keys. They must have slipped out of Rose's pocket without her noticing. Even though there was no one to share in my triumph, I did the same happy dance I used to do for Rose when I correctly answered one of her questions.

'I've still got it, Rose,' I said aloud, holding the keys to the ceiling.

Buoyed by my success, I spread the other charts out on the table. These were more obscure, with one bearing the words '12th house'. Had Rose received the same threats I had, and if so, would she have mentioned it to Nina or Gordon? Would she have kept the messages? If someone had been making threats or plotting against her, she'd expect to find them in the twelfth house – the part of the chart that signified secret enemies …

In this chart, Mercury ruled the twelfth house and was

in … I traced around the chart with my finger … Pisces, which – I consulted my exercise book – was the sign of its fall. In other words, in the context of this chart, it was up to no good. And next to Mars could behave rashly. That was all very well and good, but what physical description did this give Rose's 'secret enemy'? For that, I'd need to consult the textbooks.

The final chart in the folder was easier to explain – Finn's birth chart. Pulling it out, I automatically analysed it the way Rose had taught me. 'Look for the patterns in the chart, Clem, the distribution of planets. Are they scattered or concentrated? What about the elements – are any missing? Is it a chart of action, fixed energy or something more flexible? What about the planets? Do they talk to each other, and if so, how do they get along? Which one is calling the shots? What are their motivations? Their ability to act? Now, close your eyes; how does it make you feel?'

I closed my eyes, and I was a teenager again, sitting on the floor in the sun, one leg splayed out, the other twisted behind me in the way my father always told me would leave me with bad knees and ankles as I got older. Rose was at the table guiding me, her voice leading me to the answers hidden within. 'What's the first thing you see, Clem?' I opened my eyes and saw the Leo sun at the top of the chart. Was Finn the Strength card in my dreams?

Before I could think too much about it, my phone rang – Miles. I groaned inwardly. 'Hi, how are you?'

'I'm good but haven't heard from you for a few days. I was getting worried. Is everything okay?'

Holding the phone out in front of me, I frowned. We often went days, sometimes a week, without talking, especially if either of us were away. Deciding not to tell him about my late-night visitor – there was nothing he could do about it from there and would only tell me to finish up and fly home – I said, 'I'm fine. In fact, I'm better than fine. The weather has been fantastic, if anything too warm. I've been ocean swimming every day and walking a lot.'

His chuckle came down the line. 'Sometimes I think you're part mermaid, but isn't ocean swimming dangerous? What about the sharks?'

I almost told him it was the sharks on land that I had more to fear but resisted the temptation. 'I avoid dawn and dusk and don't swim out too far. Besides, plenty of others are doing the same thing and a little further out than me, so if there are any around and they're tempted to nibble, the odds are it won't be me they choose to nibble on.'

'Right you are.' A momentary silence ensued. 'You asked me to call you urgently. What's the problem?'

'Fortunately, it wasn't life or death, given it's taken you over a day to call me back,' I snapped.

'I've been busy,' he said defensively.

'Not so busy you didn't make the time to call Martin Cosgrove and tell him I wanted to sell the cottage to him.' I made no attempt to hide my anger as I bit the words out.

There was a short pause before he spoke. 'I thought I was helping you out, darling. Of course you don't need to sell to him, but from my research, the Cosgroves are the biggest developers in your neck of the woods, and Martin told me you guys were friends at school.'

I snorted my laughter. 'Friends at school? That's a laugh. Although you are right in one aspect – I don't have to sell to Martin; in fact, I don't have to sell to anyone. Plus, whether or not I sell has nothing to do with you.' I paused and then blurted out the rest. 'You know what, Miles? When I said I needed space to think about us, well, I've thought. We're done.'

'You're still angry about me cancelling Bali, aren't you?'

Inhaling deeply, I squeezed my eyes shut briefly. 'I'm serious, Miles, and it isn't just about Bali. You must've noticed how we've drifted apart over the last couple of years? We're more like flatmates these days than partners, and I can't remember the last time we had sex.'

'Is that what this is about? The fact that we're no longer at it all the time?' His voice held a sneer which tested my temper.

'All the time? Once every so often would be nice.'

'I didn't realise we were keeping track. I'll make more of an effort.'

Sighing heavily at the passive-aggressive tone, I tried to bring the conversation back on a more even keel. 'Perhaps we should be having this conversation face to face.'

'That's a bit difficult to do when you're swanning around up there.'

'Swanning around up here? Do I need to remind you that you're the one who thought it would be a great idea for me to come up here for a couple of weeks?'

'Yes, to pack up and arrange the sale of your aunt's house. Instead, I hear …' He broke off.

'What do you hear?' A bubble of anger made its way up from my stomach to my throat.

'Nothing. It doesn't matter.'

'Miles …'

'I was talking to Martin Cosgrove, and he mentioned that you'd gone to a barbecue at his house with some barista guy. Martin says he's a troublemaker and, apparently, doesn't have the best reputation where women are concerned.'

As he spoke, the bubbles multiplied and expanded; it was all I could do not to hang up on him. Instead, I counted to ten. 'How did you just happen to be speaking to Martin?'

'He called me. And whether or not you sell does have something to do with me. I thought it could be the push we need to sell our apartment and buy something down by the water, seeing as how you love the sea so much. I was only thinking about you.'

By now, the red mist had well and truly descended. 'Weren't you the one who insisted on that clause in the prenup? We maintain separate bank accounts, any inheritances and superannuation accounts are separate, and the only assets that are subject to division are jointly owned assets such as property and furniture. Remember that?'

'Of course I remember that,' he spat. 'I'm only just bringing my super back up to scratch after I had to give so much to my ex-wife.'

'And, if I recall correctly, the inheritance clause was there to protect you for when your parents passed away, which they haven't done yet. So what was supposed to happen, Miles? I sell Rose's house and her shop—'

'You didn't mention a shop.'

'Because I didn't know until I got here that she'd bought the shop she used to work at, but I'm surprised Martin didn't mention it, given he wants to buy that too. So tell me, Miles, what was your plan? We'd invest the proceeds from the sale into a new house in Brighton which we'd then split the proceeds on when we broke up?'

He drew in his breath sharply. 'You're the only one, *darling*, who is planning on separating, and if you think so badly of me, maybe we *should* call it a day.'

In the ensuing silence, I contemplated apologising. It was a cheap shot, and Miles had never given me any indication to believe he'd act like that, but then, why would he? He earned substantially more than I did, his annual partner bonuses more than many people earned in a year. We'd always avoided arguments about money because we simply never spoke about it. We each contributed to a single joint account that paid the mortgage, household expenses and groceries, and after that, our respective incomes were our own concern.

'Do you think we started out not trusting each other and never really moved on from that?' I asked.

'What on earth are you talking about?' Now he sounded perplexed rather than affronted.

'With the prenup. We signed that before we even moved in together, and while it's meant we haven't had to argue about money, we've also not had to trust each other either.'

'You know why we needed the prenup,' he said. 'And you know how badly I was burnt the first time. I wasn't going into another relationship without one.'

'I understand that, but it also means the stakes are lower for each of us, and I wonder now whether that's a good thing. It's easy for us to get out or to ...'

'Or to what? Are you now going to accuse me of cheating? Or are you projecting your own behaviour onto me? You still haven't explained the barista.'

'No! Of course not. Just that ...' I didn't know how to finish the sentence. How did I tell him that having a get-out clause had made it unnecessary for us to trust the other completely? It made no sense, and he wouldn't understand. 'As for Finn – the barista – there's nothing to explain. He was a friend of my aunt and now he's my friend too. He's helping me with ... You know what? Let's talk about this when I'm home, and in the meantime, I'd appreciate it if you let me handle the sale – or otherwise – as I see fit. And, just so you're aware, neither Martin Cosgrove nor anyone else has made me an actual offer to accept or decline.'

A shop silence and then, 'I didn't realise … I was under the impression that …'

'Please, Miles, let me deal with it. We'll talk when I get home.'

I rang off and sat there for a little while longer, my head in my hands. Miles and I had loved each other once, at least I thought we did; perhaps I owed it to him – and us – to go home now and talk it through. If I did, he'd somehow manage to convince me to stay – after all, Miles earned the big bucks because of his ability to win an argument. He'd probably also talk me out of coming back here to finish investigating Rose's death and could even persuade me there was nothing to investigate.

While I couldn't deal with Miles right now, I could put Martin Cosgrove back in his box.

CHAPTER EIGHTEEN

Martin's office overlooking the marina and the yachts moored there was everything I expected it to be – all white-timbered Hamptons-style.

He looked up from where he was perched on the edge of his secretary's desk when I flung the door open, his million-dollar smile matching his million-dollar view. 'Clem, this is a lovely surprise.'

I, however, was in no mood for pleasantries. 'I thought I made it clear to you the other day that discussions regarding my aunt's property were to be held with me, not my partner.' Martin's smile slid away. 'Ever since I've arrived in town, there's been an expectation that I'll sell Rose's property to you, yet no one has named a price, and you've gone behind my back to Miles.' I planted my hands on my hips, my shoulders straight, my jaw square. 'So you know what? Don't bother making me an offer. How could I conduct business with someone I can't trust?'

Without waiting for a response, I whirled around and headed back down the timber steps.

'Clem, wait!' He clattered down behind me, catching me at the bottom. 'There seems to be some misunderstanding. How about we have a drink and talk about this?' The smile was back, his tone conciliatory.

'What is there to talk about? I told you, I thought, quite clearly, that Miles would have nothing to do with any decision I made, yet at the first opportunity, you're on the phone to him.'

'Aaaah.' He nodded slowly as if a penny had dropped. 'You're angry because I told him about you and Finn.' He sighed. 'I'm sorry, Clem, but that was for your own good; Finn Marella is trouble, and I thought Miles needed to know.'

'Really? Seriously? My relationships are none of your business, and if I were you, I'd worry more about your own.'

His smile slipped again. 'What's that supposed to mean? There's nothing wrong with my relationship.'

I shrugged a shoulder. 'Well, you have nothing to worry about then, do you?' I suppressed a grin as uncertainty flickered across his face. 'You barely know me, and you don't know Miles at all, so don't tell me you're concerned about our relationship and expect me to believe it. Your only reason for jumping on the phone to snitch to Miles – because that's exactly what it was, Martin, snitching – was for Miles to order me to come home where I belong.'

We were standing in the middle of the central courtyard, and Martin looked around nervously to see if anyone was paying attention. 'Let's have that drink.'

'What's wrong? Were you worried I'd look into your development plans too closely? Or maybe I'd fall back in love with Whale Bay and decide to keep the house as a holiday house? Or is it that you want me gone because I'm questioning the circumstances of Rose's death?' My gaze narrowed as a mask dropped over his face. 'Did you leave the note on my doorstep last night?'

'What?' He shook his head emphatically. 'I have no idea what you're talking about. Rose's death was an accident. The case is closed, and I don't know anything about any notes.'

'Was it, though? An accident?' I paused, my eyes not leaving his, just long enough for my words to sink in. 'Don't go behind my back again, Martin. If you want to buy Rose's cottage, you need to make me a proper offer; by that, I mean your best offer. I'm not interested in negotiating, and I will be getting valuations—'

'I can help you with a name,' he offered, his sales persona restored.

I scoffed at that. 'I'm sure you can, and I'm sure they wouldn't be in your pocket.' A thought occurred to me, a distasteful one, one I didn't want to say out loud but knew I had to. 'Had you promised Miles a commission if I sold to you?'

Martin dropped his eyes, his smile wavering.

'Oh wow. Wow.' I shook my head in disbelief, and as he went to open his mouth, I raised my hands, my palms towards him. 'No, Martin, you don't get to say anything more.'

Turning on my heel, I stalked away from him, waiting until I was across the road before calling Miles.

'I know about the commission Martin offered you,' I spat out as soon as he picked up. 'Don't call me again, Miles. We'll sort out the legal bits and pieces when I get home.'

And then I hung up.

Even though I was still fuming as I walked back to New Moon, one step inside the shop and the combination of the incense and tinkling water from the Buddha fountain in the corner, my heartbeat immediately slowed.

This shop was an oasis of calm, and suddenly, I couldn't allow it to be turned into a fine diner or a glossy wellness retreat (or whatever it was that Lauren had planned). There had to be a way of making the shop profitable without impacting its integrity.

Nina looked up from her appointment book and smiled that calm smile of hers. 'Bella,' she called to the teenager unpacking books onto a shelf. 'You haven't properly met Clem yet, have you?'

The girl looked around shyly, not quite meeting my eyes. 'Hi.'

'How long have you worked here, Bella?' I asked.

She glanced across at Nina before answering. 'A couple of years. Rose gave me a part-time job while I was still at school ...' Looking again at Nina, who nodded, she continued. 'My dad died, and Mum had four of us at home, so the money from here really helped. When I left school, Rose gave me more hours.'

'And you didn't want to do any further study?' I asked gently.

She lowered her eyes again, but not before I saw the sadness she'd tried to hide. 'Mum needs me at home.' She shrugged.

'I see.' Bella was obviously another one of Rose's rescue missions. What would happen to people like Bella and Nina if she sold the shop? No, I wouldn't allow that to happen.

Bella smiled politely. 'It was nice to meet you, Clem, but I'd better get back to it.'

'Let's do this reading.' Nina led me behind a crimson velvet curtain into the reading room. The room had been painted a rich blue, against which sat accessories in jewel-bright colours, light coming from lamps in the corner and flickering candles. The effect was one of entering another world, an exotic world as far away from Whale Bay as possible – a world of magic and mystery.

'It's lovely in here now.' I picked up a large piece of amethyst from the collection of crystals on the table. 'Back in my day, this room had about as much personality as your average department store fitting room, but now …'

'The three of us decorated it together.' Nina's smile was sad remembering Rose. Recovering quickly, she handed me a deck of cards. 'As you shuffle these, how about you talk me through the dreams you've been having?'

Knowing I could speak freely to Nina without fear of judgement, I told her about the tarot dream with the mermaid. 'It was like she was a younger me, beckoning me back to Whale Bay. As for the other cards, change, death, inheritance, it's all there. The weird thing is I'm not having the same dream anymore.' As I spoke, I pulled the cards from the deck and laid them in front of me.

'You don't need to – you've followed the meaning of it. You said you'd had a mini reading in Melbourne. What did she say about the cards?'

I relayed the conversation, and once I'd finished, Nina agreed. 'I think the High Priestess is you too. Rose always said you had an intuitive flair for reading but that when you left here and went home, logic took over. And it seems to me that in your chosen career, you've made a conscious choice to listen to logic and reason more than your heart. That's understandable, but this card is saying you need to follow your intuition now, regardless of what reason says. Look for the signs that are around you.'

An image of the magpie and its mate flashed through my brain.

'What are you thinking?'

I hesitated slightly, more to ensure I had the events straight in my brain than from any reluctance to tell her. 'The other day, I was sitting in the swing chair – you know the one under the fig?' When she nodded, I continued. 'I asked Rose to send me a sign that I was on the right track and doing the right thing – more because I thought that's what she would do rather than any certainty that a sign would be sent. Anyway, a magpie popped down and began pecking around, and then its mate arrived. I remembered the old rhyme Rose used to say about magpies. When it looked at me, it really felt like it was looking at me, if you know what I mean.'

She nodded. 'I do know what you mean, and I know the rhyme: one for sorrow, two for joy. Magpies are often seen as spiritual birds, especially if seen after death. In many pagan faiths, they're associated with death, but not just the physical death of a loved one, but also the kind of death that brings change and transformation.' She tapped the Tower and Death cards. 'Much like these cards. The symbolism goes further than that, though – the black and white being the duality of head and heart, good and bad, masculine and feminine – it's a reminder that one can't exist without the other.' She looked up from the cards and met my eyes. 'It's also a reminder that there are two sides to every story.' She pushed the cards towards me. 'You said the Emperor fell out during the reading?'

I nodded and pulled that card from the deck too.

'The Emperor is a card often associated with Aries – you only need to see the ram's heads on his throne to see that. The red of his robe signifies power, passion and vitality. The sun is, as you know, exalted in Aries, and this card is all about bringing peace through dignified yet courageous actions. Tell me, what other cards have come up since you've been here?'

'Strength and …' I inhaled deeply and looked at the star-painted ceiling before deciding to trust her. 'And the Fool … which was found beside her body.'

Nina covered her gasp with her hand. 'How do you know that?'

Another deep breath. 'I've seen the police report.'

She held my eyes for another beat, maybe two. 'I see.' She tapped the Emperor. 'Rose trusted you.' Another little pause, and then, 'Can you please lay out the Strength and the Fool cards and fan the rest face down?' I did as she requested. 'Okay, now please draw another card and lay it on the Strength card.'

I drew the Lovers, and a smile spread across her face. 'Strength is what it says it is, but it's inner strength as well – the sort that comes from the heart, from emotional vulnerability. It's also very often a Leo male.' As my face flamed, she said, 'I'll leave that with you. The card of the Lovers signifies love, but it also represents choices that need to be made. One more card, please.' I drew the King of Pentacles. 'This is the other man – wealthy, influential, possibly materialistic. Is any of this resonating with you?'

'Yes, it is.' Finn and Miles, the lion and the king. Pushing aside my love life, I focused back on the Fool. 'I don't know why, but I feel as though the Fool has something to do with what happened to Rose.' I picked up the card and traced its lines. 'Do you know if Rose received any threatening letters or notes in the weeks before she died?'

'I think you're right about the card; as for the notes?' Nina picked up a piece of clear quartz and passed her thumb back and forth across the jagged edges. 'There was an envelope she gave me the day she died; she asked me to put it in the locked cabinet for safekeeping. Draw another card while I go find it.'

An envelope for safekeeping the day before she died? Could Rose have known what was coming? I drew the Knight of Swords and sat it on the Fool.

'Aaah, the Knight of Swords,' said Nina, returning to the room. 'A young man, driven to succeed, but this is upside down, so this person is not thinking straight, could be more talk than action. Another one?' I placed the Seven of Swords on the pile. 'And he's untrustworthy.' Nina passed me a large yellow envelope, a concerned look on her face. 'Be careful, Clem.'

'I will.'

Bella popped her head through the curtain. 'Excuse me, your next client is here, Nina.'

Resisting the urge to open the envelope, I stood. 'Thank you, Nina, that's been interesting.'

'You're welcome, but for people like us, the cards clarify what we're thinking rather than telling us what to think.' She gave me a quick hug. 'Trust what you know and look for the signs the way Rose taught you.'

I turned back, my hand on the curtain. 'Just so you know, but please don't say anything to Bella yet, I won't be selling the shop.' As she went to speak, I held up a hand to stop her. 'I have no idea how we'll make it work, but I'll need your help, and we can work the details out. I just wanted you to be the first to know.'

Nina's eyes filled, and she raised her hands to her chest in prayer. 'Rose chose well.'

Unable to say more, I nodded briskly and left.

Next door at Brewz, Finn was busy with the post-lunch rush. On seeing me, he gave a little wave. I waved back and crossed the road to the beach. Sitting cross-legged on the sand, I slid my finger carefully along the envelope's seal. Inside were sheets of paper bearing typed messages similar to the one left at my house last night:

Sell

If you don't sell, you'll be sorry

You've been warned

This is your last chance

A chill ran up my spine as I read them. Why hadn't Rose taken these to the police? Ted respected her and would've taken her seriously; I was sure of that.

Replacing the messages in the envelope, I rested back on my elbows and tilted my head towards the sky, the sun warm on my face, the rhythmic lapping of the waves calming and centring my mind. What had Nina said about signs? Something about remembering what Rose had taught me.

'Clemmy,' she'd say, 'if you see or hear something once, it's a nice to know. If you come across it again, take notice. When it happens a third time, be prepared to act.'

The magpies … What were they trying to tell me? Springing to my feet, I brushed the sand from my bum. Whatever it was, I wouldn't find it here.

CHAPTER NINETEEN

Maggie and Justin were the first to arrive that evening, followed soon after by Finn and the dogs, with Siouxsie breathlessly bursting through the door a few minutes later. 'Have I missed anything?'

'Everyone's only just got here,' I assured her.

'Excellent.'

Drinks poured and cheese and dippy bits out, we got underway. Siouxsie and I took up our position at the murder board – me asking the questions and her with her marker pen and Post-it stickers.

'Okay … suspects. I think we all agree Martin still is the prime suspect; his motive is the clearest: if Rose isn't around, he'll be able to pick up this property, and once he has this one, Gordon and Brian will sell too.' There were nods all round. 'I have a new suspect I'd like to put up, though. Maureen Peterson.'

'That grumpy shrivelled-up old cow?' Siouxsie grimaced. 'I hope she did do it. I'd like to see her go down.'

'Siouxsie!' chided her mother.

'Come on, Mags, you can't say you weren't thinking it, too.' Mother and daughter exchanged cheeky grins.

'Okay, you got me there, but why do you think she had it in for Rose?'

I told them what Maureen had said about Rose and what I'd found out from Gordon. 'She hated her – so much it was almost like an obsession.'

'But when you hate someone that much, you wouldn't want to see them dead because you'd lose so much of your purpose,' pointed out Finn. 'Maureen, and yes, I agree she's an old cow. The weird thing is, she probably misses Rose now she's gone. There's nowhere for all that dislike to go.'

'I wouldn't be surprised if she's transferred it to me,' I said wryly. 'So what do we think? Should she go on the board?'

'Hell yeah!' Siouxsie drew a cartoon figure with a frown and pinched mouth and stuck it at the top of the board. 'Just because she's a grumpy old shrivelled-up cow.'

'What's her motive?' asked Justin. 'Dislike doesn't seem enough.'

'It's always love or money,' said Maggie.

'In Maureen's case, it's love and money.' I topped up the glasses. 'She wants Brian to sell so he can give some of the money to Chris – who she absolutely idolises. But would she kill for that? I don't think so.'

'There's no way she could move a body or a ladder on her own, though.' Finn wrinkled his nose and itched idly at the back of his head. 'There's nothing to her. Even if she has a motive, she'd need an accomplice.'

'And no one likes her enough to be her accomplice,' said Maggie.

'I'm not sure.' Finn drained his beer. 'But we have space on the board, so let's pop her there.'

I tossed the ball of wool to Justin. 'What have you found out?'

He caught it neatly and grinned. 'Is this the murder board equivalent of an offsite thought ball where whoever catches the ball has to come up with an idea?'

'Something like that,' I admitted with a chuckle.

'Right, well, council the other night was full of talk about you coming back. Ray Cosgrove was talking as though the sale was a done deal and how quickly they could push the development through once you agreed to terms. The plans haven't yet come to council, but the way Ray and Bob were talking, that work has already been done in the background.'

'I bet it has,' I muttered.

'Have you received an offer from them yet?' he asked. 'Because it sounded like they had some inside knowledge of your intention to sell.'

'No, but like you said, it's assumed I'll take whatever they do offer. And the inside knowledge' —I ducked my head— 'came from Miles.'

I told them about my conversation with Miles and Martin earlier today, leaving out the part about Miles being offered what was essentially a 'finder's fee' for helping get me over the line. That part was way too humiliating.

'Oh, Clem, I'm sorry.' Maggie reached for my hand and gave it a short squeeze.

I mumbled my thanks and busied myself with the cheese board.

'How did Martin react when you hinted Rose's death mightn't have been an accident?' The question came from Finn as he reached over me to slice some Red Leicester.

'That's the weird thing. You know what Martin is like – all toothy salesman smile – but it was like a shutter came down, and for a second it felt as though I was seeing the real him. It also made sense of something Chris said—'

'Chris? Not Chris Walker?' Maggie sent an unreadable glance to her husband.

'Yes, Chris Walker. We went for dinner last night.' I narrowed my gaze. 'Why?'

Justin pursed his lips. 'It's probably just gossip.'

'You and I both know it's not.' Maggie straightened her shoulders.

'Will someone tell her already?' Siouxsie said impatiently.

'Well …' Justin began. 'Did he happen to mention that he looks after the accounts for the Lindsays and the Cosgroves?'

'Yes, he did. He said they keep him busy. He also said he has his own business in Brisbane.'

'With the Lindsays and Cosgroves as his only clients.' Justin raised his eyebrows. 'I heard that he left his last firm in Brisbane under a cloud of sorts. Nothing could be proven, but there was a suspicion of what we accountants like to call "irregularities" in some of the accounts. The money was repaid, so nothing else was said, and the next thing you know, he's looking after the financial interests of Bob and Ray.'

'What Justin hasn't told you,' added Maggie, 'is that the assumption is Bob and Ray loaned Chris the money to repay his "loans"' —she used her fingers to make air quotes— 'which means they now own him.'

'Their own tame accountant who can turn a blind eye to any of their dodgy dealings,' I said sardonically. 'He did tell me his financial future was tied to the successes of theirs.'

'None of this has been proven though,' Justin rushed to add, frowning when Siouxsie drew a cartoon figure, labelled it Chris and stuck it on the board. 'So I don't know if we should be putting him on the murder board as a suspect.'

'He doesn't seem the murdering type,' I mused. 'In fact, he struck me as being, I don't know, a bit weak?'

'I agree,' said Maggie. 'Sure, he's as dodgy as all get out, but he's always been all talk and no trousers, if you know what I mean.'

'Which could make him the perfect accomplice for either Maureen or Martin,' I said. 'There's something else we need to know about Chris – although I'm not sure how this fits with motive – he's having an affair with Kylie Cosgrove.'

As far as mic drops went, this was a good one. Siouxsie was the first to break the silence. 'No. Way! Serious?'

I nodded, a smug smile on my face.

'Kylie and Chris Walker?' Maggie finally found her voice. 'Are you sure?'

'Maybe he has more balls than I thought,' muttered Justin.

As for Finn, he laughed – a laugh that began all the way down in his belly and erupted out. 'So that's why he didn't look happy the other night when I was flirting with her and Lauren?'

'Yep. I thought it was because problems in the Cosgrove marriage could have flow-on effects to Cosgrove-Lindsay developments, and according to Chris, Martin isn't a nice man when he's thwarted.'

'Neither, if you believe the gossip, is his father,' commented Maggie. 'Besides, we saw what Martin was like at school.' She exchanged a glance with me, and I knew what she wanted to say was how Nick had been nothing like his brother or his father.

'As unbelievable as this is, Chris would be ruined if Martin ever found out,' Justin began.

'He said Martin would kill him if he found out, but then he clarified that he'd kill him professionally,' I added.

'I have no doubt about that, and Kylie certainly wouldn't hang around if the money ran out, but I can't see how this information links to Rose's death.' Justin realised he was still holding the ball of wool and tossed it to Maggie.

'What if …' Maggie mused. 'Everyone knows that if Rose sold, Brian and Gordon would too, so what if Chris needs his father to sell so he will get some of the sale proceeds? It could be enough to pay his debt to the Cosgroves and keep Kylie happy.'

'Knowing Kylie, that would only be a couple of months. Besides' —Siouxsie leant forward, resting her elbows on her knees— 'when I was at the cocktail bar down at the wharf the other day, she and Lauren were there, and they were talking loudly about how Martin was going to send them on a trip to Paris fashion week when the Finz deal came through.'

'Chris mentioned that to me too,' I said. 'As much as he says he loves her, he thinks it's in everyone's best interest that she stays married to Martin.'

'So, he is all talk and no trousers,' concluded Justin.

I shrugged. 'In any case, he stays on the board.'

Our board was now looking full. In terms of suspects, we had Martin, Chris and Maureen – although none of us really believed she had it in her. We also had plenty of Post-it notes and connecting wool. There was, however, something about the scene photos that didn't seem right. I went to sip at my wine and realised it was empty.

Finn was standing beside me and topped it up. 'What are you seeing?'

'Or rather not seeing.' I tilted my head to the side, studying the board. 'There's something about these scene photos ...' I shook my head. It would come to me, just not right now. 'Maggie, you've got the thought ball of wool; anything to report?'

'I'm glad you asked ... You know how you asked me to look at any properties Kylie owned. Well, aside from a joint share in the marital McMansion on Nob Hill, the vacant block in Wharf Road – the one directly behind Brian's house – is in her name. I did a company search on her too, and she's listed as a director on four of their companies.'

Once more, I turned to face the board, tapping my finger against my lips; this was beginning to make sense. 'So ... if she split from Martin, she'd need to sell to Martin for Finz to get over the line. She could potentially use that as leverage to get the divorce settlement she wants.'

'And all of this requires Rose to be off the scene,' added Justin. 'If Rose is gone, Brian will sell and if Brian sells, so will Gordon.'

'The only real block in the plan is you,' Finn said sombrely. 'I'm worried that if someone is prepared to kill for this development, you might be in danger too, especially since you told Martin, who still has to be the prime suspect, that you won't sell to him.'

'There's something else.' I didn't turn from the murder board, not wanting to see the concern on their faces. 'I had a visitor last night.'

'Who?' Justin's voice was laced with concern.

'I don't know. It was around eleven, and by the time I got out of bed, they were on their way out the gate and heading towards the shops. They were dressed in black, it was dark, and I have no idea whether they were male or female, but they left this.' While I'd given the original to the police, I'd taken a photo of the note. 'And before you ask, I gave it to the police this morning. There's more, though. Rose received similar notes in the weeks leading up to her death.'

Finn's frown had deepened. 'She never mentioned anything.'

'No, she didn't say anything to Nina either, but she gave her these to take care of the day before she died.' I passed across the plastic sleeves containing the notes Rose had received.

'This is clearly designed to frighten you into leaving.' Finn looked up from the threats, concern furrowing his brow. 'Have you been to Ted about this?'

'No, but I will. I didn't know about these when I took my note in this morning. I'll—'

A knock on the screen door interrupted me. Before answering, I inclined my head towards Siouxsie who, quick on the uptake, picked up the wrap I had hanging over the back of a chair and draped it over the murder board.

'Tyson!' exclaimed Maggie. 'What are you doing here?'

'Hi Mum, Dad, Siouxsie … Finn …' He cast a suspicious gaze around the room. 'What are you all doing here?'

'Just a few drinks and nibbles to welcome Clem to town.' Maggie popped an olive in her mouth.

'You're welcome to join us; can I get you a beer?' I pointed in the direction of the kitchen.

'No, thank you, but I am actually here to see you, Clem.' His eyes caught the covered noticeboard. 'Do I want to know what's under that cloth?'

Justin shook his head. 'No, son, I don't think you do.'

He looked at this mother and sighed. 'I don't think I do either.' He took a breath. 'Clem, I need you to come with me. There's been a break-in at New Moon.'

My stomach flip-flopped, and Finn immediately came to my side, a protective arm around my shoulders. 'Nina? Was Nina there?'

He shook his head. 'Nina is okay. She wasn't there, but we need you to identify if anything is missing.'

'But I wouldn't know—' I rubbed at my forehead. 'I've not spent a lot of time in there yet.'

Maggie gripped my free arm. 'You're the registered owner, Clem; they'll need you to be there as they search the premises. You know that ...'

'Of course. I'll come, but we've had a few wines ... I can't drive.'

'I'll take you,' said Tyson. 'But you'll need to put some shoes on; there's a lot of broken glass.'

'Of course.' I slid my feet into my rubber thongs.

Tyson watched me, frowning. 'Maybe not those ... the

glass.'

I nodded mutely and traded the flip-flops for sneakers.

'I'll come with you; the dogs will be okay here,' said Finn.

Again, I nodded.

'We'll pack up and lock up and then see you down there.' Maggie moved to stack the cheese knife onto the board and used a serviette to mop up some biscuit crumbs from the coffee table.

'Thank you.'

Suppressing a giggle, I allowed Tyson to lead me out to the police car, wondering what Maureen Peterson would think if she were looking out her window about now. Then a more sobering thought took over – Carmen Lindsay's comment about how New Moon was one disaster away from being in the red. It looked as though that disaster had arrived. Could this be the end for Rose's beloved store?

CHAPTER TWENTY

This morning, I'd been so sure that no matter what I decided about Rose's house, I'd make sure this shop, this sanctuary of calm, continued to trade. Tonight, though, it was anything but calm and as far from a sanctuary as possible. Approaching the shop, my shoes crunched on tiny cubes of the glass that had been our front window. Inside, it was worse. Whoever had broken into the store had done so with the express purpose of causing as much damage as possible. Stock was strewn all over the floor, and the Wheel of Fortune, which had been spun for decades, had been ripped off the wall and was in pieces. I stifled a sob, and Finn wrapped his arms around me, his warmth doing its best to soothe my jangled nerves.

As I stood there, surrounded by the debris of Rose's dream, Ted strode out of the office. Wearing silicon gloves and a dark frown, he held out a piece of paper.

You were warned.

'Do you know anything about this?'

Stepping out of Finn's protective embrace, I nodded.

'Yes, I received something similar on my doorstep last night. I dropped it in this morning … and I found a collection of them here this afternoon that I was going to tell you about tomorrow. Rose had been receiving them and had given them to Nina for safekeeping. I think she'd been keeping them in a lockable cabinet.'

'This one?' Ted pulled aside the purple velvet curtain that separated the office space from the rest of the shop.

Taking a step forward, I was surprised when my foot landed in water; the Buddha mini fountain had been upended, and the contents had spilled into a basket of discounted books.

'Yes.' I gingerly stepped over a jumble of small crystals tipped randomly around the store. 'She said she'd kept them in the lockable…' My voice trailed off when I saw the drawer had been jimmied open. 'At first glance, it doesn't look like the culprits have taken anything. This is more wilful damage than anything else. Do you think they were looking for the messages sent to Rose? The break-in might have been staged to cover that.'

Ted had taken a seat behind Rose's desk; his fingers steepled under his chin. 'You didn't mention any threats to Rose when we spoke on Tuesday.'

'That's because I didn't know she had received any until this afternoon.'

If someone wanted to remove evidence of the threats to Rose, did that mean they knew we suspected her death wasn't an accident? As if he'd followed the direction of my thoughts, Ted said, 'Does anyone other than the Kings and Finn know about your suspicions?' As I was about to ask how he knew that, he added, 'Tyson said they were all there at your place tonight.'

'No, I haven't spoken to anyone about it … Oh, hang on' —I slapped my forehead lightly— 'I might've said something to Martin Cosgrove this morning – not that I actually said anything, it was more of a hint really – I just wanted to see how he reacted.'

'You've decided Martin Cosgrove is your prime suspect, have you?'

'Yes, he has the strongest motive.'

'He also has a cast-iron alibi; he and Michael and their fathers were at a Chamber of Commerce event I also attended on the evening Rose died.' When my eyes widened in surprise, he chuckled mirthlessly. 'Yes, Clem, after I spoke to you, I knew you'd have him in your sights, so I checked. And' —he added as I would've opened my mouth— 'before you ask, Chris Walker was supposed to attend but was held up in traffic on the Bruce Highway south of the Sunny Coast. I was there when his text came through just after six, saying he'd been on the road for over an hour and wouldn't make it.'

'Oh.' Suddenly deflated, I sank into the chair opposite him, lowering my head to the table. All my suspects – other than Maureen, who wasn't really a credible suspect – cleared in one fell swoop.

More gently, he said, 'I know you want to think Rose's death wasn't an accident, but have you found any evidence to support that?'

'No, we haven't. There's the lack of torch, the timing and the placement of the ladder – which Rose couldn't have moved on her own – but I know you're going to tell me that's all circumstantial.' I looked up, and he nodded. 'Then there are the threats … I brought them with me …' I rummaged in the tote bag I'd thrust the plastic-covered envelopes into on my way out. I watched him closely as he read the messages. 'The one left at my place, where it refers to ending up like Rose, that has to be a death threat, surely?'

'Perhaps, or it could be someone wanting to pressure you into leaving and selling.' He held up the notes Rose had received. 'That's what these are – someone trying to frighten her into selling.'

I scoffed. 'They didn't know Rose well then, did they?'

Ted chuckled. 'They certainly did not.'

A thought occurred to me. 'Hang on. If whoever broke in here didn't find the notes, they might think they're still at Rose's. And with me here …' My mind went to the murder board. 'Finn, can you ring Maggie and get them to stay there until I come home?'

'Sure. Hopefully, they won't have left yet.' His mind must've gone in the same direction as mine.

Once he'd left the room to make his call, Ted said,

'Have you decided what you're going to do?'

'No. There's probably no reason for me to hold on to the house, but I was going to keep the shop. I thought I could get Nina to manage it and see if we can't make it work. But now?' My gaze took in the carnage. 'I don't know if we can come back from this and certainly not in the time I have left here.'

He stood and walked around to where I sat, laying a hand on my shoulder. 'Would Rose have given up on the shop?' I shook my head. 'Then if you feel that strongly about it, maybe you shouldn't give up on it just yet either, eh?' Patting my shoulder, he said, 'I'll get Tyson to take you home. We'll finish up here and put a watch on the place for tonight, but I suggest you arrange some emergency glass replacement for tomorrow; you should be able to claim it on insurance.'

'If Rose's insurance was up to date,' I muttered.

'Indeed,' he said. 'But you won't know until you look.' He patted my shoulder once more. 'I'll let you have a few minutes alone.'

As Ted left, Finn walked back in, the two men exchanging brief nods. 'Maggie and Justin are still at the house and will wait there until we get back.'

'Thanks. I just need to call Nina, and then we can head back.'

Nina must've been waiting by the phone for news and picked up on the first ring. 'How bad is it?'

There was no point lying to her. 'It's bad. The shop is in a mess, but I don't think anything has been stolen.'

She was silent for a few seconds. 'They just wanted to cause damage? To persuade you to sell?'

'I think so.' I hesitated and then decided she deserved the truth. 'I also think they were after the messages you gave me yesterday – the ones sent to Rose.'

Another short silence. 'Clem, you don't think Rose's death was an accident, do you?'

'No, Nina, I don't.'

'I see. I thought that might've been the case but hoped I was wrong – the cards you were seeing … What happens now? It's the end, isn't it? For the shop?'

Uncertainty was in her voice; she had to be wondering whether this meant she'd be back on the road living out of her van again. The same would go for Bella – her family relied on her income to help make ends meet. This wasn't just about me or Rose, it was bigger than that. Ted was right: Rose would not have given up on the shop. In fact, rather than letting this beat her, she would've fought back with everything she had.

'No, Nina, it's not the end. In fact, I think this is the opposite – it's a new beginning for New Moon. And I think between the three of us, we can make it even better than it was before.' I looked at Finn and saw a wide smile spreading across his face. 'So, what do you say, Nina? Are you with me?'

'I sure am, and I know Bella will be too.'

'Excellent. Let's meet here tomorrow and get this place cleaned up. Say ten?'

If whoever was behind this thought I could be beaten this easily, they had better think again. I'd been sad and guilty when I found out Rose had died, determined to get to the bottom of what had happened when I suspected her death wasn't an accident. Now though? Now I was angry.

Back home, Maggie had tidied away the food and washed the glasses and dishes. Siouxsie had booted the dogs off the sofa and had stretched out on it and Justin was at the table writing on the notepad I'd been using earlier.

'What did Ted say?' Maggie asked.

I shrugged. 'He says the notescould be seen as pressure to sell and don't constitute a threat. He didn't argue with me, though, when I suggested the break-in might have been staged. He also said that Martin and Michael were both at an event the night Rose died and that Chris was supposed to be there too but got held up in traffic. Ted was there when his text came through.' I took the cloth off the murder board. 'Ted's right, we don't have anything.'

'The text means nothing; he could've sent that from anywhere,' Siouxsie muttered from the sofa.

'What was that?' Finn looked up from the floor where he'd been wrestling with the dogs.

Siouxsie sat up. 'If Martin was going to be safely

out for dinner, Chris might've already been in town and meeting Kylie for some afternoon delight.' She waggled her eyebrows suggestively.

'And just because he was seen out publicly doesn't mean Martin wasn't able to be involved with whatever happened to Rose,' added Maggie.

'Plus, there's something else I didn't get a chance to mention before Tyson turned up.' Justin looked up from his notes. 'Rukmini in the planning department told me Michael Lindsay had a meeting last month regarding building approval to convert an existing retail space into retail plus therapy rooms.'

'New Moon?' I asked.

'It's only hearsay, but she thought so.'

I turned back to the murder board. 'If Michael wants to buy New Moon for Lauren even though we know he has the same alibi as Martin, maybe he should be on this board too? Do we even know if he made Rose an offer to purchase New Moon?'

Justin shook his head. 'If there was an offer made, Rose didn't mention it.' He glanced at his watch. 'It's getting late, and I think we should wrap it up there.' He glanced at Maggie, who nodded. 'Clem, I don't think you should stay here alone tonight; come home with us.'

I shook my head. 'Thank you, but I'll be fine.'

'I'll stay with you.' Finn jumped up from the floor. 'I can sleep on the sofa, and the dogs will certainly let us know if anyone comes near the house.'

'Are you sure?' He might be able to sleep on the sofa, but I wasn't sure I'd do much sleeping knowing he was on the other side of the flimsy wall. I couldn't, however, deny that I felt better knowing he and the dogs would be there. 'Because if anyone wants to search this house, they only need to wait until I go swimming each morning.'

'No arguments, Clem.' His eyes met and held mine.

'Okay, you win. I'll find you a pillow and a blanket.'

CHAPTER TWENTY-ONE

For the first time since I'd been in Whale Bay, I slept through sunrise, waking with a start when I heard the front door slam and the dull flip and flop of rubber thongs and scrabble of dog's toenails on the wooden floorboards. With my heart in my mouth, I sprang up in bed before remembering Finn had stayed over.

Glancing at my watch, I saw it was nearly seven, and groaning, reluctantly got out of bed, wrapping my dressing gown tightly around me. Still yawning, I emerged into the kitchen, where Finn was whistling as he emptied the contents of a paper bag onto a plate. 'Hmmm, coffee and croissants, two of my favourite things in the world. Why aren't you at Brewz?'

Cosmo (or was it Beans – I still got them mixed up occasionally) ran across the floor to me, jumping up in pleased welcome, followed closely by Beans (or Cosmo?).

Finn looked up and smiled a smile that had all my lazy, just-woken-up hormones standing to attention. 'Good morning to you, too. I leave the weekend to Lainey – her sister helps out. Did you sleep well?'

'Thank you, I did.' I accepted the coffee he handed me, closing my eyes briefly as I inhaled its rich, almost nutty aroma. 'You?'

'Not bad, although we had another late-night visitor. You must've gone out like a light if you didn't hear it.' He chuckled, the warm throaty sound wrapping around me, so at first, I didn't comprehend what he'd said.

'Sorry ... we had another intruder?' I hadn't heard a thing.

'Yes, not long after we'd gone to bed.' A little thrill ran through me at his turn of phrase. Get over yourself already, Clem. 'I heard the gate creak open, but it sounded as though they were around the side of the house, near the swing chair. Anyway, I let the dogs out and whoever it was ran off quickly when they heard them.' He grinned. 'I looked in on you when I came back inside, but you were snoring happily.'

'I don't snore!' I ducked my head towards my coffee, allowing the little curtains of hair to hide my flaming cheeks. 'The side of the house, you say, near the swing chair?'

He nodded. 'I had a quick look last night, just with the torch on my phone, and couldn't see that anything was disturbed.'

Sipping my coffee, I wandered across to the murder board. What wasn't I seeing? I tilted my head to the side. The magpies ...

'I think I know what they were looking for.' Unpinning

the photo from the board and pulling another two beetroot gloves from the box I'd left on the table yesterday, I said, 'Are you coming?'

He shrugged, a look on his face that was part bemusement, part amusement and part curiosity. 'Lead on.'

The dogs took off barking as soon as I opened the back door, heading straight for where they'd found the intruder the previous night. At their approach, the magpies pecking for breakfast flew up into the branches of the fig tree.

'What are we looking for?' Finn stood with his hands on his hips.

'Look at the photo.' I handed him the scene photo and walked across to the swing chair, the grass dewy wet under my bare feet, and looked up at the magpies. 'Thank you,' I mouthed.

'There's a rock missing in the photo,' he finally declared. 'But the border is complete now.' He looked across at me, comprehension dawning in his eyes. 'Someone must've replaced it after Rose died but before you moved in. And then whoever was here the last few nights has been trying to get it back.'

'That's what I reckon too. If they've found out I'm questioning the accident, they must also know there's a possibility the police will look more closely at the scene photos.' I snapped a photo in case we were questioned later, pulled on the gloves and joined him at the rock border. 'Which one do you think … This one?'

'I reckon.'

Crouching down, I could see the dirt wasn't as tightly packed around this rock as it was around the others and the rock came out of the ground easily. Holding it in one hand, I carefully brushed the dirt away with the other. 'Is that …?' My eyes met Finn's.

'Blood? You know, Clem, I think it might very well be just that.'

While Finn rang the police, I stood there holding a blood-stained rock in my beetroot-gloved hands, a rock I suspected had killed my aunt. I should've felt vindicated that my suspicions had been correct, but as I stood there with my aunt's blood literally in my hands, all I felt was rage.

Once Ted arrived and examined the rock I was still holding, which he had to almost prise from my hands, things moved quickly. Tyson and Selina taped around the area and took multiple photos from every angle.

News had travelled fast, and Maggie, Justin and Siouxsie were there, as were Gordon, Maureen Peterson and Chris. Even Brian had struggled out using his walking frame. Within an hour, we had quite a crowd of spectators.

Chris caught my eye and called me over to where he stood with his family. 'What's this about?'

'It's about Rose's death not being an accident.' I was deliberately blunt and to the point, watching their faces carefully for any reaction.

Chris paled, but Maureen stood firm. 'What a load of codswallop,' said Maureen impatiently. 'I expected this level of amateur dramatics from Rose but didn't realise you'd inherited the same tendencies. They might be useful in the courtroom, but that sort of carry-on has no place here. Chris, Brian, we're going home.'

'What have they found?' Chris asked me as Maureen led his father home with one last scowl over her shoulder for me.

'A rock with blood on it.' I tried not to scowl back at Maureen; instead, I gave Chris my full attention. 'It looks as though it was replaced in the border some time after Rose died.'

'So it's true, they no longer think Rose's death was an accident?' Between his baseball cap and his sunglasses, I couldn't see his expression.

'How did you know that?'

He shrugged. 'Martin mentioned something about it yesterday. I think he was worried because if it was true, it could tie up the property for another few months or at least until the investigation is over.'

'Do you think it will take that long to catch whoever did it?'

'Of course – whoever it was would be long gone by now.'

'You don't think it could be a local? After all, that

rock was replaced sometime between when the scene was photographed and when I moved in.'

He shrugged. 'I hadn't thought about it that way.' He frowned. 'How do you know what was in the scene photos? Have you seen them?'

Tyson interrupted us. 'Sorry, Clem, the senior needs to talk to you.'

'No problems. I'll talk to you later, Chris.' He nodded, his eyes on the rock border.

'What was that about?' asked Tyson as we walked back to the side of the house where Ted stood with Finn. 'Is Chris a suspect on this murder board of yours?'

I paused and faced him. 'You know about that?'

He shrugged a shoulder. 'I know my mother, I know Siouxsie and I saw a cloth-covered noticeboard and a ball of red wool in your lounge room. I don't need to be a master detective to work out what's under it.'

'Fair call.' I had to give him that.

A loud male voice called, 'Where is she? Clem? I hope you're not questioning her without her lawyer present.'

Groaning, I covered my face with my hands. 'Miles! What are you doing here?'

Miles had pushed his way through the crowd gathered out the front, past Tyson and Selina and through to where I stood with Finn and Ted.

'And who might you be, sir?' Ted puffed his chest out, a stern expression on his face. 'Ms Carter was just about to tell us how she came to find—'

'Miles Blackburn, I'm Clem's partner; I've just flown in from Melbourne. I'm also her lawyer.'

Ted raised his eyebrows and turned to me. 'Is this man your lawyer?'

I shook my head in a mixture of exasperation and disbelief. What was Miles doing here? 'No, he's not my lawyer. If I needed one – which I don't – I'd be calling on Maggie King. And, for the record, he's no longer my partner.'

'A simple misunderstanding that I'm here to clear up.' Miles was trying on his best don't-you-know-who-I-am lawyer voice.

'A simple misunderstanding? You went behind my back to Martin Cosgrove and were going to take a commission from him if I sold this cottage! That's not a simple misunderstanding; that's an underhand betrayal!'

Conscious of our audience on the other side of the fence, I somehow kept my voice to a loud hiss. Even so, I wasn't sure if Finn's startled gasp was surprise that I'd dumped Miles and not told him or what Miles had done to finally prompt the dumping.

If Ted was surprised by my revelations, he certainly didn't show it, his expression every bit the working policeman with an inherent distrust for city lawyers whose role was to discredit him on the witness stand. 'Is that true, Mr Blackburn? Had you done a deal with Martin Cosgrove to take a finder's fee on the sale of Ms Carter's cottage?'

'What?' Miles blustered.

'The question is a simple one, Mr Blackburn: did you or did you not have an arrangement with Martin Cosgrove regarding a commission on the sale of this house?'

Beside me, Finn was shaking with suppressed laughter. Miles glared at him and did a double-take when he finally clocked what I was wearing – a floral kimono-style dressing gown that reached just below the hem of the striped boxer-style shorts and singlet I'd slept in. 'Good God, Clem, what on earth are you wearing? You don't even have shoes on!'

'What's wrong with what I'm wearing? I'm decent. Besides, I'm rather proud I can still fit into these.' The sleep shorts I'd found in the drawers in my bedroom had been much more comfortable for sleeping in than the silky nighties Miles had always preferred.

'Can I just add that you fit into them very nicely?' Finn had gotten over his initial surprise at Miles's appearance and was now enjoying himself.

'Thank you.' It wasn't just the sun that was making me feel warm. 'I think it's all the swimming that keeps me fit.'

Miles, having just realised Finn was part of this morning's story, drew himself up into courtroom posture and looked down his imperious nose at Finn. 'And who, might I ask, are you?'

Unabashed, Finn held his hand out. 'Finn Marella.' Miles automatically shook his hand. 'I own the coffee shop down the road – Beach Brewz. It looks like you stopped there on the way through this morning.' Finn indicated the empty coffee cup in Miles's hand. 'A wise decision not to go to Bron's – she's the baker in town. Plenty of newcomers' —a conspiratorial smile in my direction— 'make the mistake of thinking they can get their coffee at the same place they buy their sausage rolls' —he shook his head at the naivety of such souls— 'but while her pastries are amazing, her coffee is, quite frankly, crap. And, as I'm sure you know – especially being from Melbourne – life is too short for crap coffee.' He ended his spiel with an open-palmed shrug of his shoulders.

Miles's eyes widened as he realised Finn was the town 'rake' he'd heard I'd been out and about with. 'What are you doing at my girlfriend's house at seven in the morning? Bringing her a good morning coffee?' He punctuated the last sentence with a sneer.

Finn sent me a wicked smile I couldn't resist returning. The sort of smile that told me he was about to have some fun with Miles, but also the sort of smile that sent all my butterflies into flight.

'Well,' he drawled, 'that's a bit yes and no. You see, the dogs and I did bring Clem her morning coffee' —he leant in conspiratorially— 'I don't need to tell you what she's like if she hasn't had her morning brew, but in all honesty, we'd also stayed the night. Now,' he added as Miles's face went red, 'I don't want you thinking anything untoward happened … I spent the night on the couch. Although' —

with another of those cheeky grins at me— 'if I'd known Clem was already a free agent, I might not have been as much of a gentleman.'

While my half shrug might've appeared casual, the air between us was fizzing with enough electricity to light the whole of Nob Hill.

That was the moment Cosmo and Beans decided they'd had enough of playing ball with Selina and came tearing in our direction, eager to welcome the newcomer who must surely be a potential friend. Miles, however, has never been a dog lover and not even Ted could restrain his laughter as Miles put his hands in the air and backed away, swearing, from the enthusiasm of two golden retrievers.

'Cosmo, Beans!' Finn called his dogs away as Miles frantically began brushing early morning muddy paw prints from his chinos and Italian loafers. 'Sorry about that, Miles,' Finn said, not sounding very sorry at all. 'They're very friendly.'

'They should be restrained,' grumbled Miles, rubbing at a particularly muddy patch on the hem of his Ralph Lauren polo shirt.

'If you're quite finished, Mr Blackburn, I need Clem and Finn to tell me how they found the item in question.' Ted crossed his arms.

'What item did they find?' Miles pushed away Cosmo (or Beans) again.

'The rock that probably killed Rose,' I said bluntly.

'Clem!' Ted chided me. 'It hasn't yet been proven that those are bloodstains on the rock you found, and if they are bloodstains, we don't know that it's Rose's blood.'

'I think we all do,' I said. 'But I'm happy to wait for forensics to prove that. As for how we knew where to look?' I thrust the scene photo into his hands. When he looked up with his eyebrows raised, I showed no contrition. 'I know, I probably shouldn't have taken a photo of the photo in your file, but well, that bird's flown now.'

'That's a photo of your dead aunt?' Miles sounded appalled.

'Miles, if you can't keep up, feel free to leave. I'm not inclined to have to stop every few minutes to catch you up on details.' I placed my hands on my hips but removed them as soon as I realised the action made my kimono gape. 'Where was I? Yes, the photo … In this scene photo, you can see there's a rock missing from the border, but in this picture I took this morning' —I handed over my phone— 'you can see the rock has been replaced.'

Ted nodded slowly. 'That's a good pick-up. Is there anything else?'

'That's why she's so good at her job – her attention to detail.' Miles flashed an ingratiating smile in my direction, which we all ignored.

'Yes, that's all – unless you want me to tell you how I think the magpies were trying to tell me about it. You see, I asked for a sign from Rose and a magpie flew down and landed just there – and then another.' I pointed to where the magpies had been.

'One for sorrow …' muttered Ted.

'Exactly. It was as if Rose was telling me where to look.'

Miles laughed as though I was a crazy woman not to be taken seriously, and Ted and Finn turned and glared at him.

'She probably was, Clem, she probably was,' mused Ted. 'We'll send this through to forensics as well as the letters and envelopes and keep you posted.'

'Thanks, Ted.'

'If it is blood and Rose's, we'll need to get forensics out to retest the ladder for fingerprints as well.'

'Because that wasn't done originally,' I said resignedly.

He lifted a shoulder. 'You know I can't say anything about the efficacy of the original investigation, although what I will say is I believe there was some pressure exerted to wrap it all up quickly so the death certificate could be issued—'

'And I could sell the property.'

'I wouldn't want to make assumptions about that either.' A wry half smile appeared on his face. 'Right.' He pulled his uniform pants back up to his stomach. 'If you're alright, we'll be off. Take care, young Clem. If what happened to Rose wasn't an accident, there'll be someone who doesn't want that to get out.'

Touched, I placed my hand to my chest, suddenly unable to speak.

'She's got people looking out for her.' Finn placed an arm casually around my shoulders.

'I'll thank you not to touch my girlfriend,' spluttered Miles.

Ted shook his head in exasperation. 'Can you deal with this one?'

I nodded. 'Yep, leave it with me.'

'Alright, everybody, there's nothing more to see here,' Ted addressed the crowd as he, Tyson and Selina made their way back to the squad cars.

As everyone slowly drifted away, Maggie, Justin and Siouxsie joined us near the swing chair.

'Who's this?' Siouxsie inclined her head towards Miles.

'Everyone, this is Miles. Miles, this Maggie and Justin, who were friends from school, and their daughter Siouxsie. Finn, you've met.'

'Nice to meet you, Miles.' While Maggie and Siouxsie wore matching expressions of surprise, Justin merely extended his hand.

'So you're the one she was deciding whether to dump.' Siouxsie looked him up and down. 'What?' she enquired innocently when Maggie scowled at her. 'We were all thinking it.'

'But we didn't need to say it,' her mother hissed.

'Actually,' said Finn. 'Apparently, she did dump him.

Something about doing a deal with Martin Cosgrove for a finder's fee when the house was sold.'

'No way!' Maggie glared at Miles. 'Is this true?'

With Maggie and Siouxsie rounding on him, he buckled in a way he hadn't done under questioning by Ted. 'Yes, it's true … alright? But I only did it because I had Clem's best interests at heart.' He turned to me, his palms up beseechingly. 'I wasn't going to keep the money, darling. It was to help us get into our dream home in Brighton – by the sea. You're always happier by the sea.'

Even Justin scoffed at that and turned away. Maggie, however, eyed him pityingly. 'If you think we'll believe you, you've got another think coming. I thought you were supposed to be a hot-shot lawyer.'

Siouxsie shook her head, disappointment written all over her face. 'You really don't know Clem as well as you think,' she said. 'If a man of mine went behind my back and thought he knew "what was best for me", I'd be dumping him quicker than you could say the word.' She clicked her fingers to demonstrate.

'Can we trust him with the …?' Justin nodded towards the murder board.

I shook my head. 'No, we can't. He's in too far with the Cosgroves.' As Miles was preparing to bristle, I waved my hand at him. 'Save the performance, Miles; I'm not interested. We do need to talk, but I'm not doing it in my pyjamas.' I glanced at my watch. 'Plus, I'm due down at the shop shortly. Your choice is to wait here and be nice to everyone while I get changed, and then while I send everyone else down to New Moon, you and I will talk. And when I say talk, I mean you'll listen to what I have to say, not just argue around the edges in a never-ending circle until I tire of it and give in. Any sign of circular arguments and I'm out of here. Understood?'

'What's my other choice?'

I thought about Miles's question for a second. 'Actually, you don't have one. If you want to talk, that's what needs to happen. Otherwise, you can hit the road and I'll see you back in Melbourne.'

'But I've come all this way.'

'That was your choice; I certainly didn't ask you to.'

He shook his head sadly. 'I don't know what's got into you, Clem.'

'I'll tell you what's got into her, mister.' Siouxsie poked him in the chest. 'Whale Bay's gotten into her, that's what.'

CHAPTER TWENTY-TWO

'So he really did sleep on the sofa?' Miles said, folding the blanket Finn had used last night.

Doing my best to ignore his mournful expression, I returned the bedding to the hall closet.

'What's under here?' He made to lift the cloth covering our murder board.

'Something that is none of your business.' I slapped his hand away. 'Now, why have you come here, Miles?'

He slumped down onto the sofa, lifted one of the throws on it and screwed his nose up at the possibility of what was below. 'This isn't you, Clem. This running around with strange men, knocking back sensible offers for a property you're never going to live in, running around the front yard without shoes *and* in your pyjamas at seven in the morning—'

Snorting my exasperation, I interrupted his flow. 'How many times do I need to tell people? No one has made me an offer to buy this house.' I stalked around the sitting room, picked up the ball of red wool from the table and slammed it back down. 'Do I need to put a sign up telling everyone that? For the last time, how can I accept an offer I haven't been made?'

'See, this is what I mean. Yelling like that – it's not you.' He shook his head sadly again. 'Martin has made me an offer on your behalf, and it's a good one.'

'What the …?' As the red mist descended, I squeezed my eyes shut and counted under my breath until the red faded. 'We've got nothing else to say to each other, Miles,' I said evenly.

'I spoke to your father about it, and he told me what you were like when you came back from Whale Bay. Black hair with green stripes! If the Law Society could've seen you then. He told me your aunt had let you run wild, and when you finally came back to Melbourne, you were a mess.' He stood and walked to where I stood and reached for my hands. 'Can't you see, darling, Whale Bay is no good for you.'

I pulled my hands from his grasp and wiped them on the back of my shorts. 'Get out, Miles,' I hissed, and when he didn't move, I yelled, 'Get. Out!'

He put his hands up in surrender and backed away. 'Okay, I'll go … for now. But I'm not leaving. You're obviously having some kind of breakdown, darling; losing your aunt and being here is bringing back the loss of your mother. I understand that, but you're older and wiser now, and together, we can get through this. You might not be able to see things clearly, but I can, and I'm here for you, darling. I'm sure this is just hormones.'

Picking the ball of wool up, I threw it at him, and when he didn't move, I followed that with a Post-it sticker pad and then another and another.

'Okay, I'm going. Call me when you're ready to talk sensibly.'

I chucked a marker pen at him. When I picked up another, he turned and ran for the front door, the screen door bouncing behind him before finally settling in a half-open position.

Ignoring it, I slumped onto the lounge, my head on my knees. I thought I'd left that girl behind – the girl I used to be – the one who was happy working beside her aunt in a New Age shop, reading astrology charts by day, swimming in the ocean each morning. The girl I'd been before my mother died and I'd had my heart broken.

It had taken years of study and hard work to reinvent myself and get my life on track, and now I was back in Whale Bay, I was beginning to feel like that girl again – but an older, wiser, no longer heartbroken version.

An image of the mermaid in my dreams flashed before me, her finger crooked, beckoning me to follow her. Ahead was the ocean, a great expanse of turquoise possibility; behind me was Melbourne, my sensible job and relationship. Should I follow the mermaid or swim back in the direction I'd come from?

Coming back here was turning my life upside down, and right now, I wasn't convinced that was a good thing.

I'd grabbed my phone and my keys and was about to head down to New Moon when there was a knock on my screen door.

'Clem, are you there?'

I stopped in my tracks; it was Michael Lindsay. Making sure the cloth was entirely over the noticeboard, I called, 'Come in, it's open.'

Stepping inside, he wiped his hands on the legs of his chino shorts. 'It's been a while, Clem.'

'Not really; I saw you only the other night.'

'No, I mean … yes, it was only the other night.' He briefly raised his eyes from the faded floorboards to meet mine before casting them around the room. 'I meant it's been a while since I was here, in this house.' He chuckled. 'I don't believe it looks any different to how it used to. You, though …' He looked me up and down and grinned. 'You're almost unrecognisable.' He stepped forward and poked his finger into one of my dimples the way he used to. 'Sorry, I couldn't help it.'

I let out a little laugh. 'You and Nick always used to do that – poke a hole in my cheek and then say you couldn't help it.'

'Yeah, some things don't change.' He shuffled his feet. 'Look, I'm sorry about the other night … I didn't talk …

we didn't talk. Lauren …'

'It's okay, Michael. I get it.' I paused and then, because I'd only just been thinking about those days, said, 'Are you still in touch with him?'

He shrugged, not even pretending to misunderstand. 'A bit. He left soon after you did – was out of touch for a bit … Bummed around Bali a bit, on dive boats mostly, then came back to Brisbane for uni – marine biology, would you believe? He's up in Cairns now but doesn't come back here much.'

'Right.' Even though Cairns was still over fifteen hundred kilometres away, just knowing he was in the same state felt too close. Even after twenty-five years. Even though I hadn't given him many thoughts over the past (at least) twenty years.

'I've always kept your secret, you know,' he said after a short silence. 'Me and Mags – and maybe Justin – are still the only people who know about you two. I've never even told Lauren. But then,' he mused, 'Lauren and I have never had that tell-each-other-everything relationship that Mags and Justin do.' He sounded almost envious of the other couple's marriage. 'I don't think even Martin knows about the two of you.'

'Thanks for that, Mick.' I slipped into the shortened version of his name. 'You always were a good guy. Better than—'

'Better than Martin?'

I shrugged.

'He told Ray, you know.' When I raised my eyebrows in silent question he clarified. 'Nick told his father about your engagement. It must have been only a day or so before you left town, and when you did leave Ray told Nick he'd offered you money to stay away and that you'd taken it.' He paused and asked a question he must have been wanting to ask me for decades. 'Did you take money to stay away?'

Aghast he could even think that, my mouth dropped open. 'Of course I didn't! It was … I left for other reasons. My mother died, remember. Up until the other night I'd never properly met Nick's parents."

Michael nodded as if he'd never seriously thought I would, but had to ask. 'Anyway, that's why Nick left so soon after you did. Ray put up a fight – you know how he likes to get his own way – but Nick stood firm. He said he wanted nothing to do with the business and Ray cut him off financially.' He laughed mirthlessly. 'Martin was quick to take his place, but I don't think even he knows what went down.' He paused and then said. 'Anyway, that's not why I'm here.'

I sighed heavily. 'Please don't tell me you're here to make an offer on this place.'

'No, that's Martin's business. I don't care whether Finz goes ahead or not, although to be honest I'd prefer if it didn't. I heard about what happened at New Moon last night and wanted to make you an offer on that.' As I would have interrupted, he held his hand up. 'Please hear me out,

Clem … I know the financials of the store, and I know things were running close to the wire, and it follows that it's going to take a concerted effort to bring the shop back from a disaster like this. The thing is, Lauren is into all that – her crystals, tarot, New Age stuff. In fact, she used to be so jealous of you because you got to work there.'

'Really?' I found it difficult to think Lauren Walker had ever paid any attention to me other than to join Kylie Lindsay in looking down her nose at me.

'She wants to turn it into something more glitzy – LA style, she said. White walls, white floors, plenty of chrome, that sort of thing. We've … ummm … had our problems. I mean, all marriages have problems, right? You're a divorce lawyer, so you would've seen it all … and I want her to be happy.' Somehow, he managed to get through his speech without looking at me, and then he named a price that made my eyes widen.

'Your mother mentioned something about this the other night,' I said. 'I must admit, I wondered whether it was some competitive business between the two anointed sons. Your mother, I don't imagine, would be happy with Martin getting all the glory.'

'Well,' he said, 'Martin is the golden boy – the rest of us can only bask in whatever light he lets us bask in.'

'That sounded a tad on the bitter side. I thought you guys were tight.'

'I suppose we are – we have to be, don't we? Our

fathers are in partnership, and it's assumed we'll carry their mantle, but to be honest, if it wasn't for Lauren, I'd be happy just running Dad's tour boats and being done with it. Mum, though, wants more for me – she always has done – and Lauren, well, she's guided by Kylie, of course.' He cast me a sideways glance as he mentioned his sister.

'Careful,' I warned, 'I might almost feel sorry for you.'

He scoffed at that. 'Heaven forbid. Seriously though, Clem, I have no idea what your intentions are regarding the shop and the house or even how long you'll be staying in Whale Bay, but if you want to sell, I'd be interested in buying. If, however, you want to make a go of the store and need any help, well, we were friends once, and I'd like to think we could be again.' He grinned cheekily, and the decades fell away. 'But it would need to be our secret. You know you're probably Martin's least favourite person in the world now your aunt has passed away. Followed closely by Finn Marella, of course.'

'Of course.'

'I know I haven't said it, but I was sorry to hear about your aunt. She might've caused my father some problems and Ray, well, Ray couldn't stand her towards the end, but her heart was in the right place, and she was always good to me.'

'Thank you.' I reached out and touched his arm lightly. 'And thanks also for actually approaching me about an offer—'

'You mean rather than go through your boyfriend? I told Martin that was a stupid idea. Just because Kylie can't think for herself, he shouldn't have assumed you'd be the same. Besides, it does him good to have someone stand up to him every now and again – none of us do.'

'Yeah, it wasn't one of the smartest moves he's made and it's backfired on him. But' —I paused and took a breath— 'as generous as your offer is, can I just say no? You see, that shop … it meant something to Rose, and it means something to me, and now it means something to Nina and Bella, and I'd like the opportunity to turn it into something that people look forward to visiting on their annual holidays to Whale Bay.'

He nodded. 'Good decision, and as I said, if I can help in any way …'

'Thanks, Michael. I need to get down there to help with the clean-up, but before I go, I don't suppose you know anything about last night's break-in?'

He frowned, confused, 'Why would I? Oh, I get it – to create a disaster so I can ride on in and make you an offer that will take away all your problems. You can't really think that I would …?' He hesitated, and under his stare, heat flooded my face. 'Actually, I can see how after dealing with Martin and his father, you might think that. I can assure you I don't do business that way.'

I nodded jerkily. 'I'm sorry, I had to ask.'

'I get it, and if I hear anything, I'll let you know. On

the subject of awkward questions, though, is it true you don't think Rose's death was an accident?'

'Yes, it's true.'

'Is that why Ted was here this morning? Chris said something about a blood-stained rock.'

'Yes, although we don't know that it's blood and we don't know if it's Rose's blood, but if it's not, it would be weird to put it back into a rock border.'

'One last question and I'll leave you to get down to New Moon – please tell me that under that cloth isn't one of yours and Maggie's investigation boards?'

My face flamed, and he burst into laughter. 'Good Lord, some things never change. You two always were trouble together.' He leant towards me conspiratorially. 'Am I on it?'

At my hesitant nod, he laughed even louder. 'Aaah, Clementine, there's never a dull moment when you're around.' He opened the screen door. 'I do hope you stick around, even if it's just to see Martin's face.'

CHAPTER TWENTY-THREE

Seeing the crowd gathered in and around New Moon, ready to pitch in and help, almost brought me to tears again. Aside from the Kings, Nina and Bella, Harry was there, Gordon, Bella's mother and siblings, and some other women Gordon introduced me to as being friends of Rose – Debbie, Donna and Sue.

'We did aqua aerobics together,' said Sue.

'… in the summer, and land aerobics in the winter,' added Debbie.

'Plus, we were in a book club together,' said Donna. 'We'd do anything for Rose.'

'Well, thank you, everyone, for being here and helping to get the store back on its feet,' I said, my throat thick with emotion.

'Once Nina put the word out that you were definitely reopening and not selling, heaps of people wanted to help.' Finn handed me a coffee. 'Alright?' The whisper of his words tickled my ear and sent shivers of sensation humming through my body.

'Yeah, it's okay. Miles is gone – for now anyway, although I daresay it's just to regroup. But just after he left, I had a visit from Michael Lindsay, which I'll tell you about later.'

'Okay, as long as you're alright.' He curled his pinky finger around mine and smiled that bedroom eye smile at me, and the humming in my veins turned into the complete string section.

'Right.' I pulled away before I could do something stupid like kiss him in front of the entire town. 'Let's get this show on the road.'

Over the next few hours, I organised my willing workers into groups. We cleaned away the broken glass and somehow managed to round up all the crystals scattered throughout the store, Bella putting her two youngest siblings to work organising them into vague colour families – we'd work out the details later. I set to work in the office and the others all dealt with the remainder of the stock, placing the damaged goods to one side for assessment.

Harry and Finn decided that while all the shelves were empty, now would be a great time to give the store a fresh coat of paint. 'Do we want to go with the same colours?' asked Harry, looking at the navy walls dubiously.

'You know what? No, let's give it the full Baroque treatment – maybe tangerine on that wall, turquoise on that one, navy on another.' What I didn't say was, 'Let's make it as far from Lauren's idea of sleek and glitzy LA style as possible.' I thought from the arch look Maggie gave me that I didn't need to say the words out loud.

Bella, who had been hanging about listening to the conversation, said, 'I love that! Can we also maybe put Turkish lamps on the counter, and if you can get me some new fabric, Mum can run up new curtains for us? Some tapestry style fabric in rich blues and greens, maybe some purple cushions … We can still keep the velvet on the reading tables, and …' Her voice trailed off, a soft pink tinge to her cheeks.

Smiling warmly at her, I said, 'I love it. In fact, why don't you and I take a drive to the fabric store at the homemaker centre tomorrow, and you can pick out what you think would work?' An idea occurred to me. 'And maybe on the way, you can tell me how you think we can use social media to attract more business.'

Bella's eyes lit up, and as she happily went back to sorting stock, Nina sidled up to me. 'That's a good thing you said to her – to trust her with some designs and ideas.' Her eyes were suspiciously moist. 'It's exactly what Rose would've done.'

That now-familiar lump moved back into my throat, preventing any words from getting through, but what I would've said if I'd been able was that right at that very moment, with the shop in disarray and so many people caring enough to raise it back from the proverbial ashes, I felt as though Rose was with me – with us – in spirit.

Bron brought over party pies, sausage rolls and cut salad sandwiches from the bakery, and Finn ensured we were all caffeinated. Slowly but surely, New Moon began to look like a shop again instead of the aftermath of a cyclone.

It was midafternoon when a red BMW convertible pulled up outside New Moon, and first Lauren and then Kylie emerged.

Lauren, in particular, seemed surprised to see the working bee underway, hesitating on the footpath outside the store until Kylie nudged her elbow. Then, as if synchronised, both women flung back their (what looked to be) freshly salon-blowdried hair, pouted their glossy lips, lifted their chins and strode into New Moon as if they were stepping out onto a catwalk – all long, tanned legs and three-inch heels.

'Do you think they spent long practising that move?' asked Siouxsie in a stage whisper.

'Only every day since puberty,' commented Maggie.

'And probably even before that,' I added.

Finn was the first to recover. 'Hello, ladies,' he greeted them with the same flirty smile he would've greeted them with if they'd come into Brewz to order a coffee. 'Are you here to lend a hand? We can do with some help with the walls. Hey, Harry, have you got a spare roller?' Then, as if he'd only just noticed the flouncy mini dresses and strappy sandals both women wore, he said, 'You'll be wanting to change, though, first.'

Kylie's tinkly laugh rang around the shop. 'We're not here to work.' Ending with a wrinkling of her upturned nose, she somehow made the four-letter word sound like another sort of four-letter word.

'We heard about the break-in and wanted to see the damage for ourselves. Although, quite frankly' —Lauren tossed her Kate Middleton tresses again— 'I'm not sure why you're bothering. After all' —with a side glance and satisfied smile at Kylie— 'I'll be getting rid of all of this when it's mine. This tacky colour, the thread-worn curtains …'

'Oh.' I injected a mixture of surprise and pity into my voice. 'Haven't you heard?'

'I don't think she's heard,' echoed Siouxsie, staring at Lauren until the other woman looked away.

'Heard what?' Kylie eyed me suspiciously.

'Can I tell her?' asked Siouxsie.

'Please let me,' said Maggie.

'No, it's my news to tell.' I brushed my hands over my already paint-stained T-shirt. 'The thing is, Lauren, I've decided not to sell the shop. New Moon will continue to trade, so if you're looking for somewhere to open your crystal and wellness centre – or whatever it is you wanted to turn New Moon into – you'll need to look elsewhere.'

'But …' Lauren looked wildly at Kylie. 'Your mother said the break-in would be the final nail, that she'd need to sell after that.'

Was that a glare Kylie had just sent her friend?

Interesting.

'Instead of which, the break-in has only made me more certain that I'm doing the right thing by keeping it open.' With palms open, I swept my hands around the shop. 'It took that to make me realise how many people care about this shop. Besides, as someone interested in crystals and tarot and the like, I'm sure you'd agree, Lauren, that a shop like this makes that accessible to everyone. Also, and you're the first to know this, we'll soon be offering classes in tarot, astrology and many other things.' I smiled sweetly at her. 'Our mailing list will be open during the week, so sign up to make sure you don't miss a spot on next month's full moon workshop.'

'Have you told Martin this?' hissed Kylie.

'Martin? Why would I? The last time I looked, I wasn't required to check in with your husband before making any decision.' There might've been a time when the likes of Kylie would've turned me into a shrinking violet, but those days were long gone.

'Maybe not,' she said with a sly smile, 'but my understanding is your boyfriend doesn't think too highly of what you've been getting up to here.' She leant in conspiratorially. 'He's staying with us, you know, and is quite the catch. I wouldn't be letting him go in a hurry.'

'Aaah, but Kylie, unlike you, I'm quite prepared to make my own money. Besides, if we're trading veiled threats, I'd be worrying more about what *your* husband doesn't know than what my *ex*-partner does.' I held her stare. 'But' —I shrugged— 'if you're happy to go down that path …'

Kylie dropped her eyes first. 'I don't know what you think you know—' she began.

'What's she talking about, Kyles?' Lauren asked plaintively.

'Nothing important,' Kylie said.

'Oh, and while we're trading secrets … or not … let your mother know that while the CCTV on New Moon hasn't been working for yonks, the cameras next door at Brewz are functioning perfectly.'

My inspired guess hit its target, and Kylie visibly blanched. 'What's that supposed to mean?' she muttered.

'If you don't know, I'm sure your mother will. Now, if you two aren't prepared to get your hands dirty and help us, I'd suggest you leave us to it.'

Kylie grabbed Lauren's elbow to guide her away, but the other woman stood firm. 'Mike said he was going to see you this morning about selling; wasn't the price high enough?' Dropping her princess act, her eyes pleaded with me to reconsider. Suddenly, I saw the girl I played happily with until she fell into Kylie's clutches.

'He did come and see me,' I said more gently than I'd spoken to Kylie. 'I explained to him I wasn't prepared to sell, and he understood why. Don't blame him, Lauren; he told me it was your dream, but, you see, it was also my aunt's, and she trusted me to hold it for her.' Kylie had stalked to the front door and stamped her foot in impatience. I ignored her glare. 'There's room in town for both of us – your shop and mine. We have different customers, and we're not in competition – remember that. You'll find the perfect place, and I suspect it's going to be down at the wharf.' I leant closer and whispered, 'And when you do, I'll visit. It can be our secret.'

She nodded jerkily and smiled a smile that was gone almost as soon as it was there.

'Are you coming, Lauren?' Kylie's toe tapped out a staccato beat.

'I think you've been summoned,' I said sardonically.

Lauren lifted her chin again, flicked her hair, turned on her heels and the pair left in much the same way as they'd arrived.

'What was that about?' Maggie was by my shoulder.

'You know,' I said, watching as the convertible roared down the road. 'I think I just saw a glimpse of the Lauren Walker we used to know.'

'Really? You mean before she decided to be one of Kylie's minions?'

'Yeah. Before that. I think I also know who was behind last night.'

'Not Lauren? I wouldn't have thought she'd have it in her.' Maggie leant on the broom she'd been using to sweep up the last of the glass from the footpath.

I shook my head. 'No, not Lauren, but the words she

used and the words Mick used when he dropped by were the same that Carmen had used the other night. I think she was behind it, and I think Kylie knows it too.' I tapped at my bottom lip. 'And Kylie knows that I know – and she'll tell her mother. I don't think we'll ever be able to prove it, but I also don't think we'll have any more trouble from them.'

'But that business about the CCTV at Brewz?'

'Oh, that? I made that up.' I waved her words away. 'I have no idea if Finn has CCTV but doubt it very much.'

'I heard my name used in vain. What was that about me and CCTV cameras?' Finn had joined us, a paint roller in one hand, a splurge of turquoise paint on one cheek I ached to wipe off.

Instead, I slapped his cheek playfully. 'Nothing you need to worry about.'

He shook his head and chuckled. 'As a matter of fact, I do have CCTV cameras at Brewz, and I reckon they'd pick up New Moon … Ted's already asked for a copy of the footage. Once I finish here, I'll have a look … What are you hoping to see?'

'Carmen Lindsay with a cricket bat,' I said, my expression deadpan.

He laughed. 'No, seriously, what are you hoping to see?'

'Carmen with a cricket bat,' I said again. 'Unfortunately, though, what I expect to see is a nondescript figure in a black hoodie who is probably already back in Brisbane with his wallet stuffed, but I'd like to see Carmen in it.' That splodge of paint was distracting.

'With a cricket bat.' He grinned that cheeky smile and his eyes danced, and suddenly, the space was too hot.

Before I could do anything as obvious as fan my cheeks, I looked away. 'What say we do a barbecue at mine after we're finished here? Sausage sangers all round?'

'That's exactly what Rose would've said.' Harry had joined us. 'Remember when we all got together to paint her garage? How else do you think the door ended up with all those mad colours?'

'I wondered about that,' I said chuckling as I recalled my thoughts upon first seeing the multi-coloured garage doors. I glanced at my watch. 'Okay, well, we've made great progress today. Let's give it another hour and call it quits for the day.'

As I returned to the mess I was sorting through in the office, Nina approached. 'Did I hear you tell Lauren we'd be running courses and moon workshops?'

'You certainly did.' I sat back on the edge of the desk, the possibility of how the shop could be unfolding in my mind. 'It came to me in that moment so I'm sorry I hadn't spoken with you first … is that a problem?'

Her smile was broad, and again, she reminded me of a younger Rose. 'Not at all. Just before she died, I'd come up with a proposal to run tarot classes, so I'm up for it if you're willing to trust me.'

'If Rose trusted you, then so will I. In fact' —a brainwave struck— 'the three of us should get together for a planning workshop before I head back to Melbourne. See if we can't come up with some strategies to make this shop thrive in the way we know it can.'

Nina's face had fallen at the mention of my return to Melbourne. 'You're still going back?'

Despite the pang of regret in my chest, I still nodded. 'I have to; it's where my life is. I have no choice.' Bending down, I picked up two tarot cards that had been frisbeed around during the break-in. Death and Judgement. The death of an old life and a life changing decision to be made? Why did I feel Rose was pulling my strings from beyond the grave?

Nina's eyebrows rose. 'I wouldn't be too sure of that,' she said. 'Something has died, and judgement, well, the Judgement card brings life, even new callings.' Even though her stare was fixed, her voice was gentle. 'Of course it's up to you whether you answer that call when it comes. You always have a choice. Head and heart, logic and intuition … look to the lessons of your past to guide you … but then, you already know the answer, don't you?'

And on that enigmatic note, she left me to it.

CHAPTER TWENTY-FOUR

The next few days passed largely without incident. Miles came over on Sunday morning to attempt to talk me around to his way of thinking but after another circular argument returned to Melbourne with his tail between his legs.

'We've been through this,' I said tiredly. 'The point is, I can't trust you, Miles, not after this.'

'I'm not giving up though, Clem,' he said. 'I still believe in us and our dream of a house in Brighton.'

'You're not listening to me. That's your dream, not mine, and if it's been such a dream, why am I now only hearing about it?' I was so weary of going around in circles. 'If it means so much to you, you can buy a place down there with your share of the apartment sale.'

'Where will you live?'

'I don't know.' I closed my eyes against his questioning and sighed my weariness of the subject. 'I'll work it out.'

That was when his tone changed to something more patronising. 'Obviously, this is some midlife rebellion, Clem, something you need to get out of your system. It could be the start of menopause, and all you need is a patch or a tablet. Come back to Melbourne, and we'll get you sorted out.' He smiled smugly. 'We can get through this, darling. A decent doctor and some medication and you'll be back to normal, you'll see.'

'For the last time, I'm not coming back to Melbourne with you!' My temper flared, and I no longer bothered to lower my voice.

Clearly, he decided there was no point in keeping up the pretence. 'If you don't come back with me now, don't think you can come crawling back later, not after you've been cheating on me.'

'For the last time,' I yelled, 'Finn and I are just friends!'

'So you say. Do I need to remind you, *darling*, that I'm in a position to make things very difficult for you at work as well?'

There it was. 'Get out.' I said flatly, and when he made no move to leave, I screamed the words again.

'I'm sure once I tell your father about this, he'll bring you to your senses.' His words were bitter and determined as he rested one hand on the door, but if he hoped they'd bring me to heel, they had the opposite effect and made me, if possible, even angrier.

'Good luck with that.' I turned my back on him, flinching when the door slammed behind him.

•

The shop had been cleaned and freshly painted, and the new curtains for the reading rooms were up – Baroque-style fabric in shades of deep blues and greens. With the addition of Turkish-style mosaic lamps and some parlour palms and other greenery, the shop now felt richly exotic and calming all at once.

On the drive down to the homemaker centre, Bella had confided that she'd wanted to study either graphic design or marketing but, due to family circumstances, had been unable to, so I put her to work on our social media accounts and the design of a new web page. She'd almost skipped out of the car and into the house when I dropped her home, and on Wednesday, when her mother delivered the new curtains she'd made for us, she couldn't stop thanking me for my kindness to Bella. It was, I explained, no more than what Rose would've done.

The three of us – Nina, Bella and me – got together on Friday night and planned a series of courses and special events, and Bella took several images she could use for our social media.

'It's such a pity you're going back to Melbourne,' said Nina, 'or you could run astrology events as well.'

'Yes, well, we can maybe schedule some for when I'm back from time to time.'

The smile she'd given me was a knowing one, and I wondered whether she was a mind reader as well as a tarot card reader. Despite knowing I had to return to the job

I'd been so reluctant to leave just a fortnight ago, I was now considering taking an extended break from work and staying around longer – not that I'd tell her that yet. While it was career suicide, Whale Bay had wormed its way back into my heart.

Aware he was shouting up the wrong tree with Miles, Martin phoned on Tuesday, inviting me to meet him for a drink. While I declined that, I accepted his offer of a coffee at one of the cafés at the wharf.

He was already there when I arrived, flashing his trademark toothie smile at the girl behind the counter who, despite being young enough to be his daughter, was responding to his charms and twirling a piece of hair around her finger. If I didn't know Martin the way I did, I probably wouldn't blame her. His once blonde hair was still intact, and with his tanned face, blue eyes, crisp white shirt and chinos, he looked every inch the successful coastal businessman. In fact, in the right light, and he had positioned himself to that effect, there was a touch of Robert Redford about Martin Cosgrove that I hadn't noticed before.

On sighting me, he said one last thing to the barista, making her giggle, before striding confidently across to me.

'Thanks for coming, Clem.' He kissed my cheek and smiled into my eyes. Having abandoned the tactic of going through Miles, he was now taking the charm offensive, and if I didn't know him as well as I did, I might even have been flattered. 'I can't tempt you with something sweet? No?'

After I'd declined, he guided me across to a table out on the deck overlooking the water, bemoaning the fact that the protected mangroves on the other side of the river precluded any development from taking place there and drawing my attention to some boats that were moored at the wharf.

'Now that one is an absolute beauty. It's owned by a Melbourne businessman, I believe, staying just a couple of days on their way up to Port Douglas. And coming in now is Bob and Mike's newest vessel.' He pointed out a sleek two-storey catamaran. 'Not bad, is it? Two bars, one hundred and twenty passengers … It's primarily for whale season, but they're running dolphin tours daily and already taking bookings for Christmas and New Year.'

'It's certainly lovely,' I commented, not surprised to hear of its popularity, but wishing he'd get to his point.

I didn't have long to wait. 'Of course these days, we're not just about whale season; we're busy all year round. This place' —he waved his arm to encompass the shops and restaurants— 'has brought life all year round to town. People travel from Brisbane to dine in some of these restaurants. Now we need to ensure they have somewhere to stay.'

'I would've thought there was plenty of accommodation; at least there's a lot more along Beach Road these days and around the surf club. And there's that lovely new resort at Sunrise Point … I imagine everyone staying there would come to Whale Bay for restaurants and bars?'

'Yes, they do, but what we're missing is luxury accommodation. I know it's a short drive down to Noosa, and sure, we have some high-end houses available for holiday rentals up in The Heights and along my parents' end of Beach Road, but an all-inclusive boutique resort offering spa treatments, a beachside bar and a lagoon-style pool' —he shook his head, a serious expression on his face— 'that's what this town is sadly lacking.'

He beamed at the server as she set our coffees down. She responded by casting him a lingering look over her shoulder as she went back to the counter.

Somehow, I managed to stop myself from laughing out loud at the theatrics of it all. 'And that, I take it, is where I come in,' I said wryly.

'It is. And before I go any further' —he shrugged and opened his palms— 'I have to apologise for the clumsy way I've acted. When your … When Miles phoned me wanting to open discussions, I was under the impression you were fully aware of that and were agreeable to me speaking with him on your behalf. I've since discovered that wasn't the case.'

My eyes widened in disbelief. 'Really, Martin? I thought I made it clear that wasn't the case.'

He lifted a shoulder again, his smile not slipping. He'd obviously created his own narrative and was sticking to that. 'Mike told me you'll be retaining New Moon … While I think you'll be throwing good money after bad, well, I respect that decision. Besides, I'll be ready to pick it up for a knockdown price when you've had enough.' He took a sip of his coffee and leant forward. 'Business is all about the long game, you see. How's your coffee? It's good here, isn't it?'

I sipped at my coffee. 'Not bad, but not strong enough either. I suspect the problem is with the beans. If she's interested' —I nodded back to the barista— 'I know Finn is looking to run some coffee appreciation sessions soon.'

His smile faltered but was soon back at full beam. 'Mike did point out to me, though, that I've never made you an offer for Rose's cottage. Well, I suppose it's your cottage now.' He slumped back in his chair and laughed at his error as though it were a joke. 'So … my offer is' —he mimed a drumroll on the table before passing me across a slip of paper— 'this.'

Pulling the paper across to my side of the table, I opened it slowly and flicked my eyes to his, surprising a self-satisfied smirk.

'Impressive, isn't it?'

'Hmmm. Not bad as a starting figure.' I suppressed a smirk of my own as his smile fell. 'Although I'll be running it by a valuer before I give you an answer.'

'Well, that's not an immediate no, so I'll take that as an almost yes,' he said with a confident laugh. 'Although, don't forget, you'll be saving on real estate and solicitor fees by dealing directly with me.'

'You can choose to take it any way you want, but all I'll tell you is that I'll think about it. Carefully. I've had some interest expressed by friends looking for a holiday investment, and I promised to consider their offer as well.' In my lap, my fingers were crossed.

Martin's eyes narrowed and his mouth twisted unpleasantly, but the expression was fleeting, and the high-voltage smile was soon back on his handsome features. 'I understand completely. Take your time, but not too long!' He chuckled again. Then, eyes darting around the café to make sure no one else was in hearing, he said, 'Last time we spoke, you hinted that Rose's death might not have been an accident.'

'That's right, I did say that.'

'Do you really believe that?'

'Absolutely.' I watched him carefully for a reaction. 'I know she didn't fall off that ladder on her own, and so do the police now.' There it was – the flicker I was hoping for.

'Do you have any evidence other than, I understand, a rock that might or might not be stained with blood that might or might not have come from Rose?' Now he was watching me carefully, and I bit the inside of my mouth so I didn't betray any emotion.

'Unfortunately,   everything   else   we   have   is circumstantial,' I admitted. Leaning forward, I whispered, 'Where were you between eight and ten on the night in question?'

Martin's laugh was loud enough to attract the server's attention and everyone else in the café. 'Oh, Clem, you crack me up. But for the record, I was at a Chamber of Commerce event with Mike, my father and Bob Lindsay.' He tapped at his cheek as if he were thinking. 'That's right, Ted Winters was there too.'

'And you didn't leave the room at any time?'

'Only to take a slash and make a couple of calls.' His laugh was confident, finding it hilarious I'd had the temerity to ask him for an alibi. 'Actually, I might've gone to the bathroom more than once.' He smirked. 'You know what it's like when the seal is broken … but to answer your question, I didn't leave the room for longer than about ten minutes, and that's not long enough to run to your aunt's house, knock her off a ladder, bury a rock, and run back.' He chuckled again. 'If you think it was me, you have nothing to go on, do you?'

I shrugged as if his answer was what I expected. 'Aah, well, if you don't ask, you don't know. Anyway, thanks for the coffee, and I will consider your proposal.'

'That's all I ask.' He was still chuckling to himself as I left.

It was only when I was walking back to New Moon that I realised whoever was involved with Rose's death replaced the rock *after* the scene photos were taken. No matter how much I'd hoped to the contrary, it couldn't have been Martin.

CHAPTER TWENTY-FIVE

As expected, the police drew a blank on the CCTV from Brewz. Instead of the hoped-for image of Carmen Lindsay with a cricket bat, all we saw was a nondescript figure dressed head to toe in black. So far, I'd watched the footage several times, and the only distinctive feature visible was a pattern on a trainer. The perpetrator, as Ted said, was probably now long gone.

'It was just your average robbery, Clem, nothing more to see,' he'd said. By the way he wouldn't meet my eyes, he didn't believe it any more than I did, but without evidence, he had nowhere to go.

'You and I both know that's not true, Ted. No money was taken, and whoever broke in had a mission to cause as much damage as they could. Plus, the file drawer has been jimmied open and everything has been rifled through. They were looking for something, and I think that something was the threats I gave you.'

'It certainly looks like the intent was to push you to sell the shop, but I can't believe Carmen Lindsay is behind it.' Ted shook his head stubbornly. 'Besides, I thought your theory was the threats were intended to get Rose to sell the house. You've already told me the Cosgroves want the house and the Lindsays want the shop. You can't have it both ways, Clem.'

'What if it was both ways? What if the wilful damage was to prompt me to sell the shop and the threatening letters were about the house?' I was struggling to join the dots. 'I'm sure Carmen organised the break-in – she would've paid someone to do it.'

'If your theory is correct, though, Carmen wouldn't know about the threats in order to instruct whoever it was doing her dirty work to search for them. I'm sorry, Clem, it doesn't make sense.' He softened his tone. 'I know you want to find out what happened to your aunt, but I don't think that and the break-in are connected.'

I sighed and scratched at the back of my head. 'Has anything come back from forensics yet about the rock?'

'No, it's not part of an active case, so I had to pull a few strings to even get it tested,' he said.

'I see.'

'Even if it does come back as your aunt's blood, they won't find fingerprints.' The look he gave me was full of pity and my spirits sank further. 'Your prime suspects have all got alibis … I think you've gone as far as you can with this.'

I pondered that as I walked back along the beach that

afternoon after a swim. Had I really taken this as far as I could? Despite what Ted had said I couldn't shake the feeling that I was letting Rose down. Again.

After a barbecue at my place on Saturday night – at some point over the last week, I'd stopped referring to the cottage as Rose's and begun calling it home – the usual band of suspects gathered around the board of suspects. With Chris Walker's revelations that he and Kylie were having a fling, the break-in at the store, and the discovery of the blood-stained rock, we'd been hopeful of a breakthrough. Instead, the investigation had stalled.

Now, though, fuelled by red wine, barbecued lamb and a selection of salads we'd all pitched in to make – I'd even cooked Rose's signature potato bake, or dauphinoise as she liked to say, complete with a French flourish – we were preparing to take a fresh look at the murder board.

'Right,' I said, taking my place at the board. Siouxsie, as always, was ready with her Post-it stickers and marker pen. 'What do we know for sure?'

'That Mick Lindsay wanted to buy New Moon for Lauren's wellness centre, and Martin Cosgrove wanted this cottage to make way for his development.' Maggie counted them off on her fingers.

'I heard at the council meeting during the week that Mick has put in a building permit for one of the vacant shops at the wharf,' Justin said. 'The one with street frontage that used to be one of those holiday agents.'

'Right,' said Maggie. 'I know the one. To be honest, that will be a much better site for what Lauren wants to do than New Moon would've been.'

'I agree. As I said last weekend, Lauren and I are targeting different markets, and there's plenty of room for both of us.' I tapped at Siouxsie's caricature of Michael on the suspect line. 'I don't think he was involved with either Rose's death or the threats and definitely not the break-in.'

Maggie nodded. 'I agree. Despite his friendship with Martin, Mick's always been a good guy, and Rose had a soft spot for him, but she never tolerated Martin or Kylie.'

'I know I've said it before, but Rose was a great judge of character,' said Finn from the sofa where Beans was lying across his lap, with Cosmo spread out on his feet – these days, I could tell the difference. 'If someone was good enough for her, they're good enough for me.'

'Plus, another thing we know is that he has an alibi for the time of death.' Siouxsie was already unpinning Michael from the top of the board and moving him down to the bottom.

'Not to play devil's avocado,' began Justin, ignoring Siouxsie's giggle, 'but so does Martin.'

'Devil's avocado?' chuckled Finn.

'Justin used the phrase devil's advocate one night, and Siouxsie thought he said avocado, so ever since, that's what it's been,' Maggie explained with a fond glance at her husband and daughter.

I laughed but quickly brought the discussion back on topic. 'But if we accept Martin's motive – that with Rose gone, whoever inherited would be likely to sell to him – he could still be behind both the threats and the death,' I pointed out. 'Besides, we don't know whether anyone had eyes on him for the whole time in question – he'd only need fifteen minutes to duck out to take a phone call, and that's enough time to run from the bowling club, deal with Rose' —I was unable to be more descriptive than that— 'and be back before anyone noticed he'd gone. Although I did ask him about that and he said he didn't leave the room for more than ten minutes, but we only have his word for that.'

'You really want it to be Martin, don't you? Anyone would think there's some history between you two.' Although Finn's words were light and delivered with a half smile, his eyes were focused on my reaction.

Maggie caught my blush and rushed to say, 'Doesn't everyone in this town?' I sent her a grateful smile. 'You mentioned you asked him. When was that?'

I told them about our meeting and his offer. 'So, as much as I'd like it to be him, he didn't know the rock was replaced after the photos were taken.'

'Or he could be bluffing,' said Siouxsie.

'I agree,' said Maggie. 'I think he still belongs on the suspects list.'

'I'd like to talk about Chris Walker.' Finn deftly moved thirty kilos of golden retriever from his lap and nudged

Cosmo off his feet before coming to where I stood. 'His is the only alibi that doesn't stack up.'

'I don't know,' said Justin wryly. 'Have you ever sat in the Friday afternoon Bruce Highway parking lot?'

'But this was Thursday,' argued Finn.

'It can be any day of the week, and just because no one saw him there doesn't mean he wasn't stuck in traffic,' added Siouxsie. 'Remember that night it took me almost four hours thanks to a prang near the Glasshouse Mountains? No one saw me there, but trust me, I was stuck in that traffic.'

'Don't we know it,' groaned Justin. 'You only bring it up every chance you get.'

'Well, it was traumatic.' Siouxsie grinned back. 'My point is, we mightn't be able to verify his alibi. Besides, he called Martin from the highway and said he wouldn't be able to make it in time for the event.'

'We only have his word that he was calling from the highway.' Finn gripped his chin as he examined the murder board. 'After all, he could've arrived earlier and, as you said the other day, taken the opportunity to catch up with Kylie.'

'It's not a bad idea; Kylie would get off on sneaking around like that.' Finn raised his eyebrows at the bitterness in my voice. 'The problem I have is that while he has a motive for wanting rid of Rose – to potentially remove his financial ties to the Cosgroves – he has no motive for what happened at New Moon and something about it tells me they're connected.'

'Okay,' Maggie said slowly. 'Let's backtrack. We know Martin, Chris and Maureen have reasons to see Rose dead – even though in the case of Maureen, the reason is lame and I think it's time to take her off the board, even if she is, as Siouxsie so eloquently put it, a grumpy, old, shrivelled-up bitch. Are we all agreed on that?' Everyone nodded. 'As for New Moon, Martin would buy it if it was on the market, but he's not desperate for it, so we can discount him there, and Chris has no reason for wanting to see it sold. Lauren wanted to buy it and Michael wanted to buy it for her – although we've already discounted him – which leaves Carmen.' She screwed up her nose and frowned. 'Can someone remind me why Carmen's on the board – aside from the fact that you don't like her, of course?'

'Because she wanted Michael to buy the shop and because she was the person who said it was just one disaster away from needing to be sold. Plus, there was Kylie's reaction when I hinted as much to her. I think Carmen was involved with the break-in at New Moon, and there was no love lost between her and Rose.' Aware of how improbable it sounded, I exhaled loudly. 'I know I'd love for it to be either of them and I truly feel in here' —I held my hand against my stomach— 'that Carmen is involved with the break-in at New Moon. But I don't think we'll ever be able to pin it on her, and I don't honestly think she had anything to do with Rose's death.'

Maggie traced the lines of red wool from suspect to clue and, standing back, shook her head. 'We need something more … There's something missing.'

'We don't know if Maureen has an alibi.' I sounded desperate, but I really needed to get to the bottom of this before returning to Melbourne.

'Good luck with that one,' Justin said, staring at the board. 'Even if she has no alibi, we've already discounted her ability to move the ladder on her own.'

Finn bit at his bottom lip and tapped his chin. 'I think we're trying too hard to link all of this together,' he finally said. 'We began with investigating Rose's death – I think the break-in at New Moon has confused us because it doesn't appear to be connected and we're trying to connect it. But what if it isn't?' He turned to me. 'We have no way of knowing whether Rose received those threats in the same way you did or whether they were left at the shop, but what I'm hearing is that Lauren only got the idea of buying New Moon when she thought it might be available, so that would mean the threats are related to the sale of this house.'

'I understand that.' I rubbed wearily at my forehead. 'But if that's the case, why was the last one left at the shop after the break-in?'

'Maybe,' Justin said slowly, 'whoever broke into New Moon wants you to think it's linked, which would point the finger at someone who knew we were investigating and someone who knew about the other threats.'

'But doesn't that mean they're connected?' Maggie's voice rose with the same frustration I was feeling.

We all stood around the board in silence, each hoping that something we'd missed would jump out and grab us.

Eventually, Justin spoke. 'We're going around in circles. Let's park this until Ted has the pathology results back and then reconvene.'

While Siouxsie was inclined to argue, Maggie and I reluctantly saw his point and agreed. They left soon after, Siouxsie commenting that the timing was perfect and she was heading to the wharf to meet friends.

Finn stayed behind to help me clean up after dinner, pushing aside my arguments to the contrary.

'You okay?' he asked.

I shrugged. 'Just disappointed. I really wanted to find out what happened to Rose, you know.'

'I know, and it's not over, Clem – we might still get there.'

His reassuring smile brought me undone, and first one tear and then another snuck out. I rubbed at my eyes with the back of my hands. 'I'm sorry, I don't know why I'm so upset.'

He pulled me into his warmth, his arms wrapping around me tightly. 'I know exactly why you're so upset – you've been fighting this on too many angles, trying to find out what happened to Rose, dealing with the break-in, overseeing the clean-up and reopening of New Moon.'

He smiled into my hair. 'And that's before Miles fronted up here. Your mind hasn't stopped since you've been here. *You* haven't stopped.'

I pulled back slightly, just enough to see his face, and our eyes met. In the depths of his, there was compassion, understanding, and something else that made my heart race and my body sing. Without thinking, I pressed my mouth against his, closing my eyes, just my lips against his for a heartbeat, for two. Long enough to taste the sweetness of Maggie's pavlova on them. Long enough to fill my senses with his scent: coffee, salt and something undefinable but perfectly Finn. Long enough to know I wanted to keep kissing him for much, much longer.

Lifting his head, he said softly, 'Clem? Are you sure?'

My gaze flicked back to his lips, and I nodded, then slowly shook my head. 'I want to be sure, but …'

'I know.' He kissed the top of my head before releasing me. 'It's too soon, and with everything else that's gone on, it's too much.'

'Yeah,' I admitted. 'Plus, I'm going back to Melbourne.' When had I stopped referring to Melbourne as home? Whale Bay felt like home, Melbourne felt like real life.

'Are you?'

'I have to – it's where my job is.'

'We'll see. In the meantime, I'm not going anywhere.' He smiled ruefully. 'Except home to bed.' He kissed my lips lightly. 'Sleep well.'

I nodded even though I didn't believe I had a hope of doing so.

That night, cards filled my dreams again: the Lovers, the Knight of Swords, the King of Pentacles, Strength and Judgement all whirling around the Tower, and in the centre of it all, the High Priestess wearing my face.

CHAPTER TWENTY-SIX

The following morning, I pulled Rose's twelfth house chart out again and some textbooks to see if I couldn't make sense of the significators. The traditional astrologers – and I'm talking about the guys who did this sort of thing centuries ago, back in the days when doctors had to learn about the planets and the elements and kings (and queens) had their astrologers on retainer – were able to produce a physical description of the man who had stolen their cow (or whatever) from the planets signifying them. An aspect to Jupiter could make the person rounder or larger, either body or spirit; in aspect to Saturn, perhaps older or thinner; Mars could be an indicator of rash behaviour … that sort of thing. Of course it was more technical than that, and I wished I'd taken the time to listen more to Rose when she spoke about it. As it was now, I'd come up with a man who probably had brown hair and was behaving impulsively. Not a lot of help. As much as I hated to admit it, perhaps Ted was right and we had come as far with this as we could.

As a result, I was relieved when Finn and the dogs dropped by just as I was heading across the road for my afternoon swim.

'Mind if I join you?' he asked.

'I'd be glad if you did,' I said, shutting the gate behind me. 'But I'll warn you, I'm not great company.'

'Anything I can help with?' He unclipped the dogs from their leads when we reached the sand.

'Not unless you can find the missing link in this investigation.' The dogs gambolled across the wet sand, occasionally splashing in the little pools left behind by the receding tide.

'You don't deal with inactivity or roadblocks well, do you?'

His chuckle brought a smile to my face. 'No, I never have. Rose used to say it was the Aries in me – wilful rather than stubborn, and needing always to be moving forward.'

We walked a little longer in silence, stopping every so often to throw a stick for the dogs.

'I know I'm probably overstepping,' Finn said, 'but what's the history with you and Martin Cosgrove? Did you two used to date?'

Stooping to pick up the stick Beans had left at my feet gave me the space to decide how to answer him.

'No,' I finally said, 'we didn't date, but I was engaged to his brother Nick … his twin brother.' When Finn's mouth fell open with shock, I turned away from him towards the ocean. 'Nick was nothing like Martin, either in looks or temperament. Where Martin has always been an entitled bully, Nick was … he was lovely.' Out in the gentle waves, a ray emerged from the water, landing with a splash. 'I'd had a crush on him for years, but it wasn't until my last year of school that he noticed me. I used to swim a couple of times a day, but one evening, there was this kid, a teenager, who'd gotten into trouble and hadn't factored in the strength of the current. I was already out there, so I tried to save him but was struggling myself. Anyways, Nick saw it all and came to help. We got talking, and it turned out he swam most days, too.' I shrugged. 'I guess it grew from there. No one could know, though – the niece of an astrologer with a Cosgrove? His parents would never have allowed it. He was supposed to marry Kylie Lindsay and join the two empires. Our best friends – Maggie and Mick – were the only ones who did.'

Turning back to Finn, I smiled tightly. 'We fancied ourselves as star-crossed lovers, Whale Bay's Romeo and Juliet. I wonder now whether that was part of the attraction – the forbidden love.' I sank onto the sand, Finn beside me. 'We used to meet here, of course, and at the cottage when Rose was at work, and then one day he proposed, and I said yes. Looking back, I don't think either of us truly believed we'd be allowed to be together, but when we were, we let ourselves dream of exactly that – a future where he was free of the business and could do what he wanted.'

'And you?' Finn's voice was quiet. The dogs had returned and made themselves comfortable beside us on the sand.

I shrugged again. 'I didn't know. The plan had always been for me to go to uni in Melbourne once I finished school. My marks had been good enough to secure a place in a law degree. I thought I could specialise in environmental law, help save the oceans and all that.' I snorted a laugh at the memory of my naivety. 'And look at me, I'm a divorce lawyer. Anyway, my parents wanted me home, but … I was in love, and that was all that mattered. So instead of doing what I was supposed to do, I deferred my place for a year and stayed here in Whale Bay, living with Rose and working in the shop.

'Dad phoned and ordered me home, told me he wouldn't give me a penny until I did – which was the worst thing he could have done as it made me more determined to stay. Besides, by then, I was earning my own money in the shop and doing readings for clients. Then Mum phoned and pleaded with me to come home. So I did, for Christmas, but we had this massive row, and as soon as I could, I came back here. I went for a few months not talking to Dad but called Mum weekly; she always sounded so sad, but only once asked me again if I'd reconsider.' A tear tracked its way down my cheek. 'I told her I wouldn't, and then I told her why.'

I took another deep breath. 'I told her I was engaged.' I sniffed and wiped at my wet cheek. With trepidation, I glanced at Finn's face, sure I'd see judgement. Instead, his features were soft, and there was compassion in his eyes. 'Anyway, after I told Mum, the phone went silent; I could hear her disappointment down the line, and I said I was never coming home until they were able to accept that.' I bit at my bottom lip, swallowing down the lump in my throat. 'It … it was the last time I spoke to her.'

The words – and my breath – were thin and ragged. Inhaling deeply, I decided to trust him. He'd either turn away from the dark, nasty truth I'd kept hidden all these years or continue to hold me. In many ways, it would be easier if he turned away, easier for me to leave.

'I went to Nick's house to tell him what had happened and found him' —I swallowed hard again— 'in his bedroom … with Kylie Lindsay.' I squeezed my eyes shut and saw them together again as if it were yesterday; she was straddling him, her blonde hair falling over him like a curtain.

'Were they …?'

'Having sex? No, they were both fully clothed, but if I'd been even ten minutes later, they would've been. I can still see her smug smile, the one that told me she'd won. I knew then if she didn't know about us, she knew how I felt about Nick.' I attempted a shrug. 'I left and ran home, and that's when Rose told me' —I stifled a sob— 'that Mum had died suddenly from a massive aneurism.' By now, the tears were flowing freely. 'And my last words to her were in anger.'

I lifted my head to look at him through blurry eyes. 'That's why I didn't come back – my heart was broken, yes, but more than that, I felt guilty that I wasn't there, that Mum had asked me to come home and I hadn't. It was only after Mum was gone that I realised I'd spent more time with Rose when I was growing up than with my parents.

'In a way, by staying away and making a success of my life, it felt like I was making it up to Mum, even though I knew nothing would ever make it up to her.' I reached out and stroked Finn's jaw, the rasp of his stubble rough against my hand. 'Rose and I never spoke about it, not properly, but I think she understood.'

He turned his head and kissed my palm.

'I hope she understood.' I smiled tightly. 'So now you know why the Cosgroves aren't my favourite people in the world.'

'Have you seen Nick since?'

I shook my head. 'No. Rose told me he'd tried to get in touch, but I told her I didn't want to speak to him. He left town soon after I did so even when I was ready to talk to him – needed to talk to him – he wasn't around. Michael said he's up in Cairns these days.' Wiping the last of my tears away, I said, 'What about you and love? Have you been married before?'

'Aaah,' he said lightly, 'the short answer is yes, but' — the dogs had decided there'd been enough sitting around— 'that's a story for another day.'

As we walked back along the sand to my place, my phone rang. My stomach flipped when I saw the caller's name. 'It's my boss,' I mouthed to Finn. 'Stephen, hello … this is an unexpected call.'

'Hi Clem, I'm sorry to call you during your holidays and on a Sunday, but where are you at the moment?'

'I'm in Whale Bay,' I said warily. 'It's a few hours' drive north of Brisbane.'

'What are you doing there? Actually, don't bother answering me. Tell me, have you seen Miles recently?'

The same something that had worried me so much during our discussion on the day before I went on leave was back in his voice. 'Yes … he was here last weekend – briefly.' I paused, not sure whether this information would have any bearing on what he was going to tell me. 'We've broken up.'

'I see.' Was that relief in his voice? 'Clem, I know I have no right to ask, but is there any chance that you could fly back to Melbourne in the next few days?'

My stomach somersaulted its way up to my throat. 'Stephen, what's this about?'

'I'm sorry, I can't explain on the phone, but it's important you come back to town.'

'Am I being investigated for something?'

'No, I assure you that neither you nor your work is being called into question.'

I released the breath I'd been holding. 'So, it's Miles, then.'

He paused. 'I'm sorry, Clem, I can't go into detail on the phone, but I'd appreciate it if you didn't discuss this meeting with Miles.'

'That's unlikely,' I said sardonically. 'We're not exactly on speaking terms at the moment.'

'That could turn out to be a good thing for you in the circumstances,' he said cryptically. 'Will you come down? You only need to stay until we complete our enquiries, and then you're free to recommence your holiday.'

I glanced at my watch. 'It's too late to leave now, but I'll leave here early tomorrow morning and should be able to be at the office by mid-afternoon. Does that suit?'

His sigh of relief was audible. 'Thanks, Clem, I knew I could rely on you.'

After he hung up, I stared at the phone for another few seconds, almost as if it were suddenly going to spring to life.

'You have to go back.' Finn's voice was full of resignation.

I slid the phone back into the pocket of my shorts. 'Yeah. Hopefully, just for a few days.'

'But isn't your annual leave over at the end of next week anyway?' He'd said what I'd been afraid to think.

I nodded slowly. 'I'll be back, though.' We'd come to a stop at my gate.

'Are you sure about that? Last time, it took you twenty-five years to come back.'

Rather than sounding accusatory, his words were sad.

'That time was different,' I said. 'I have to go to Melbourne and deal with whatever it is Miles has gotten himself in trouble over, but I'll be back. I promise. Even if it is just for another week or so.'

He lifted my hand to his lips and kissed each knuckle. 'Good, because I might just be missing you already.'

'Yeah,' I said softly, falling back into the promise in his eyes. 'Me too.'

He kissed me then, and this time, it felt different. This time, it felt as though I wasn't just falling into his eyes but also falling in love with him.

'Take care, Clem,' he whispered and turned to walk back up Beach Road, the dogs beside him. I watched until they were out of sight. Only then, with a resigned sigh, did I go inside to book flights.

CHAPTER TWENTY-SEVEN

'Miles did what?' Lara's reaction was almost exactly as mine had been when Stephen broke the news to me earlier this afternoon. 'I thought my husband was the dick of the century, but Miles has taken it to a whole new level of dickery.'

One of the last things I'd done yesterday afternoon was to message the girls and arrange a catch-up.

'He's been having an affair with one of the juniors who used to work with us,' I said. 'Stephen originally told me she'd gone to Fair Work complaining about hours and unfair expectations—'

'Which is why he said he wanted you to take some leave,' said Andi, looking more pregnant than I thought anyone could look without actually delivering the baby on the spot.

'Yes. Apparently, the allegations she also made were around harassment from Miles.' I still couldn't quite believe what Stephen had told me – that Miles and Helen had embarked on what had begun as a consensual affair that had turned into something very different when Helen had tried to end it. 'There's more, though; apparently, the firm had received an anonymous tipoff about Miles making side deals regarding commissions on some of the acquisitions he's been working on. And that's the real reason Stephen needed me to be away from the office – so they could investigate the claims without my interference and the possibility of word getting back to Miles.'

'You're kidding! And you had no idea?' Goldie's mouth hung open, her eyes wide.

'None at all.' I'd spent the last few hours this afternoon being questioned by Stephen and one of the other senior partners along those lines. 'I thought he was in Singapore working on a deal for one of his clients – and sometimes he was.' There had been other dates, though, where he'd told me he was calling me from Singapore and had instead been holed up in a hotel room in the CBD with Helen. 'How could I not have had any idea?' A memory of the arrangement he'd tried to make with Martin Cosgrove drifted to the surface.

'What?' asked Andi. 'What have you remembered?'

'You know how I told you about my aunt Rose in Whale Bay?'

Andi nodded. 'You emailed and said something about how she'd passed away and had left a beachside house to you.'

'Yes, well, Miles went behind my back to a local developer and attempted to negotiate a sale involving a finder's fee for him. I'd already told Miles I needed a break, but this was the final straw. Maybe,' I mused, 'that's what he's been doing on the side.'

'Perhaps. Will you tell Stephen about it?' Lara's nail tapped at the stem of her wineglass.

'Absolutely. If it comes out later and turns out to be important, I'll be in trouble for keeping it to myself.' I sipped at my wine.

'Are there any clauses in your prenup relating to inheritance?' asked Goldie.

Andi looked at her pityingly. 'This is Clem we're talking about; her prenups are legendary.'

I chuckled. 'Absolutely. The only way he could access any inheritance would be if I used it to buy a property held in joint names. Then, if we sold that property, he would be entitled to half the total proceeds. Miles said he wanted me to sell Rose's cottage so we could buy a new place down in Brighton. If we did that and then split up, he'd essentially be getting half of the extra I'd put in. According to our prenup, it's the only way he'd be able to touch it.'

Lara signalled for more drinks. 'Did you know he was having money problems?'

'I don't know for sure that he is – we keep separate accounts. I've had to give my authority to Stephen to have a snoop through mine just to be sure I'm not involved, but even being associated with something like this is damaging to my career.'

'Hold that thought – I need to pee again. This baby is disco dancing on my bladder.' Andi all but rolled out of the chair and waddled to the loo.

Once she was back, I filled them in on what had been happening in Whale Bay, from the investigation into Rose's death to the break-up with Miles, the break-in at New Moon, and finally, the feelings I was developing for Finn.

'Ummm, Clem …' began Andi. 'You've only been away a little over two weeks, and it seems as though your whole life has changed.'

I couldn't decide whether it was concern or something else I saw on her face, but I chose to ignore whatever it was. 'It really has. You know how last time I saw you I was asking whether cases like Cametti v Cametti were all there was to life? Well, I can see now that it's not.'

'You mean you want to give up the law and manage a New Age shop doing astrology readings?' Goldie put a hand over mine. 'Are you sure this isn't a …' She searched for the right words.

'A midlife crisis? You can say it, you know, and perhaps it is. I don't know. All I know is I'm not ready to return yet.' I rested my chin in my hand. 'I've felt more over the past two weeks than I've felt in years. Sure, I'm being healthier – I swim and walk every day and eat regularly – but it's not just that. Running this investigation, putting together the business plan for the shop – it feels as though I'm doing something worthwhile.'

'What we do *is* worthwhile,' Andi said.

'Sometimes, yes, but at other times, I don't feel good about it at all. Sure, the money is amazing, and I'm not saying I'm going to step away from the law. I'm just saying I want the opportunity to see if there is anything more.'

'And you think you'll find that in Whale Bay?' Lara sounded sceptical.

'I *know* I'll find it in Whale Bay.'

Andi nodded slowly. 'I think I understand, it just—' Wincing, she placed her hand on her belly. 'Maybe I should go home.' Standing, she reached for her bag, her eyes widening as a gush of water ran down her legs. 'Oh. That's not good.'

'No,' said Lara slowly, 'that's not good.'

'Should we ring for an ambulance?' asked Goldie, her eyes wide with panic.

'It will be quicker in a taxi.' Lara pulled out her phone.

'I can take her. You guys get home, and I'll keep you posted.' Swallowing my panic, I grabbed our bags and put my arm around Andi. 'Come on, let's get you a taxi.'

'But Todd?' She seemed bewildered.

'You can call him from the cab.' I clutched her head between my hands. 'Sweetie, he won't have time to get into town and back out to the hospital. He can meet us there. Okay?'

'Okay.' She nodded, fear in her eyes. 'Will we get there in time?'

'Absolutely.' Lara clasped Andi's shaking hand. 'It's a first baby; you should have plenty of time.'

Lara had injected so much positivity into her voice that Andi began to relax. Only Goldie and I saw the concern in her eyes.

'Come on, Andi, you've got this,' I said as I led her out of the bar. 'Besides, how glamorous are you going to look marching into the maternity ward in your Louboutins?'

'Life's too short for bad shoes,' she said, some of her bravado returning.

'That's my girl.'

Andi's labour was well along when we arrived at the hospital, so I stayed with her until Todd rushed in an hour later.

I left them to it and, too weary to deal with the possibility of Miles at our apartment, checked into a hotel in the city for the night. Todd texted just before eleven to let me know their son had arrived safely and to thank me (again) for getting Andi to the hospital. I messaged Lara and Goldie with the news. Only then did I sink onto the bed and give in to the tears that had been threatening ever since Andi's waters had broken.

Back when I'd gone into labour, it had been Rose who'd taken me to the hospital and Rose who'd sat by my side, holding my hand as the pain split me in two. Rose who'd held me as I sobbed when they took my baby away.

I'd had no choice about giving her up. By the time I'd

realised I was pregnant – or admitted to myself I could be – it was too late to do anything about it, and keeping the baby was out of the question. Rose was the first person I told and she immediately flew down to Melbourne to be with me, rarely leaving my side until the baby was born.

'Does Nick know?' she'd asked me.

I'd shaken my head and told her about catching him and Kylie together.

'He still has a right to know,' she said, and something that could have been regret flashed across her face..

After I nodded my agreement Rose tried to contact him, but he'd left town without telling anyone where he was going.

'Maybe it's better he doesn't know,' I'd said.

Now, I reached for my wallet and pulled out the photo that sat at the back – the one that had been folded and unfolded so many times it was almost in four pieces. My baby – mine and Nick's – would be almost twenty-five. What sort of woman had she grown into?

I traced the tiny face and wondered, not for the first time, where she was, whether she was having a nice life, and whether I'd done the right thing in giving her up the same way my birth mother had given me up. Then I wondered whether my daughter ever thought of me the way I'd thought about her. Had she ever tried to find me? Did she resent me or, worst of all, did she not care?

My thoughts turned to my own birth mother. Was she

out there somewhere hoping I'd come to find her in the same way I was now hoping my daughter would look for me? Even as I knew it wasn't rational, I'd worried that any attempt to track her down would be seen by my parents as being ungrateful for the life they'd given me – a life she, for whatever reason, hadn't been able to. Maybe it was time.

As I lay down and closed my eyes I tried to conjure up an image of the woman my daughter had grown into, but the only face I saw was Rose's.

CHAPTER TWENTY-EIGHT

The following morning, I returned to the office to tell Stephen about Miles and his actions with Martin Cosgrove and to advise him I intended to take all the leave currently owed.

'Are you sure?' he asked. 'What you're proposing is a long time to be out of circulation.'

I couldn't help but laugh at that. 'Really, Stephen? Only a few weeks ago, you sat in this same office and told me the firm was actively trying to reduce people's leave accruals.'

'But that was because—'

'You needed me out of the way. Yes, I know. The thing is, I need a break; I hadn't realised how disillusioned I'd become until I was no longer at work.' I didn't remind him that if I'd taken maternity leave, I would've already had at least six to twelve months away from the office, presumably without destroying my career.

'Are you sure this isn't a reaction to Miles?' Frowning, he tapped his Waterford pen against the desk. 'I wouldn't blame you if it was; depending on what happens, it will be difficult. The good news is you never married him so don't share a surname.' He grinned. 'Silver linings and all that.'

'I was already considering taking a sabbatical of sorts before you called me the other day, but in all honesty, this has helped make the decision easier.'

'As long as you're sure. Now, do you need any help with the separation from Miles? I know you've got an ironclad prenup, but even so ... Staff rates, of course ...'

'You're incorrigible, Stephen.' I chuckled. 'But yes, please, the sooner the separation is formalised, the better. I would've used Andi, but as of yesterday, she's on parental leave.'

'Excellent. I'll get Mark to call you, or better still, you can drop in there on your way out. I know he and Meera would like to see you – Marta Cametti wants to negotiate a postnup agreement.' He grinned. 'Best possible outcome in the circs.'

My final task before leaving town again was to visit my father and Prue; there were things that needed to be said.

Prue greeted me in the over-friendly way she always did – as if she were walking a tightrope between treating me as family and also being conscious that I'd never really regarded her as such. I, however, greeted her with a hug so warm that when I stepped back, her eyes were suspiciously moist.

'Well' —she bustled me through the hall— 'we were

just about to have a drink out on the patio; I don't suppose you'd want to join us?'

'That would be lovely, thank you, Prue.' Her gratitude was so obvious it filled me with guilt at how dismissively I'd treated her. 'While it's just us, can I say thank you and sorry? Thank you for loving my father and sorry for not being more welcoming to you over the years. I know I'm two decades too late, but I wanted you to know.'

She swallowed, her eyes filling with tears and grasped my arm. 'Thank you for saying that, Clem. I know it was hard for you and being the age you were and with everything else …' She nodded once. 'But thank you.' With a little shake, she pulled herself together. 'How about you head out and see your father? I'll be through in a jiffy.'

'Clem, this is an unexpected surprise. Miles finally drag you back, did he?' My father rose from his chair to kiss my cheek. 'You're looking tanned.'

'Thanks. Yes, Miles did drag me back – in a fashion.' I drew in a breath. 'I know you liked him, Dad, but Miles and I broke up a week ago.' As Dad frowned, I rushed to fill the silence. 'At first, it was no one's fault; we'd simply grown apart, but the final blow was when he went behind my back to do a deal with Martin Cosgrove to sell Rose's house.'

Prue was back and handed me a gin and tonic – the same as what they'd been drinking – and placed a plate of cheese and crackers on the white, glass-topped wicker table. I smiled my thanks.

'I don't understand; I thought it was your intention to sell the house.'

'Perhaps, but in my own time and to a buyer of my choosing. Miles had a plan, though, whereby I'd sell the house and use the proceeds to buy something, meaning he'd pocket half of the inheritance when we split.' I sipped my drink. 'Under the terms of our agreement, it was the only way he could benefit from it, you see.'

'What do you mean, "when you split"?' Dad's eyes were narrowed.

'Miles has been having an affair, and I've just found out he's being investigated at work for some underhand dealings – it's why they insisted on me taking leave.'

Dad rubbed at his forehead. 'This is a lot to take in, Clem. Are you sure? He was only here the other day asking me to convince you to sell the cottage. He said something about how you were running wild up there, having some sort of midlife crisis. I told him, of course, that I wouldn't interfere, that I was sure you'd do the right thing. I remember, you see, how broken you were when you came back after Grace passed away. If it wasn't for Rose taking charge then …' He cleared his throat. 'That's the sort of thing Grace was good at. The thing is, Clem, I was wrong to try and force you to come home then; I can't help thinking that if I'd left you to do things in your own time in your own way … You always were so much like your mother. She used to say it was the Aries in you – wilful and courageous. Well, you've always been that.' He swallowed a mouthful of his gin. 'What are you going to do now?'

There was something in what he said I didn't quite catch. 'I've taken extended leave from the firm – all my long service leave and my annual leave, and I'm returning to Whale Bay. That's the other thing – as well as the house Rose left me her shop.'

'I wondered if she still had that,' he said. 'She wrote and told me when she bought it.'

'She told you?' It had never occurred to me that she would've told my father and not me. 'I didn't realise she communicated with you.'

'Just the occasional letter. She wanted to keep up with what you were doing, especially after that business with the baby.' He looked at me keenly, as if he'd told me something I hadn't understood and was waiting for me to catch up. 'But then she would, wouldn't she …'

A thought occurred to me, an idea I was almost afraid to say out loud. 'You said before that I was like my mother, but I remember Mum being calm, practical and compliant, and we can't pretend I've ever been any of those things.'

'No.' He chuckled. 'You've never been any of those things.' He cleared his throat again. 'But you are like your birth mother.'

He waited as if wanting me to fill the gap, to say the words so he didn't need to.

'I … I didn't know you knew who she was.' Even

before he said it aloud I knew what was coming.

'You've always been like Rose,' he said.

My throat closed, and I gasped for a breath that couldn't get through, tears burning behind my eyes.

'I'm sorry, Clem, I always thought you knew. Grace used to say she'd tell you when the time was right, and that year you decided to stay in Whale Bay, well, I assumed she'd told you, and that's why you'd insisted on staying there.'

'I didn't know … Mum never said.' I picked up my glass to have a drink, but my hand was shaking – from anger or emotion, I didn't know, and it didn't matter. 'Rose never said. Why didn't you tell me?'

'I didn't know how to – not once your mother … when Grace had gone. You really had no idea?'

I shook my head miserably. 'None. I always loved Rose – of course I did. She felt like a mother to me. Sometimes it felt as though I had two mothers.'

'You did, Clem. You had two mothers who loved you.'

My father wasn't known for his tact or displays of physical affection so I wasn't sure whether it was the gentle tone in his voice or the way he reached over to grasp my hand that brought tears to my eyes.

'That's why I never went back to Whale Bay,' I said. 'I felt as though in loving Rose and choosing to stay with her, I'd been disloyal to Mum. It's why I never searched for my birth mother – not, as it turns out I needed to.' My indrawn breath was ragged. 'I don't understand how … why …'

Releasing my hand he sat back in his chair. 'Grace and I, we'd hoped to have children, but as the years went by, it became clear it wasn't going to happen. When Rose fell pregnant while she was in London on a gap year and decided she couldn't keep you, we stepped in. We loved you as if you were our own, you know. I've always felt as though I was your real father. Plus, Rose could still be involved in your life. It was the perfect solution.'

'Do you know who my father is?'

He shook his head. 'I'm sorry, Clem, we never knew his name, but your mother … Grace … said Rose had loved him very much. He was the love of her life, she said, but he was already married. As far as I know she never told him about you.'

Somehow I managed to stop the weird and inappropriate giggle from sneaking out. Talk about history repeating itself … I too had a child whose father knew nothing of her existence.

'And that's why you were so comfortable leaving me with Rose when you were overseas?' I couldn't help the bitterness that snuck into the words.

He nodded. 'I'm truly sorry, Clem.' He reached for my hands again and held onto them. 'Truly sorry.'

Tears shone in my upright, uptight father's eyes, and it felt like I was seeing him clearly for the first time. It was no wonder I'd loved Rose as I had – part of me must have known.

'Rose's death wasn't an accident, Dad. She was either killed deliberately, or it was made to look like an accident.' I blurted out the words.

'Are you sure?' Dad gripped my hands more tightly.

Biting at my bottom lip, I bobbed my head. 'Some friends have been helping me investigate it, but we've hit a dead end.'

Sitting back in his chair he crossed his arms, his lips pursed. Then in that same gentle tone as before said, 'How about you talk me through what you've got and let's see if we can find the missing piece.'

'I'd like that.'

'Prue, we're going to need paper, pens and some more gin.'

CHAPTER TWENTY-NINE

That Tuesday afternoon, Dad and I talked more than we ever had about the things we'd never spoken of, and in going through the investigation with his clear eyes – and Prue's help – I could finally see the entire picture.

'Let's flip what you know on its head,' he said, shuffling the papers on the table. 'You've been looking at a motive as being the sale of the house, but what if there's another?'

When I continued to look blank, he said, 'What would you say is the cause of most relationship problems – based on the clients you see?'

'That's easy – money and love ... or, for that matter, love of money. Obviously, there are usually underlying issues, but it almost always comes down to money and love.'

He nodded. 'Exactly, so what if Rose knew about Chris and Kylie? After all, you only have Chris's word that no one else knew and the way I see it, Kylie has a lot to lose by being involved in an ugly divorce ... Would it get ugly?'

'Absolutely! And it wouldn't be just Martin and Kylie involved. Given their respective fathers are in business together, it would be their entire empire. Besides, I can't imagine Kylie divorcing Martin for Chris – no matter what Chris might like to think or say. She likes her lifestyle too much for that. No, if she was to divorce Martin, she'd set it up much better than that. She'd make sure she had a bargaining chip, and that block of land behind Brian's would be an excellent one. She might've always been a mean girl, but she's not a stupid one.'

Prue rejoined us with fresh drinks, which she placed on the wicker table. Looking over my father's shoulder at the replica I'd drawn of our murder board she said, 'Do any of the women have alibis? After all, women can kill too.' She raised her eyebrows to emphasise her point. 'Here's a scenario for you. What if Rose knew about the affair between Chris and Kylie, and Kylie came over to try and talk her out of telling anyone? You did say that Rose had no time for any of the Lindsays and Cosgroves, so presumably she might use the information later if she needed to?'

'That's right, she didn't have time for any of them – although she always quite liked Michael and Nick. But as for whether Rose would use the information? If she thought she needed to, she might.' Where was Prue going with this?

'Okay,' she said. 'Here's how it might've happened. Kylie comes over to try and convince Rose to stay quiet. They get into a scuffle, and Rose falls, hitting her head against the rock.'

Biting at my top lip, I thought it through. 'That makes

sense. Kylie certainly wouldn't want to be seen at Rose's, and with Martin out for the evening, no one would need to know she was there. The only thing is, I don't think she'd have enough strength to move the body.'

'You'd be surprised at the strength most women have when they need it.' A knowing smile crossed Prue's face. 'You'd have enough strength to do it – and you'd be able to move the ladder too.'

I supposed I would, and Kylie did look after herself with regular gym and yoga sessions. She was slim, but she was strong too.

'Or,' added Dad, 'she calls her boyfriend and gets him to help move the body.'

'Yes.' Prue kissed the top of his head. 'That's exactly what could've happened.'

Dad reached for her hand and held it against his chest. How had I been so wound up in myself all these years and missed what Prue and my father had built? He'd had every right to find happiness again and Prue had softened some of his more abrasive edges.

'And now' —Prue warmed to her theme— 'Kylie has something else over Chris.' She glanced at me. 'You did say she was that type of person – to use people to her own ends.'

'Oh yes, Prue, she's that type of person.' I was beginning to see where she was going with this.

'She sees an opportunity to get her boyfriend to break into New Moon. You said whoever did it was there to cause wilful damage? Plus, he's just helped her cover up a death, so he'll do anything for her.'

'I think he was in so far he already would've done anything for her,' I muttered, and Prue shot me a sideways look, suspecting correctly there was more to my history with Kylie than I'd let on.

'What reason would Kylie have for breaking into the shop?' asked Dad. 'Surely it's nothing to her?'

Prue smiled a complicit smile at me. 'No, but it means something to Clem.'

'Kylie always liked to have whatever was important to me,' I confirmed. 'And if she could get me to sell the shop to her brother, so much the better.' I grinned at Prue. 'It fits.'

'But what about the threats?' asked Dad. 'How are they connected?'

I stood and walked over to the railing. The sun had gone down, and the solar-powered lamps in the garden beds had taken over, casting an almost magical light.

'Through Chris,' I said, turning back to face them. 'I think Chris wrote the original threats to both Rose and me. Martin had told him I didn't believe Rose's death was an accident, but I hadn't mentioned the threats to anyone. He'd be afraid that if the police reopened the investigation, the existence of those threats would get out, so if Rose had kept them, he'd need to find them.' I warmed to my theme. 'He was unable to get into the cottage to look, and he would've known I had guests that night so took the opportunity when breaking into the shop to look for them … and to leave another note to make it appear as though the threats related to the sale of the shop rather than the sale of the cottage. After all, he had no reason to want the shop sold – that was all on Mick and Lauren.'

Moving back to where I'd been sitting, I picked up my glass. 'I think we're almost there. There's just something … something about the scenario that doesn't quite fit, but what?'

Dad said quietly, 'What would Rose say if she was here?'

I sipped at my drink thoughtfully. 'She'd tell me to stop thinking about who I want it to be and to stand back and look at the patterns. Then she'd ask me what I know in my gut rather than what I know in my brain.'

'Who do you want it to be?'

Without hesitating, I answered, 'Either Martin or Kylie, I'm not fussy. And I rather like Prue's idea of how it happened. Unfortunately, I don't believe it was either of them.'

'And what about when you close your eyes?' Prue leant forward in her chair, her voice softening.

'I think I know who did it.' I opened my eyes and smiled widely. 'I also think I know why and how.' Excitedly I turned to Prue. 'You were almost there, but I think it was Chris who confronted Rose and Chris who made it look like an accident. I also think it was Chris who broke into the shop but, I suspect, at Carmen's bidding. I'm just not sure how to prove it.'

'And that's where the lawyer in you needs to come out.' Dad squeezed my hand. 'Use your training now and follow the evidence you do have.'

'Well,' said Prue. 'Thank goodness you've got there – dinner is well and truly ready!'

I ended up staying two nights with Dad and Prue, waiting until I knew Miles wouldn't be home so I could pack my things into my car. Even though I'd calculated it would take me three long days of driving, if I was going to stay in Whale Bay, I'd need my own transport.

On Wednesday night, I called Maggie to let her know what was going on.

'Hey you, what's with leaving and not saying goodbye? Finn seemed devastated when I called by on Monday … Speaking of which, did anything happen between you two on Saturday night after I left? He's not saying, but I get the—'

'Maggie!' I laughed at how she hadn't let me get a word in. 'I didn't get to say goodbye because it was a really sudden thing.'

'Something to do with Miles, Finn said, but he didn't say anything else about it.'

'Yes, it's a long story, and I'll fill you in later. I was wondering, though, is there a way we can find out whether

Chris was on the Bruce Highway when Rose died or if he was in town either shagging Kylie or killing Rose? Does he have a secretary we could ask?'

'I imagine he would. I'm on it, or rather, Siouxsie will be. Hey' —she paused— 'you are coming back, aren't you? I mean, last time…'

'Last time I left, it took me twenty-five years to return? I'll be back, Maggie. I need to settle whatever this is about.'

'For how long, though?' In a quieter voice, she added, 'You know Finn has fallen for you.'

Her words filled me with warmth, and a flashback to our goodbye sent a shiver of delight up my spine. 'I'm not sure about that, and I'm not sure how long I'll be back for. All I can commit to at this point is that I will be back.'

Maggie called me on Thursday evening as I was settling into my hotel room in Canberra, glad I'd thrown a jumper into my overnight bag rather than one of the harder-to-access suitcases. 'Where are you?'

'Canberra. I—' I didn't get any more words out before she squealed down the line so loudly I had to hold the phone away from my ear.

'That means you're on your way back! And if you're driving, it means you intend to stay!'

'Maggie … Maggie! What are you doing?' There were all sorts of whooping and hollering in the background.

'Siouxsie and I are doing a happy dance, and Justin is

pretending he doesn't want to join in, but we all know he really wants to.'

'Well, before you get too carried away, I've taken all my leave, so it's for a few months – not forever. Maggie … did you hear what I said?'

'Yeah, yeah, yeah. After a few months, you won't be able to imagine life without us. You certainly won't be able to imagine life without Finn.'

I didn't tell her she was probably right.

'Anyway, you were right about Chris Walker – he wasn't on the highway when he said he was. His secretary, who, incidentally, has resigned because he owes her money, said he left at noon that day, so he would've been in town by no later than three. Surely someone saw him between then and when Rose died?'

'If he came straight to Whale Bay, that is.' Something Dad said last night came to mind.

'What are you suggesting?' Maggie asked.

'What if they didn't meet in Whale Bay? Kylie and Chris, that is. What if they used a hotel in Noosa? Kylie's always ducking down there for lunch or shopping or whatever. If we can find out where she likes to stay – or even where she likes to lunch – we might have enough to prove he was with her for at least some of the time and what time they left. And I'm sure I can get Maureen to talk about him … All we need is to prove he could've been here by eight on that Thursday night.'

'That could just work,' mused Maggie. 'Siouxsie knows Lauren's daughter and says she's always bragging about where Lauren and Kylie go … Oh my god, you're right, Siouxsie! Kylie and Lauren fancy themselves as social media influencers. We only need to look at their feed to see what they've been up to and where. Leave that one with us.'

'Fantastic idea! Right, well, I should be home—'

'Awww, Clem, you just referred to Whale Bay as home. I think I might cry.'

Chuckling, I continued. 'As I was saying, I'll be home Saturday afternoon, all going well, so—'

'Pizza, red wine and murder board at yours!' Maggie finished. 'Now, for goodness sake, ring Finn. He's been going spare wondering what's going on.'

'I will,' I promised.

'Now!' she ordered and hung up.

Finn picked up on the first ring, so I hadn't had time to think about how I would start the conversation.

'Hey you,' he said. 'Maggie texted and said you were going to call.'

Even though no one was in the room to see, I rolled my eyes. 'Of course she did.' I'd literally only had time to arrange the pillows on my bed into a backrest of sorts and make myself comfortable.

'How are you?' The low, slightly raspy timbre of his voice curled around me, warming me from the inside out.

'I've missed you,' I said impulsively.

'Good, because I've missed you too. Where are you?'

'In Canberra, I'm on my way back.'

'In Canberra? Does that mean you're driving? Because if you're driving, it means you're staying.' The hope in his voice sent a lump to my throat.

'It does, Finn – well, at least for a few months, and then we'll see …' I hesitated briefly before trusting him with the information I wasn't yet ready to tell anyone else. 'I wanted to call you, but … my father told me …' To hell with trying to find the right words. 'Rose was my mother, not my aunt.'

He was silent for a second and then another. 'Oh, Clem, that's big. How are you?'

I crossed my legs and propped another pillow behind my back. 'You know what? I'm good. I'm really good. For the first time, things are making sense and … I'm good.'

'Tell me about it,' he urged.

So I made myself even more comfortable, and that's what I did. And it felt better than good.

Saturday night saw our little group gathered around the murder board with the promised pizza and red wine. Despite having an audience of three, when Finn walked through my front door I stopped midsentence and ran into his arms for the kiss I'd been missing since he last kissed me, emerging only when Siouxsie began making faux vomiting noises and Justin cleared his throat and Maggie said, 'Get a room!

Actually don't, we have a murder to discuss first.'

'Alrighty,' I said, taking my place at the board. 'Before we get going, there's something I've discovered in the last few days that I think you need to know.' I glanced at Finn, who gave me a thumbs up. 'Rose was my mother, not my aunt.'

Maggie's hand flew to her mouth, but not quickly enough to stop her gasp of surprise from emerging.

'So while this was always important, now it feels even more so,' I finished.

'Oh, Clem, I don't know what to say.' Maggie rushed to hug me. 'It makes so much sense in retrospect, though.'

'Yes,' said Justin. 'It really does. And now I know, it's easy to see the family resemblance.'

'All the more reason to nail the dude,' added Siouxsie. 'Or dudette, as the case may be.'

Blinking back grateful tears, I brought our meeting back to order. 'Exactly. So, what did we find out from Kylie's socials?'

'First, that Kylie does nothing and goes nowhere without it being recorded for Instaposterity,' said Siouxsie. 'But these photos have all been taken by a pool or at the restaurant attached to one particular hotel in Noosa.' With no room left on the murder board, she laid the images on the dining table. 'From the tags, I could identify the hotel, and from her posts, we have the dates. Dad and I' —she sent a fond glance to her father— 'have married these dates up to Chamber of Commerce, council meetings or other business events when Martin wouldn't be home until late. And the best news is, she posted from there on the afternoon that Rose died.'

'Excellent work, Siouxsie! Now all we need to do is prove that Chris was there too and therefore not more than a thirty-minute drive away from Whale Bay rather than stuck on the Bruce Highway as he said he was.'

I looked at the images of Kylie pouting into the camera in the classic poolside pose: chest out, torso slightly angled, one long tanned leg in front of the other, blonde hair arranged artfully over one shoulder.

'I'm going to talk to Kylie,' I announced. 'Tomorrow.'

'Are you sure?' Finn's eyes held concern.

'I am. And it's something I need to do alone.'

CHAPTER THIRTY

On Sunday morning, I swam while Finn walked the dogs on the beach. My heart skipped when I strode out of the water to see the three of them waiting for me. 'Better?' he asked as I tied a towel around my waist.

'Much.' I leant across and kissed him. 'It's good to be home.'

Over coffee at Brewz, he made another attempt to dissuade me from seeing Kylie. 'If you have to see her, at least let Maggie or me come with you. She might still have been involved.'

'Thanks for your concern. I need to do this myself, but I'll compromise and meet her here.'

The decision was made, and I fired off a text to Kylie.
Me: We need to talk.

Her reply came through quickly.
Kylie: About what?
Me: About Hotel Tropicana, Chris Walker and where you both were on the night Rose died.

Grinning at Finn as three dots appeared and then

disappeared in the message panel, I said, 'She's hooked.'

'You think? She's taking her time about replying.'

'All part of the game. I might, however, hurry her up a tad.'

Me: I could always ask Martin.

Kylie: Where?

I held my hand up and Finn high-fived me.

Me: Brewz. Today at 10.

Kylie: I'll think about it.

Finn raised his eyebrows. 'One thing you can say about her is she's got guts.'

'Perhaps,' I acknowledged. 'But so do I.' I searched through the contacts in my phone and selected one.

'Who are you calling?' Finn tilted his head in an effort to see the screen of my phone.

I held up a finger as the call was answered.

'Clem, I wasn't expecting to hear from you. Have you considered my offer?'

'I have, Martin, and we need to talk.'

In the booth beside me, Finn's shoulders shook with suppressed laughter.

'Absolutely. The coffee shop at the wharf? Tomorrow at ten?'

Imagining the smirk he was probably wearing at the thought of an impending victory, I said, 'No, Brewz at eleven tomorrow.'

'But …'

'I'll see you there.'

As I hung up, my phone pinged with a message.

Kylie: I'll be there.

Finn was still chuckling. 'Remind me not to get on the wrong side of you.'

'I've dealt with worse than Kylie Cosgrove on the witness stand. But I have to say' —my grin was cheeky— 'I rather enjoyed that.'

He pushed a lock of wet, salty hair behind my ear. 'Sometimes I think you really are half mermaid and have come out of the ocean to tempt me away.'

'Would you follow me back in?' I teased.

'In a heartbeat.' He kissed me gently. 'I know this isn't the time or the place, but I think I'm falling in love with you, Clementine Carter.'

'It's exactly the time and the place,' I said and kissed him back.

If it wasn't for the fact that I had less than an hour to get home, get showered, changed and back down to Brewz to meet Kylie, I could've skipped – I possibly did skip a little. As romantic gestures went, a declaration of falling in love in a crowded coffee shop was hardly up there, but from Finn with his coffee bedroom eyes and his coffee-rich voice, and the faint taste and smell of coffee lingering in his skin, it was about as perfect as it could've been. And that made it worth skipping about – even if skipping was undignified behaviour for a forty-four-year-old Melbourne family lawyer.

Once home, I had a quick shower, dressed in denim shorts and an old, softly faded T-shirt I'd left behind and was just running my fingers through my hair when I heard the screen door shut.

'Finn? Is that you?' When there was no answer, I said it again, this time with trepidation. 'Finn?'

Holding perfectly still and straining to listen, I heard the soft tread of sneakers on the floorboards in the sitting room and the rustling of paper. Bugger, the pictures of Kylie were on the dining table, as were the copies of the threats Rose and I had received.

Glancing at my watch, I saw it was still fifteen minutes before I was due back at Brewz, so fifteen minutes before Finn would miss me. What to do? It could be nothing, but if Kylie had made a call …

Pulling my phone from my back pocket, I dialled Finn's number and immediately replaced it, praying he had picked up. If it was nothing, I'd call it a pocket call, but if it was who I thought it would be, Finn would be able to hear everything and know if I was in trouble.

Taking a deep breath, I ventured out of my bedroom. 'Who's there?'

Chris Walker had taken the cover off the murder board and was tracing the red lines from suspect to clues and back again.

'Chris, what are you doing here?'

Without looking away from the board, he said, 'Shouldn't I be asking what you've been doing here with this … what would you call it? A murder board?'

I forced out a laugh and casually said, 'Oh, that thing? I was just following my curiosity. It's just a bit of fun.'

He turned to look at me, his eyes cold, his face without expression. 'Is that why you wanted to meet Kylie today? For a bit of fun?'

He pulled a Post-it sticker from the board and read from it. ' "Confirmed – Chris left work at midday – no alibi. Kylie at Tropicana – were they together?" Is that what you wanted to ask her?'

My heart hammering, I inhaled deeply. If I could keep him talking and hold my ground until Finn got here – if he'd picked up the call, that was …

'Yes, as a matter of fact, that is what I wanted to ask her.'

'So why don't you ask me instead?'

He picked up the ball of red wool and unravelled it, wrapping one loose end around his wrist and tightening it into a taut string. If his action was meant to unnerve me, it succeeded.

I attempted a nonchalant shrug. 'Okay … where were you on the day Rose died? I know you weren't stuck in traffic on the Bruce Highway.'

'Where do you think I was?' He stretched the wool out further.

'I think you spent the afternoon in bed with Kylie at the Tropicana and the evening here in Whale Bay killing Rose,' I said bluntly, watching his face for any flicker of reaction. Seeing none, I continued, 'Not that I think you did it deliberately.'

'How did you know? About the hotel?' His eyes still on me, he leant across to grab the scissors on the dining table and snipped the wool, dangling the scissors from his pinky finger. 'I'm interested.'

'Your secretary told us you left at noon. As a note to self, if you want your staff to confirm your alibis, you probably should make sure you pay them on time.'

The corner of his mouth twitched. 'I'll bear that in mind, but at the time I wasn't aware I'd be needing an alibi. Go on.'

'As for the hotel, Kylie can't resist posting photos for her adoring fans.'

'You don't know I was there with her.' A pulse throbbed in his jaw.

'If you weren't, she would've called my bluff, but she didn't. For the useless book of knowledge, were you there?' Surely he could hear the thumping of my heart.

His head bobbed slightly. 'I was. And the rest – how do you think that went down?'

I grimaced. 'That I'm not so sure about. I'd just be speculating.'

'Give it a go.' He waved the scissors menacingly in my

direction. 'Let's see how close you are.'

Resisting the urge to check the time, I clenched and unclenched my fist to stop my hand from shaking. 'You know I'm expected down at Brewz. Finn will come looking for me as soon as I don't show up on time.'

He glanced at his watch. 'That gives us enough time to finish our conversation and for me to decide what to do with you.'

He held the wool between his hands and pulled it tightly until there was no slack. He was between me and the front door, but I might be able to make it through the kitchen and out the back door.

'Oh, and in case you're thinking of making a run for the back door, I took the precaution of locking it. The key's in my pocket.' He pulled it out and dangled it in front of my face before slipping it back into his pocket. 'So tell me, Clem, what do you think happened next?'

Swallowing hard, I said, 'I think you left Kylie sometime around seven or eight and came straight home. You park around the back so no one would see your car. After that? Something brought you here that night to see Rose. I think you wanted to frighten her, maybe reinforce the message in the threats you've been leaving her.' I tilted my head to one side with more bravado than I felt. 'Did I tell you I found the notes and gave them to Ted? He's having them checked for prints.' Ted wouldn't mind a little white lie in the circumstances. 'He's also had someone out to check the ladder. I can't imagine why they didn't do that in the first place, but there you go.'

Something that could've been fear or uncertainty flashed across his eyes. 'Just get on with it,' he growled.

'Well, as I said, this is only a guess, but what I think happened is that you had a blue with Kylie – maybe she dumped you – and you've come home thinking if only you had more money, if only your father would sell the house to Martin, you could talk him into giving you your share of the proceeds now rather than waiting until he dies. After all, Maureen would've been only too happy to take on that battle. In fact,' I mused, my finger tapping at my bottom lip, 'that could be what happened. You came home, and Maureen was carrying on about Rose and Gordon's fling and why Rose had interfered and stopped Brian from selling. She might've even said if Rose wasn't around, your father would sell. You would've been upset with Kylie for dumping you – did she at least wait until after you'd had sex? Knowing her, it would've been as you were both getting dressed. What did she say? "It's been fun, Chris, but you can't afford me, so it's over?"'

Surely, if he was coming, Finn would be here by now.

'Go on,' Chris urged gruffly, his fist clenching around the wool.

'So you've got Kylie in your ear, and then Maureen in your ear, and you storm out and come over here, but Rose hears you. You threaten her, and she takes a step back and trips, hitting her head against the border. You check her pulse, and she's dead, but you panic and see the ladder propped up against the garage. The silly old woman was climbing and fell – it happens all the time. So you move her and place the ladder beside her – by the way, that was your second mistake: the ladder was placed too carefully.'

'What was my first mistake? Hypothetically, of course.'

'Imagining that she'd climb a ladder in the dark dressed as she was and without a torch … but that's by the by.'

There was a movement at the window. Finn gave me a reassuring wave, and beside him was Michael Lindsay. Finn held up a hand to indicate I should keep Chris talking.

Trying not to show the relief that had coursed through me at the sight of their faces, I said to Chris, 'How am I doing?'

He gave a little nod. 'Keep going.'

'But now you have another problem – you have a blood-stained rock that's been knocked from the border. You pick it up and move it to one side, intending to replace it, but you either forget or can't find it.' The corner of his mouth twitched again. 'Yes, I think you forgot all about it. And when you did remember, it was too late. Luckily, though, the police weren't here for long and you were able to sneak back and replace it later. You must really have thought that you'd gotten away with it – and you nearly did. In fact, if it wasn't for your biggest mistake, I probably would've discounted you as being all talk and no trousers.'

What had Nina said about the Knight of Swords

reversed? She'd only described Chris.

'So tell me, what was my biggest mistake?' His eyes still on me, he placed the scissors and the wool on the table and reached behind the murder board for a knife he must have stashed there when he first came into the house.

At the window, Finn made a move, but Michael held him back, a finger to his lips. My heart sped up again.

'Why, leaving the note at New Moon after the break-in, of course. Although I wasn't sure about that until I saw the design on the side of the trainers you're wearing now, but the CCTV images will confirm it was you who broke into New Moon.' His eyes strayed briefly to his shoes. 'Only someone who knew about the previous threats would've gone looking for them in the office and attempted to throw the scent in a different direction by leaving another. The why of this one had me bamboozled for a while, I must admit,' I said conversationally.

'Really? Why's that?'

He flicked the knife against his finger, drawing blood. Despite knowing I had cavalry at the ready, I sucked the air in.

'You had no motive for doing over the store, although Mick did because he wanted it for Lauren. Then I remembered that you and Mick had always had a similar competitive relationship to Kylie and me. You couldn't resist setting him up as a potential suspect, could you? Especially when Martin told you I was making noise about

Rose's death not being an accident. As for the rest, my guess is that Carmen found out about you and Kylie and perhaps suggested New Moon was one disaster away from closure. Not that she would've asked you outright, of course. Besides, it gave you an opportunity to look for the threats you'd sent – in case Rose had held onto them, that is.'

He glanced at his watch. 'This is all very interesting, Clem, but sadly, there's no one else who'll get to hear your little story.'

'Aaah, but, that's where you're wrong.' I pulled my phone from my back pocket. 'You see, I took the precaution of dialling Finn as soon as I knew someone was in the house. He and Mick have heard the whole thing.' Acting more bravely than I felt, I waggled my fingers in a wave at the men at the window.

'You …' As Chris lunged at me with the knife, Tyson and Ted burst into the room.

I pushed the murder board towards Chris and bolted for the hall and the front door and into Finn's arms.

'Smart thinking, that trick with the phone,' he said, holding me so tightly I could no longer feel myself shaking.

'It all happened so quickly,' I said. 'One minute I was in my room getting changed and the next …' I shuddered at the thought and Finn's arms tightened around me.

Pulling away slightly, I turned my attention to Michael. 'How did you end up here?'

'Purely accidental. I was at Brewz picking up some

coffee – I might be forced to drink from the café at the wharf during the week, but life's too short for bad coffee on the weekends. When Finn got your call and took off, I followed, and he filled me in on the way. What about Kylie? Will she get dragged into this?'

Stepping out of Finn's arms, I inclined my head towards where Chris was being led out of the house by Tyson. 'I think that depends on Chris. Legally, she's done nothing wrong, and I can't see there's any reason for the affair to come out unless Chris chooses to make it public.'

Ted followed them out, pausing to lay a hand on my shoulder. 'Are you okay, Clem? That was some quick thinking on your part to keep him talking.'

'I'm fine, thanks, Ted. To be honest, I don't think he would've hurt me. He didn't seem to know what to do with me, and Rose's death was an accident.'

'Be that as it may, he'll be facing charges, and we'll need you to come down and give a statement.'

'No problem. We'll follow you down.'

As the squad car drove away, my phone pinged with a text.

Kylie: Well, I'm here at Brewz – where are you?

The laugh bubbled up from my belly, and once it was out, I couldn't stop it. I showed Finn the message, and soon he was laughing with me.

'What's so funny?' Michael looked confused.

'Nothing – it's your sister … I'll explain later.'

•

'So it was as you thought?' asked Maggie.

After giving our statements, we'd met the others for a late lunch at the pub on the wharf. Once he'd been arrested, Chris broke down and confessed everything.

'Pretty much. Chris was the one sending the threats to Rose. He was sure that if Rose could be persuaded to sell, Brian would follow. Not only did he owe Ray Cosgrove for repaying what he'd embezzled from his last firm, but he also had other debts. His idea was that Lauren was settled and financially secure, so why couldn't he have her share, too?

'That night he and Kylie had parted – she'd dumped him – and he'd come home upset and convinced he could have hung onto her if his finances were healthier. Because he'd been managing the Cosgrove accounts, he also knew Kylie owned the land behind Brian's and figured they could force a better price out of Martin and make a life together. Kylie wasn't having any of it, though. It's quite sad, you know, I think he really loved her – and always had done – whereas for her, it was a fling. Money and love – it always comes down to that.'

At the pier, one of the Lindsays' boats was unloading passengers from their daily seafood lunch cruise.

'Why was he at Rose's that night?' prompted Siouxsie.

'He was upset from the fight he'd had with Kylie and

had come home to hear Maureen going on about what Rose had been up to and how if she wasn't around, they'd all be better off, so he went around to see her. He said he wanted to talk to her, but I think he wanted to threaten or at least scare her.' Remembering how he'd gripped my wrist that evening we'd had dinner, I shuddered at how he might have attempted to 'talk' her round. 'She heard him, though, and came outside. The rest happened as I'd guessed: Rose tripped and banged her head. Chris moved the body and arranged the ladder but forgot about the rock. The next day, he was playing golf with Martin and Michael so was unable to replace the rock until later that evening.'

'When Rose's death was signed off as an accident, he must've thought he'd gotten away with it,' said Justin.

'Until you came back to town and began sniffing around,' added Maggie with a grin. 'What about the shop? How was he involved with that?'

'The version he told police is that Martin had told him I doubted the accidental death verdict and he began to panic that if the case was reopened and the threats resurfaced, he could find himself without an alibi. Although I think he was also worried that his affair with Kylie would be discovered. He said he overheard Carmen telling me that the shop was one disaster away from having to close, so when he went looking for the notes, he figured he might as well create that disaster. I still think Carmen knew about him and Kylie and possibly suggested he might like to find a way of persuading me to part with New Moon, but I'll never be able to prove that.' I lifted one shoulder. 'And that's it, really.'

'Well,' said Maggie, 'I'd like to propose a toast to Clem for having the guts to voice her concerns, rope the rest of us in, and see the investigation through – and get justice for Rose.' She held her glass up. 'To Clem.'

I waved her words away. 'Thanks, Maggie, but this was a real team effort, and I couldn't have done it without you guys. So if we're toasting, I think we should be toasting each other.'

'Agreed,' said Siouxsie. 'To us!'

As I lowered my glass back to the table, there was a sharp tap on my shoulder.

'We need to talk,' Kylie Cosgrove said. As always she was dressed to impress, her arms folded, her toe tapping.

'Sure.' I waved her towards an empty seat.

'In private.' Without waiting for a response, she stalked off to a vacant table.

With a grin for the others I followed her and sat in the chair opposite her. 'What did you want to discuss, Kylie?'

'I don't know what you think you know,' she began.

'About you and Chris? I know quite a bit as it happens.'

'Are you going to tell Martin?'

At the realisation that her overly confident pose covered a very real fear of exposure, I suppressed a smile and delayed my response long enough to see uncertainty flare across her face.

Lowering her eyes to the table, she said haltingly, 'I know we haven't been close over the years, but Martin … he wouldn't take it well, and I like being married to him.'

'Then why cheat?'

She shrugged one shoulder. 'To prove I can, that I still have it.'

She raised her eyes and met mine, and I understood that for a woman who'd always used her looks for power, getting older and potentially losing that power must be frightening.

'Your affair with Chris is none of my business, Kylie. I was only ever interested in finding out what happened to Rose.'

Before she could say more, I smiled tightly and joined my friends.

'Okay?' Finn laid his hand on my thigh.

'Absolutely.'

I leant across and kissed him lightly on the lips. It was good to be home.

EPILOGUE

Two weeks later ...

Rose's backyard memorial was exactly the event she would've loved.

Finn had spread the word with the regulars at Brewz, Nina did the same at New Moon, and Rose's book club ladies made sure everyone at the keep-fit classes they attended together knew about it.

Whale Bay turned on a corker of a day with clear blue skies and one of those warm but not too warm days you get in early May in South-East Queensland – the days that conjure up the sorts of slogans about perfection day after day tourism departments love. Across the road, the water shimmered in the sun, and here in the backyard of the home where Rose had lived for so many years, eskies full of ice kept the beer, wine and soft drinks cold while trestle tables groaned under the weight of salads, bread rolls and other contributions from people whose lives she'd touched.

To feed the masses, I dragged out Rose's barbecue,

Gordon wheeled his in from next door, and Maggie and Justin brought their portable kettle-style barbies. Manning the barbecues and balancing beer and tongs were Justin, Finn and Harry, and I was kept busy chatting with everyone who had a story or a memory of Rose they wanted to share.

While the senior Cosgroves and Lindsays hadn't made an appearance, Michael and Lauren did, Lauren going so far as to lose some of her acquired airs and graces throughout the afternoon. Chris's arrest had hit her hard, and both Maggie and I suspected that if Kylie hadn't been involved to the extent she had been, Lauren could easily have been ostracised by association with him. As it was, Kylie had stood beside her publicly, so the circles they mixed in had no option but to follow suit. While Mick knew of his sister's involvement with Chris, we'd agreed that was something we'd keep to ourselves.

Also missing were Brian Walker and Maureen Peterson. The day after Chris was arrested, Brian called by to apologise for his son's actions, balancing precariously in his walker as he stood at the front door.

'Come in, Brian,' I urged. 'I'll put the kettle on.'

'No, pet,' he said, his face having aged another ten years almost overnight. 'I won't stay. I just wanted to tell you how sorry I am for the part my Chris played in what happened to Rose and how he damaged the shop.' He shook his head, his words faltering. 'I don't know where we went wrong, but we all spoilt him and now …'

'Don't blame yourself, Brian. This was all on Chris.' I reached out to pat his arm to bring comfort, but he shook it off.

'But it is my fault – he's my son. And while I know he didn't set out to hurt Rose, his need for money has meant that's exactly what's happened.' He paused, his eyes moist. 'The irony is, I'm selling the house now. I can't live here any longer.'

'Oh Brian, I'm so sorry to hear that. Where will you go?'

'Maureen and I will go into a retirement village on the Sunshine Coast – separate villas this time. She hasn't yet accepted her part in what's happened. She pandered to the boy all these years, and I allowed it to happen. I've since found out she gave him most of the money from when she sold her house in Brisbane, and he frittered that away too – it's why she couldn't afford to buy into a villa here. I'm glad you've come back, Clem, and I'm even glad you took it upon yourself to investigate Rose's death. Now we can all get on with things.'

Touching his head in a mini salute, he laboriously turned and made his way back down the path, through the squeaky front gate and back to his house at the end of the road. He seemed so small and frail within the metal frame of the walker.

Although I felt deeply sorry for Brian's pain, I had no sympathy for his sister. Maureen had blamed me for all that had occurred. 'That girl has always been as much of a troublemaker as her aunt – she should've just kept her nose out of things.' But no one was prepared to listen to her.

Lauren took me aside during the afternoon and apologised, too. It felt, though, that she was apologising for more than her brother's part in Rose's death – it felt as though she was sorry for abandoning our friendship all those years ago and the mean girl cruelty she'd inflicted on Maggie and me at school. I doubted we'd ever be close again, but her brother's fall from grace had given her a perspective she'd been lacking.

'I can't believe Chris was trying to pin suspicion onto Mike and me by messing up your shop so it would look like we'd hired someone to do it,' she said after I'd waved her apologies away.

Maggie and I looked at each other and decided to keep her mother-in-law's part in that to ourselves. Chris had taken the entirety of the blame, and there was no evidence that could ever be proven about Carmen's role. It was, however, satisfying that Carmen was aware that we knew of her involvement in the break-in at New Moon and would be wondering if or when we'd use that information against her.

As the sun began to sink and the crowd dispersed, I found Gordon on the swing chair under the old fig tree. Sitting beside him, I clinked my bottle of beer against his.

'I miss her, Clem,' he said. 'But it's a comfort knowing part of her will still be here.'

'You know, don't you?' I asked.

He nodded. 'She told me many years ago.'

My breath caught in my throat. 'Are you …?'

He smiled gently. 'No, although I'd be proud to be. Rose and I only began seeing each other in the last few years.'

'Do you know who my father is? Dad only said she came back from her gap year in England pregnant, but I wondered …'

He bit his bottom lip and shook his head once. 'No, I don't know who your father is. Rose never told me, although I have my suspicions. But before you ask me, suspicions are all they are, so don't ask me to share them.' He drank deeply from the bottle. 'Even if she hadn't told me, I'd know – you're the image of her, you are, Clem. Maybe not in the mirror so much, although you do have the look of her, but your heart is as big and as strong as hers was. In everything that matters, you're your mother's daughter. God rest her soul.'

With tears streaming down my face, I clinked his bottle again. 'To Rose,' I said.

'To Rose,' he echoed.

As we tipped our bottles to drink, a magpie flew down and began pecking about near our feet.

'One for sorrow,' said Gordon.

Its mate flew down to join it. 'And two for joy,' I replied, looking to where Finn stood watching us. Even in this light from this angle, I felt rather than saw love in his eyes.

When I first drove into town less than a month ago, I hadn't imagined any of this. My intention was to see what needed to be done to the cottage to place it on the market, stay a couple of weeks to have a well-deserved holiday and then head home. Instead, I'd inherited a shop (and some willing workers), been involved in the investigation of a suspicious death, reconnected with an old school friend, discovered my aunt was my mother (and vice versa), and fallen in love. My whole life had changed, yet somehow it felt like it had all turned out exactly as fate – or Rose – would have it.

'Thank you for bringing me home, Rose,' I whispered to the birds.

'What was that, pet?' asked Gordon.

'Nothing, Gordon, I was just talking to the magpies.'

BEFORE YOU GO ...

If you enjoyed *One For Sorrow* I'd love it if you left a review in the usual places. If you'd like to stay up to date with what Clem and the crew from Whale Bay get up to next, you can sign up for my newsletter at my website: https://joannetracey.com.

You can also drop by and see me – virtually speaking, of course – here:
My blog: https://andanyways.com
Facebook: https://facebook.com/joannetraceywriter
Instagram: https://instagram/jotracey

ACKNOWLEDGEMENTS

It was my friend Deborah Cook who first suggested I write a series based on astrology. Deb and I spent a lovely afternoon on my daughter's lawn at Urangan, Hervey Bay, with K'Gari (Fraser Island) in the distance, drawing what I imagined would be a storyboard for this, the first Whale Bay mystery. Then I began writing something else and misplaced the sheets of paper we'd been working on.

But Clementine Carter refused to go away. She didn't seem all that keen on the story I'd planned for her, nor was she fond of the supporting cast I'd created. Instead, three years after she was first envisaged (and inconveniently while I was in the middle of a major relocation project at work) she decided, in the space of six weeks, that I'd write the story she wanted me to write. Characters, I've found, have a habit of doing that.

Thank you, Deborah, for both the inspiration, your friendship and the shared wines (and whines). This one is dedicated to you.

While you won't find Whale Bay on a map of South-east Queensland, it really is a combination of two places I adore – Hervey Bay, on the Fraser Coast (the whale-watching capital of the world), and Mooloolaba, here on the Sunshine Coast. The latter I'm very familiar with (as followers of my Instagram would know), but I've only gotten to know Hervey Bay in the three years since my daughter moved there. So thank you, Sarah, for giving me a reason to regularly visit a town I now love. Sarah also says she deserves credit for listening to me talk through the plot as I was writing it. Hmmmm.

As always thank you to my editors – Nicola O'Shea and Jo Speirs. In you I have the dream team. Thank you also for rolling with it when you get sent a book that's completely different than the one I told you I'd be writing.

Thanks to Louisa West for another fabulous cover, and to Keith Stevenson for turning this manuscript into a real live book.

To my early readers – my sister-in-law Pieta, and the ladies from the Simply Stunning Bookclub (did you enjoy your cameo?) – thank you for your friendship and for being my personal cheer squad.

The usual thanks to my family – Grant, Sarah and Kali (aka Adventure Spaniel). I couldn't do what I do without you.

Mostly though, my thanks go to you, my readers. Thank you for helping make my authorial dream come true and I truly hope you enjoy reading this first Whale Bay mystery as much as I enjoyed writing it.

ABOUT THE AUTHOR

Joanne Tracey lives on the Sunshine Coast in Queensland Australia with her husband and a cocker spaniel who takes her role as resident flop-dog and guardian of Jo's office very seriously. An unapologetic daydreamer, eternal optimist, and confirmed morning person, Jo writes contemporary romance, romantic comedy, women's fiction and cosy crime. When she isn't writing, Jo loves baking, reading, long walks along the beach, posting way too many photos of sunrises on Instagram and dreaming of the next destination and the next story.

Jo's life goals (apart from being a world-famous author) are to be an extra on *Midsomer Murders* and to cook her way through Nigella's books.

Milton Keynes UK
Ingram Content Group UK Ltd.
UKHW010840190424
441445UK00001B/7

9 780645 958751